Jack Martindale

Snapshot

Austin Macauley Publishers™
London • Cambridge • New York • Sharjah

A CIP catalogue record for this title is available from the British Library.

ISBN 9781788785457 (Paperback)
ISBN 9781788785464 (E-Book)

www.austinmacauley.com

First Published (2018)
Austin Macauley Publishers Ltd™
25 Canada Square
Canary Wharf
London
E14 5LQ

Jack Martindale is a guy with whom you never know quite what to expect. Akin to his writing, his natural level of introspection has only been intensified and enhanced through the experience that he recounts in *Battling a Brain Injury: The Life That Jack Built*.

Going forward, having attained a BA 2:1 in English and Politics from the University of York, Jack's main take on life is that as long as you don't take things too seriously, your life should be all right!

SNAPSHOT is his latest and first purely fictional work to be published, dealing with the joys, trials and tribulations of the millennial transparently for all concerned.

To Sarah

Acknowledgements

For my friends and family.

What I have for you here is a collection of life entries to help me try to try and understand things from various stages of my mid-twenties. Rest assured that I was never enough of a dick to keep day-to-day diaries or ever to share whatever I may have been eating or places I may have been entering at any given time through social media and whatnot. Indulgent, as you may feel, for what I have done here, it really is what it is. You'll probably see things about my character that I'm completely oblivious to and I'd like to believe that I'm an all right guy with many all right friends and all right aspirations. I'll admit that as a pretty introspective guy with a big enough ego, I at least know that I'm nothing more than a delusional façade. This is, truthfully without actually caring any less. Although lessening with age, what people make of my fragility is a genuine concern.

One

1. Day 1: In a Beach Bar

Call me whatever you shall, though given that I had only first crossed paths with him barely 10 minutes ago, I consciously snubbed much of the further tedious conversation with Stephen or whatever he was called. All that we seemed to have in common was that it was our first visit to this beach and, indeed, country. He was the sort of guy that quickly seemed more than capable of making any destination banal.

This pretentious adjective that I use to describe Stephen may seem especially rich when I have to own up to it coming from Darren Brown. And yes, that is me as opposed to that magician guy, on whom I don't really have any real opinion, let alone knowledge. The fact that I remain close to my wonderful parents, despite being given the name that goes better with somebody conceived in something like a Volkswagen Golf in a Beefeater pub car park, just proves that you really can't read much into a name. Or so I assure myself anyway.

Here I was in Sri Lanka, which is all too widely and accurately regarded as the first calling point for many middle class visitors to the diamond of the Indian Ocean. Mount Lavinia Beach is an easy stop-off first calling point of many travellers in their onset of exploring the luscious and magical island. As always with the plane's lowering into our landing point, the landscape inevitably differs from whatever mental picture that I have painted, which, after at least ten hour's air borne, was embossing itself as far less than anything at all vivid. Whilst the greenery made for a welcoming descent, my cynical inside—which I've long given up trying to suppress—couldn't help but prepare me for plenty of rainfall during my trip of just less than a month. I'm a Brit going abroad, after all.

I had arrived at the resort with almost worrying ease, and from my first impressions I was relieved that I wasn't intending on being around the place for more than a night. Already from glancing around at the young crowd, it seemed a valid concern that I may be bumping into some of the same people that I could run into at my Peckham supermarket.

For the second time, I was travelling on my lonesome. One of the most salient things that I remember from my first little bourgeois solo expedition to South America—where the delight of independent adventuring and the dismay of feeling lonely happened at similar speeds—was vowing to never go backpacking on my own again. It just felt like too much effort and expense for the reward to ever again be much justified.

Still, that was over half a decade ago and after having come out of (or more realistically being ditched from) yet another meaningless fling, the time to clutch at straws and cling to the hope of some worthy life-enhancing experience had certainly arrived.

I had no real commitments other than yet another meaningless flat share, in South London this time actually. Although, apart from at university, I'd always lived in the capital, this was to be my first time going this side of the river. In the meaningless charity sector, I also doubted that the new job that I had lined up in should be any different from my last tedious job. The fragrant smell of the tropical monsoon, only increased my craving for some escape.

It appeared that the inane conversation with monotonous Stephen thingy had not quite concluded, as he fired off, 'have you stayed at this hostel before?'

Glugging the local beer—which was tasty and smooth enough (here, at least)—I merely offered some sort of nod, as I was far too preoccupied with simply revelling in my new found freedom and knowledge that the bulk of the next month could be passed as I pleased. This is certainly more than dunking a toe in the water, although I've been lucky enough to have been away for far longer periods in the past. Still, it felt long enough so that I didn't have to be too intense about cramming in as much of this appealingly beautiful part of the world as possible.

Basking in my lack of responsibility, it was a pleasant surprise for a sucker for nostalgia like me to hear *Devil Within* by the *Midnight Juggernauts* blast out of the loudspeaker. Having not heard this music, or even anything by the band in some moons, this tenuously mirrored my feeling of an excitable unknown sense of adventure occurring against the securing backdrop of some vague familiarity.

What I was not anticipating was for this perspiring (though in fairness, he was overweight and did have one of those ever shiny faces) oaf named Stephen to quip, "I fucking love this song, going to go and pull some shapes!" I immediately thought, 'Spherical is the only real shape that you could muster you big fat fucker.'

Words failed me at this point. It is almost fair to say that I would even have exchanged the song choice for some comprehensive primary school 6–8 P.M. disco music of Whigfield's Saturday Night, the Macarena and maybe Chumbawumba if we were lucky. This is for Stephen suddenly dropping dead. Well, just going away from me and leaving me alone is all that'd be necessary if I'm being kinder.

Part of me was already dying inside and cringing for poor hapless Stephen from Northampton which was a place that he provided the perfect metaphor for, in my crassly generalising eyes. Though being refined and far more pitying than abrasive, I believe that I only replied with a response that my friends tell me is all too common. This is a hybrid of bewilderment and an attempted smile that looks more akin to a grimace. And as I grow increasingly over the hill of my mid-twenties, it seems progressively to be my response to many topics of people's conversation. He was being selfish to humanity and misrepresenting manhood in appearing so shameless as to represent the stinking sloth that he did though.

It all too often seems that as I gain more life experience and my outlook supposedly matures, I am forced to feel what would be classed as the contrary.

As I'm in the mood to cast things in boxes, I have a twinge of envy for those naïve little bright eyed and bushy tailed guys especially, who along with feeling that they are God's gift generally often exude the persona of having done it and experienced everything all before. Even daring to audaciously believe that they actually have a clue how this world operates. The fact that I can confidently state how far from having any real idea about anything hopefully segregates me from their insecurities masked by audacious feigned wisdom as a by-product of their disingenuous anxieties. Or just the intellectual vacuums that they all must inhabit.

Mine is certainly not the image of this age that I had any vision of; life should get easier unless you were an absolute moron or, unfortunately, living within some crisis. Being invincibly convinced that neither of these misfortunes should ever apply to me, I felt that I was entering the stage of fully controlling my life. Well, it's not all bad and it's certainly far from anything all good, but my mid-twenties is certainly not what I ever anticipated. Ha, not that I'm bitter.

Being heart-broken more than once and being a not so proud carrier of syphilis, it'd be a delusional lie for me to claim to ever have fulfilled any expectation that I had of myself. Perhaps, I'd burned the candle from both ends (not that I properly know or even understand what that means anyway) for a little too long, and although I never had any real idea of where life was taking me, I'd have thought that I would be more sorted than I am now.

"Another drink then?" Stephen wistfully enquired, almost as if he had some untoward designs. Not caring one iota what this sycophantically sweaty drink provider felt or thought about anything, drinking really was the only way forward. If I had to tolerate more of his tedious company, I obliged and resigned myself in allowing him to get me another beer. Then I'd have to reciprocate the deed, as I mean he did keep buying me drinks, and please allow me some credit where credit's due. It was a pleasant gesture which was only enhanced by his pleasant addition of a jaeger bomb.

Smoking and drinking relentlessly was something that Stephen's company seemed to beg of me as I dealt with it in my own way. The former, as I found it to be a useful tool in buffering the conversation by substituting any input expected of me with smoke; and the latter, as any further detachment from reality was necessarily marooned in his more than mediocre level of company.

Nonetheless, whether it was principally due to the heat, increased inebriation and other people around seeming to be having a joyous time, Stephen was becoming increasingly hard work. This comfort was reaching its pinnacle when he delved into further uncouthness with his bold and beastly question of 'so, have you shagged many girls since you started your trip?'

Clearly, this query from an impertinent wretch was not met with any response. This failed to deter shitting Stephen from regaling me with his supposed numerous exploits with these poor so-called 'lucky ladies' made by this hideous creature. My mind automatically conjured the anachronistically patriarchal expression, 'Damsels in distress'. All that I could wish for were obviously for him to shut up leave my side and quit subjecting me to his tirade or verbal diarrheic tales, and that Rohypnol had not had to pass through any of these girls' lips for Stephen to have his wicked way.

Needless to say, I was incredulous at Stephen's supposition that we could go about tonight being 'partners in crime'. Given that I could not under any circumstances ever use date-rape or desperation as a catalyst to any of my actions, along with beginning to actually loathe this limp excuse for a man and all that he represented, there were few things that I could entertain as a more repulsive idea. Not to mention how demeaning I'd find the concept of 'going out on the pull' anyway. I just feel too old for such tom-foolery; having to shake-off the slight depression that this makes me feel.

Thinking on my feet with my synapses moving their fastest in terms of how my—yes—it was at the stage to confirm it to be—drunken state should allow. I'm okay with the odd white lie, and 'I'm actually gay, Mate' seemed to be the most tactful response that I could manage in ridding myself of this pitiful amphibious company.

Given that Stephen has all of the makings of an ignorant bigot, I was convinced that I should soon be rid of this imbecile. Oh, how things can be misinterpreted, as it was with shock and anguish that I digested his response.

"I see, well me and Kayleigh over there have been toying with the idea of having a threesome with another man and I could suggest that if you like?" I could read a few things into this ridiculous, if not just bilious, proposal. The first being that this more conventionally attractive Kayleigh had said that she could only go to bed with him provided that another man was involved too as a joking attempt to rebuke him for his delusional and ill-founded belief that she'd ever touch him with a barge pole. Stephen's notion that anybody who I found remotely attractive should ever go anywhere near him amazed me, if it was not just something that I found appalling. Stephen would have to practise necrophilia to have involvement with me in any sexual context.

Confirmation that Stephen was a repressed gay shouldn't particularly shock me in the least, but his arrogance in believing that he could come anywhere near me made me feel nauseous. If he had been battling with his sexuality, I'd try to be more empathic for this situation, but his suggestion was something else.

From all that I'd already noticed from the hostel pool's communal changing area soon after I arrived, he was one of those people who loved to parade about, letting all there was of it hang out. Granted, I rely just on the small towels provided by the hostel and don't mind the odd slip out, but I don't follow Stephen's lead in feeling the need to prance around on full display to everyone else's misfortune.

In my experience, these type were nearly always both old and wrinkly… or just trying to prove that they were comfortable in being ugly as sin. Stephen definitely fell into the latter camp.

Instead of relating another, I quickly just quipped, "Nah, Mate, definitely not, I think that you'll just have to make do with using your left hand again whilst here." Stephen scrunched his eyes together and his brow looked crestfallen, although, bless him, he did feign an attempt to join in a bit with my effortful laughter. I did feel that I'd been a bit mean though.

Rather than taking his leave—as I'd hoped—he did what I'd deemed more likely realistic, if truth be told, and in attempting to further coax me into this revolting act, he went on with, 'Well that's what they all say!" Too right, I thought. Only, he didn't do what any sane person should and stay clear of me, but he relentlessly badgered me and along with being satisfied that he was well over half-cut, I was desperate for him to KO.

Part of me was thinking that he was almost certainly a virgin. An insecure one at that. But then, going with my long streams of almost semi consciousness, I was convinced that he'd find absolutely no shame in forking out for it. Where we were, this was seemingly a particularly easy pie to make. In fact, I felt some of what I can only imagine must be the victimisation that many, if not all, girls have to be subjected to: being prey. It was almost a level up, if possible—almost like being required to pay to have your leg over. Escaping, rather than in any way partaking, was always my only motive in these instances. It's so sad that so many Westerners, not to mention locals, go in for these sorts of thing and, worryingly, it's not even seen as soul-destroying in any way; half of these viciously pimped (as if there any other way) prostitutes were clearly way under our age of consent.

Then, although I was relieved that he stayed clear of sex from this point in the conversation, his replacement for it was hardly more preferable. Some switch inside him had definitely been flicked and certainly not for the better. As Stephen started, for some unbeknown reason, talking about the family that he was leaving behind back in England. I really did not need this.

Still, he rambled on anecdotally, akin to a grandparent, reeling off no end of stories with no real beginning, middle or end. These were what could be called home-truths, and I certainly can't claim to have retained a great deal of what he was divulging. This sums up Stephen's character to me, as there is normally nothing that I relish more than finding out about other people and what makes them tick. No information responsible in any way for the formation of Stephen is something that I could find at all interesting. It was mostly just white noise.

With this, it was all just in one ear and out the other. The few snippets of information that I retained relate to him having some older brother who'd surpassed everything that he's done, now separated parents and the fierce nature of his dad apparently relating to turmoil in the Falklands War of 1982. Marital breakdown and even 'compassionate leave' then followed. The fact that we were poles apart was not something that I liked to think I'd have allowed myself to act as a reason not to identify and empathise with this guy, it's more that he just seemed to be a complete fool, who I would not suffer gladly.

Then it transpired that his dad had died sometime in the recent past. Perhaps, I am an overly morbid person, but this was the first thing that Stephen had said which was of any interest to me. "It was due to our garage in the field becoming on fire whilst he was in it and the loss adjustors supported the theory of it being set off by too much pressure upon faulty wires." Well, I hadn't asked one single thing about it, though this was pretty engaging. "Though a brunette was witnessed by a youth too young to be identified—probably poaching or committing arson around the field—leaving our driveway around the same time."

Without even needing to have to put on some act, I was pretty engrossed in this. It's quite a gripping story for me to listen to, without feeling the necessity to feel any turmoil, let alone having much sympathy for. Anybody partly responsible for producing Stephen and unleashing him on the world could not, in any way, be that worthy of much of my grief anyway.

A glisten of a tear is something that I saw reel down the side of Stephen's flabby cheeks. Witnessing a fellow person cry is never in any way pleasant, but in all honesty, if I was with somebody that he did have some respect for, I'd probably join in, as a refreshing blubber is something that I think should do me a world of good at the minute. Like pissing yourself, it happens once in a while, but never needs to be shared with polite society. Thankfully, I cannot remember the last time that I engaged in either activity whilst still at all sober or otherwise. Stephen continued to harp on relentlessly; surely, Stephen was about at the passing out stage. I wished.

When Stephen elaborated upon how he was not actually on speaking terms with his father when he died, it seemed much more likely that I would nod off to sleep before Stephen passed out. Jeez, I thought that we'd done with his home truths. It often seems when travelling that you end up hearing loads of confidences from people that you'll almost certainly never cross paths with again. Often, this is fine and perhaps, it provides the exact release that many people like me are looking for whilst also enjoying the supposed detachment of travelling. From people that you enjoy being with, then obviously, it's all part of the game, but having to encounter it from people you've no interest in it is inevitably complete and utter ball ache. Hearing about Stephen once 'nearly' having to bump into his father in a Tesco metro's car park, really was amongst my pits of my social existence.

Boring backstory's never fun, especially when lots of paint could dry during the tale. At times like these, I feel that I can be way too tolerant and thus have become an expert at resigning myself to inane conversations with those who I'm almost convinced my enviable pals never have to encounter. A slight silver lining to being granted access to somebody's pitiable unloading is that there is absolutely no need to feel the need to do anything beyond smoke—especially when you could smoke inside as in prior to the depressing July 2007—and drink with maybe the odd bit of *paraphrasing* once every couple of minutes if I was feeling generous.

Increasing levels of fuzzy apathy is still all that I could feel towards any of Stephen's circumstance. Perhaps one of the perils of being a screaming child of Thatcher was that, although I'd like to think that I had fair empathy, I really could not afford to devote much of my precious time to the concerns of strangers.

At least I admit it, having completed my Government and Politics degree from the University of East Anglia (UEA) gaining a 2:1, I can't say that I've ever felt more apolitical or indifferent to much the whole crony political process that I once so wanted to be part of. A bit sad if I consider what I used to be like.

Don't get me wrong, I pretty much always vote for the red coloured ones, but beyond that, I can't say that I've got the self-importance, interest or yearning for satisfaction to feel the need to engage much within any political organisation. Disenfranchised rather than disengaged, if I'm being pretentious, seeing it as little beyond rah de rah de rah followed by a load of blah di blah if I'm being honest. And that's whether you're Theresa May, Jeremy Corbyn, or especially that particular of his string of old squeezes, Hackney North and Stoke Newington's Dianne Abbot. Being amongst the first three black MPs to get elected in 1987—all for the Labour Party, obviously—is admirable, but can't she go away now that she's had her fun snuggling up to former foe Michael Portillo on the Politics Show and being able to send her son to public school? #hypocrisy

Anyhow, you know that politics is quite dry isn't it; once you've come to terms with the reality that your life is subconsciously a political game, it seems pretty limiting and even unimaginative to devote your life to this particular discipline. It's all just people having a wet dream over their egos whilst exchanging their often ill-thought-out opinions, having feuds and engaging in social calamity. Not saying that I could do any better, but many of them too should have just stuck to the day job. Obviously, I'm not saying that it should revert back to centuries ago, when they weren't paid for what they did, but at least it'd give some honesty to the fact that it's usually all just about the rich looking after the rich. The ruling class look after the ruling class and a lower middle class (going with the lingo!) kid from Higham's Park doesn't really feel at home in this world. Fluctuating between sharing some of my dad's shame at just how much better off I am that many of the working-class that I most wish to identify with against the backdrop of how little power or influence I feel that I, in truth, command.

I'd choose almost anything above publicly politicising my life any day. Life's just not something that is healthy to take that seriously, is it? Wreckage and inevitable humiliation, without wanting to dwell on ay particulars, is sufficient reason in itself for me to distance myself from the political domain. Always having been lumbered with Iain Duncan Smith as my MP, I may once have felt compelled to enter politics out of a delusional conviction that I could better things, or to placate my disillusionment at having being raised under a Tory MP. Think that he's a Thatcherite example of 'working class made good'... Or is that more John Major from Brixton? They're both equally dated and past their sell-by date selfish men anyway.

At any rate, I felt tired and ready to hit the hay, gazing over Stephen reeling out plenty of verbal diarrhoea as he tried and instantaneously failed to chat up misfortunately selected girls, who, given that they both had a pulse and their own teeth, were miles out of his league. So, as I left Stephen with his own stupidity and delusions, he told me what a pleasure it had been meeting me after we shook hands. Obviously, this turn of phrase could by no means be reciprocated, but I smiled, which hopefully did not appear too pitying.

On the short trip made in the pitch black back to the hostel, I went via a convenience shack which was able to supply me with a local spirit to lull me into a deep sleep and a 20 deck of cigarettes. To confirm that I am just the Brit abroad, although it was substantially cheaper than back home, they was dearer than the shameful little Englander arrogance inside me may have hoped.

It was as I stumbled away armed with my supplies, I witnessed some young guy (he looked about 10, but what do I know?) take a tumble off of his moped thing. After a painful second or so of wondering whether he had met his untimely end, he clamoured back onto the long worn vehicle wearing an expression that seemed indifferent to the incident. A sad hopelessness wept over me when I was forced to have to think of how many scores of young guys tumble off of a motorbike every hour and aren't half so lucky. Part of the issue must be that so many are trusted at the command of a motor before their balls have even dropped.

It's not as though I felt particularly horny, but especially given how much booze I had by then consumed, I couldn't help but feel a little pleasantly surprised to catch the eye of one of the 'babes' that Stephen had shamelessly cast his rotund eyes upon. She seemed what could be described as 'lightly flustered', though this was probably a misinterpretation. Part of me wished to be the knight in shining armour, whilst more of me was reverting to my ridiculous penchant for catastrophising things. Anyway, she introduced herself as 'Helen'.

The voice Helen had could, I thought, perhaps be described as mild Scouse—an accent that I've always found attractive—and this turned out to be pretty accurate as it transpired that she was from the Wirral and therefore, on the posh Cheshire side of the Mersey. With mounds of auburn hair draped all over a freckle-less pale body; I instantly thought her pretty hot. The gravelly voice that she had certainly helped rather than hindered the ever sexier image that I had made of her.

Conversation was effortless and instantly of the type where a few passing minutes could easily become an hour. The only thing about her that particularly surprised me was learning the fact that she had never before done any proper travelling and had decided to come alone having spent the entirety of her adulthood in an 'unfulfilling relationship'. My guess was that she'd perhaps be a couple of years older than me, though I wasn't so crude as to ask.

Nonetheless, she soon volunteered her age and it turned out that she'd be hitting 'the big 3-0 during this adventure'. Looking good on it. Other than Phoebe—the only girl that I'd ever claim to be in love with—older girls were my usual preference. This Helen only really got hotter during our conversation and her having spent over a decade in being controlled within a 'controlling' relationship just seemed more and more out of character. This Nicholas that she had 'belonged to' just sounded like more and more of a bastard.

Still, she was out of that old mess now; the main lasting adverse effect of the relationship appeared to be the fact that this working-class lass from Liverpool way had never completed her undergraduate degree in English Literature from Cambridge. This bloke that I'll have to call 'Nick the prick'—whose professional expertise was in banking—obviously felt threatened by Helen's intellectual prowess and was seemingly obsessed with being the alpha-male breadwinner.

Helen was evidently not fool enough to just take all of this on the chin and do nothing. Using the Open University, she had obtained a degree in English combined with Linguistics and had become an accomplished speech therapist working at one of the big London hospitals.

Speaking with her was a delight and before too long, I had imagined that we were together travelling the world hip by hip; Helen utilising her transferable speech therapist skills and me... Making money by blogging or something equivalently indulgent. Jeez, I'm a sucker for quickly conjuring elaborate fantasies, but hey, why not?

Life being what it is, Helen had already passed the vast majority of her expedition abroad—for a ginger person, she was obscenely bronze—so beyond exchanging Facebooks, there was relatively little chance of us ever crossing paths again. Still, I'd definitely been reinvigorated and I was back to being able to have fun as we poured gin and lemonades down our necks. This overly sweet and pretty dull beverage is justified principally by the unfortunate difficulty I'd found in getting any tonic water.

All in all, I was in a positive and pretty jovial frame of mind, other than the inevitable chain smoking and ethanol's presence in my blood-stream. That I was in a fine place by the time that I either took myself into a deep sleep or just passed out into bed is neither here nor there.

2. Day 2: The Dorm and Beyond

Unlike when my iPhone alarm startles me when I'm back home in London, for whatever reason, I can just never lie down to much extent when I'm consciously trying to relax. Something about being in a shared dormitory—at least a third cheaper—must also inhibit me from being able to properly unwind.

Also this morning, I am soon made aware that I have been bitten to smithereens by some mosquitoes. Naturally, I was just far too inebriated to bother applying any of the supposedly strong repellent that I had packed with me, luckily this green island had managed to banish any chance of contracting malaria for quite some time. Perhaps, my absence of any recollection from whatever I had dreamt on this occasion was largely due to the copious amount that I had drunk. Though some of the dreams that I'd had over the previous few days as I had been getting tanked up on the preventative tablets had been pretty vivid. It's just a shame that mosquitoes apparently find me to be so delicious.

Phoebe had actually even featured in the most recent dream that I could recall and this is a feat that had almost much never have happened before. As a general rule, I try to never pay a morsel of attention to anything that I conjure up as I'm sleeping. Instead of any of that dream diary bollocks—the kind that wishy-washy travellers are just the type to practise—I tend to just view dreams as just your mind sorting stuff out and filing things in its own way. Reading anything in to your dreams is beyond boring, surely, and it seems the height of indulgence to actually believe that anybody else should have any interest whatsoever.

The more that I travel, the more dubious I am of bothering to spend money taking these preventative medicines when I'm lucky enough to ever see far flung places. The rabies injection has always seemed like the most pointless waste of money, as having it would only prolong slightly the time needed to get medical help, rather than prevent you from needing to have further hospitalisation. Amongst plenty more inane conversation, I'm pretty sure that Stephen mentioned having had it and I responded with: "I'll just do my best to get bitten by a dog, Mate!" He was one of those people whom I could only seem to tolerate conversation with on any level if I played the part of a smug arsehole.

And I bet that Stephen hadn't been bitten to anywhere near the extent that I had, despite probably having at least twice the skin surface area to choose from with him. Still, Stephen's skin probably tastes more of gristle and fat as opposed to my scrumptious skin.

Still, believe me, if I could have erased the last—at least the last 3 double G+T equivalents then I would—but then I'd never have crossed paths with Helen. Although I've never seen her again since this little episode. Attractive as she was, with the baggage that she clearly still carried from her Nicholas, and given the amount of a sleaze that I undoubtedly would have appeared, I'm grateful that all between us just remained purely platonic as I was lying there in the abyss of my drinker's dawn, itching and scratching relentlessly.

Hold on, I had some remnants of some skin soothing cream left over from a previous trip. Magic, how it felt. Instantly after its application, I felt like a new man and my foggy head lifted immediately. Only for the itching to return again in about 5 minutes.

Also, I had been lucky that the dorm that I had chosen to spend the first night of this trip in had been and still remained so quiet. Glancing around, I noticed several other, apparently, fast-asleep people and at least 2 of the beds had been unoccupied. This was a mixed-sex room; they were again always less money and didn't stink, like the all-male dorms, which always seemed to reek slightly of something slightly untoward.

The only other active person in the room, at this time, was some almost middle-aged looking man. Whilst I don't remember what his name was—if we ever even actually introduced ourselves—he did notably just seem like a bit of a dick-head. This was mainly because, although our conversation was pretty brief, I gauged that he was one of those guys who would always have had to at least claim to have done and tried everything and beyond what you ever claimed to have experience. I really just do not have time for this.

I thought with relief that I'd not have to be spending so much as another night in this Pearl something, whatever it was called, hostel, as I had luckily managed to secure some late night bus tickets to my next port of call. The journey was, I think, only scheduled to be for 6 hours or so, but that would save me one night's stay at a hostel.

I had lunch with a couple at a basic local beach café who were friendly enough, if not slightly bolshie young Canadian tourists from Toronto. Mike and Cas-aan-dra were clearly more than the 'just good friends' that they'd insisted, but although they were fine company, I possessed absolutely no interest in learning anything whatsoever more about either of the pair. In the most amicable way possible.

Running with the apparent theme of the day, their most annoying trait was that of fervently trying to trump just about every tale that you shared with them with something 'more impressive' that they had done. This one up-man-ship and petty point-scoring was beyond boring and always depresses me a bit. Especially as it's a trait that I first remember observing in my schooldays, and although I always felt that it should have finished by the next academic year, it seems to be something that never leaves people. Including myself a little bit. Probably.

These two Toronto's had apparently 'nearly' experienced just about everything that I shared. Part of me wanted to fabricate that I was on the run for attempted or, even carried-out, homicide, just to see how they would one-up me on that. You know by now as well I do that this isn't what I bothered doing.

Their fruitless tales ranged from the insanity of accidently walking out of some shop carrying the dress that Cassandra was wearing, which looked as though it was made out of seaweed, to 'shamefully' getting caught for drunk driving. Whether the shame was in the arrogance of risking innocent people's lives through doing this or in getting caught, I have no idea or even real care.

After my mushroom pizza and nasty, mushy, ludicrously thick chips—along with taking a bit of a down turn about the negativities of the globalisation that I was shamelessly fuelling—I retired to pick my stuff up from the grotty and basic, yet sanitarily functional Pearl Palace.

The dorm room was deserted and although this solitude was exactly what I felt that I should need, something inside of me was stirring that meant that I could not even focus on my paperback book that I was trying to read for the first time since leaving the plane. Rather, that awfully soul destroying spell came down upon me where you start to reflect and analyse your position in life. It felt as though I was wasting my life waiting for my genius to be fully realised. And appreciated.

Instead, it was dawning upon me abruptly just how little my life was meaning and how different my existence was from anything that I had envisaged as an aspirational child. I felt winded, rather than put at ease, by being on my own, though it wasn't at all as if I was usually at all unhappy in my own company. The huge, yet vulnerable, ego that I carry around with me felt as though it was wearing out.

Although generally trying to be positive, I'd still say that I was enjoying life overall, it definitely felt as though I was approaching a hole with little to show for even having been out of it. Okay, nothing was categorically awful about my life, but it wasn't half what our consumerist and fierce capitalist society tells you that it could and should be. So, I'm in work and don't find it too dull and I'm pretty close to, although yet to quite crack, the 25k salary barrier; I have no dependents and can afford some luxuries, such as this trip. Although my job is not feeding in to any career that I properly want to do—whatever that is—and my potential limited prospects are haunting.

Normally, I'd have 37.5 hours a week taken up by trudging through my job. Although this predominantly involved trudging through one menial task followed by the next, it at least ensured that I didn't have any time to mindlessly wallow. It is hard not to feel resentful at times. As part of the tested generation, we were fed the old spiel that if you worked hard enough, you could achieve anything. Being a conformist sucker, I guess that I believed this myth. Perhaps this was true for my parent's generation, who first entered the grisly world of work in London in the early seventies succeeding full employment and just missing out on Ted Heath's 3 Day Week of the early '70s. They had it so easy, being able to buy a house and get awarded a mortgage, seemingly with as much ease as it now is to pass your driving test and get a motor. Even idle hands could work towards a limited, yet clear merit.

Christ, I was a sublime dolphin, jumping pretty effortlessly through just about every hoop that could be tiringly placed in front of me to get to the next phase of life as quickly as possible. Youth is wasted on the young, indeed. Always having a fairly firm grip on life always seemed to be effortless; whereas now, I have no real idea what life or anything else is all about.

This is not something that I tend to mind, and although it is far from perfection, I'm far more contented in my late twenties than I have been at any previous phase in my life. I've been incredibly short of all brass before and had my heart broken more than once if I'm honest. But people nostalgically wishing that they were still in the school playground or being leader of the pack of their school clique are the ones that have really fucked up, as if this horrid period of adolescence was the highlight of their pitiable lives. Each to their own, I guess.

I was just enjoying a nice first and solitary cigarette of the day on the balcony watching the calm azure sea rippling along as two females walked past me and we smiled at each other and then they looked at my smoking disapprovingly. The conscience I have, which can be the bane of my life, was on the verge of apologising, but before I knew it, they were both cackling in what sounded eastern European and I was obviously excluded from any conversation that could be had with them. We never got anywhere near as far as to introduce ourselves to each other. Still taking leave downstairs, I had soon settled up at this Pearl hostel and was had soon found my way to be in a taxi for the ride to the bus station.

The price of the hostel was pretty cheap overall, but I'd have resented paying so much as a penny more for these lodgings that were closer to a dive than any sort of palace. As for the standard of many hostels that I had shelled out more money for, the Pearl Palace wasn't too bad. The fact that 'palace' is a suffix not dis-common for many of the hostels that I have stayed at and it always acts a bit like salt in the wound for parting with the dosh that you're shelling out as backpacker hostels—as pleasant as they so often are—do not offer anything remotely close to any palatial lodgings!

Most of what I was looking forward to at this point involved breaking my increasingly ample hunger and listening to some music with my headphones for the first time on this entire trip.

At the coach station came flea market for various tit-bits I bought a packet of crisps and some kebabish type stick of meat, which wasn't the healthiest breakfast really. It was relatively painless to find out which part of the station my coach went from, and even the airport-security-style queue wasn't half as strenuous to go through as I know they can be. It was as I made my way towards the coach that—as always, I had that inkling that it might in fact be the wrong one; oh, my neurosis—was supposedly destined for where I wanted to get to and I ran into this guy called Phil.

Disappointingly, he was another Brit and after having introduced himself as 'Phil', I was determined not to let the fact that I'd have to resent my child to give him this name, as every Phil that I've ever had the chance to meet had always ended up being oafish and drab. Determined to keep an open mind, I entered into conversation with Phil (never knew his surname), but I couldn't help but question the seeming coincidence that I was even sat next to the only other white person on the coach, who was this buffoon.

Of course, I didn't quite know that he was so sheltered and naïve at this stage, only it didn't take long to work out that his PhD from Cambridge didn't quite translate to appearing at all cultured or civilised. He actually asked me what type of food 'bouillabaisse' (however that came up) was and also whether cocaine ever caused you to go 'crazy'. Oh dear, I thought. Not that I like to judge, but for somebody with a Master's degree in…something electronics-based, I think, to have such a shielded and unexposed turn of phrase. Call me a snob, or whatever you like, but I just think that there are certain things that you'd hope that people had experienced or at least were slightly familiar with, by the time they'd reached a certain level of maturity.

Phil was just a big C word. This is in terms of being conventional, cocooned and conservative with a small 'c'. Travelling alone for the first time in his life—obviously fair enough in itself—he was determined to have a 'good' time. What constitutes a preferable time is something that I felt was different in both of our eyes. First and foremost, Phil clearly took life way too seriously to engage in many activities that I'd call much, if any, real fun.

Still, he was more than bearable to talk with and was inoffensive to the blandest degree. He was unsurprisingly single and at just a few years younger than my fine self, seemed well on his way to securing a well-paid job and wanted to get married along with having children before too many more years passed. We really were from completely opposite ends of the spectrum on just about everything. It was principally the fact that we were such poles apart that made our conversation bearable in my eyes. Otherwise, it would have been boring with a capital B, the only shred of attraction stemming from the fact that I'm so interested in finding out about different walks of life and learning what makes other people tick.

Still, it continued to be hard work. The most interesting fact about Phil that I can maintain is that he was from Jersey, and although I've never been to the Channel Islands, at least it gave him a trait fairly exclusive. Though, perhaps it says most that is the only aspect of Phil that I'd automatically ever be able to recall. Even his hair colour and style were pretty non-descript. In fairness, he was in standard scrappy trainers, though to see him in socks and sandals wouldn't have even shocked me to any great degree. It was tiring me as I had always been convinced that there was some type of chat that I'd be able to do with anybody! Apparently not.

I put my iPod onto shuffle, though probably only actually listened all the way through to one in every 10 or so tracks that came on. On long journeys I'm no stranger to getting pretty reflective and pondering on all ranging from the healthy, the dark and the aspects of the world and my life that make little sense. Oh no, unfortunately, I was not given any chance to do so on this trip because Phil could witter for England or even Jersey combined once he got going.

It's not even that Phil was effeminate, only—perhaps because our parting was still so fresh—many of his mannerisms and traits of as good as monosyllabic conversation brought to mind my most recent summer fling with Holly. It was the sort of brief fling that when I was in it, soon felt as though it had gone on forever.

Holly was and I'm sure still is 'nice' enough, only originality, variety and a thousand other qualities that I crave were a long way away from her radar. Credit where credit's due, she did want fairly frequent sex, only as with everything else in her life, it felt as though it was running by clockwork, and it'd be hard for me now to separate any of the times that we had it from the previous or next.

Perhaps fittingly, this can make me sound pretty soft, but one of the least attractive qualities that Holly had was that she seemed a bit overly into me; I live for the chase. Maybe these 'commitment issues' are the main reason why I am continually single, only I'm not being made to compromise. Yes, lots of people sagely say how you need to 'compromise' for anything productive to ever happen, which in the case of New Labour or the Good Friday Agreement of 1998 in Northern Ireland may be true; but I think that the age of 27 is still a bit too young for such a depressing realisation.

Credibly, and a bit depressingly, I've come to think that this may be the exact same thing in reverse that Phoebe's doing to me now….though in reality, I know that this cannot be true. First off, I'm far more buoyant than Holly ever was about any potential misgivings or insecurities with respect to where I live, my friendship circle and the vast majority of people I know well. Our only ever being together intermittently is a result of circumstance, and the drive we each had to only be dictated to by ourselves and to do our own thing. She just seemed too inflexible to ever immerse herself in anything, if you know what I mean.

Juxtaposed to Holly in just about every respect is my Phoebe. I'm hers.

Strange though it may seem in light of the picture we present to the outside world, not unexceptionally, but generally, we are the first person that either turn to in any time of crisis, bereavement or major milestone. The majority of important decisions that we make are told—rather than consulted—to each other. Even ridiculous stuff, such as inane anorak information like snippets from days of the week when we were born, where and how we lost our first tooth, to when and where we had our first orgasm—and no, it wasn't together—are shared.

People have speculated shamelessly and usually with some unbeknown authority as to how 'you can't love each other that much, or you'd be together' and even 'she's obviously playing you, wake up and smell the roses, mate'. I mean, I love socialising, but en-mass—take the general public—people just couldn't be more stupid or selfish, could they?

In fairness, I may have been an innocent, bright-eyed and bushy-tailed virgin when we first met, and my comparative naivety and lack of experience could too easily have been used against the conceited and possibly even aloof sixth former that I was at the time. Though, this is the best part of a decade ago and my familiarity with all things exciting and dangerous has more than caught up, if not even triumphed Phoebe.

Phoebe may still be somewhat more promiscuous than me, but what's the odd notch on the bedpost between lovers and friends? Some less liberal friends, who are nearly always male, seem to see it as something lacking in my masculinity that I find Phoebe's breadth of romantic experience—I've never taken part in an orgy, for example—a bonus.

Many just do not, by any means, understand my obsession with Phoebe. Yet this narrow-minded chivalry just masks whatever sexual insecurities they may have, or even just jealousy that they've never experienced the openness and confidence that Phoebe and I share.

Although sounding smug or arrogant is the last thing that I'd want, it is fair to say that whilst individually we're nothing beyond babes who understand a fair bit, whereas together we could easily triumph over the world.

Jeez, it is at the end of this reflection that I notice that Phil is still rabbiting on and producing more of his white noise. I smile and nod at the rare occasion when I can be bothered; sometimes, I even go so far as to repeat the last word that he has said, part out of trying to give the false impression that I actually am listening and partly so as not to fall asleep.

This journey is taking far longer than I had anticipated. An arrival time at Aluthgama was never actually specified and isn't printed on the ticket, although I was pretty sure that I heard that it was just about 5 hours. Darkness had fallen and it was that sort of tropical black that leaves you with absolutely no idea where anything outside is. This situation is not at all unfamiliar to me and although I am no stranger to this situation, I'd be lying if I said that even the company of Phil was something of a welcome relief, without wanting to sound too bitchy.

As—especially given the head that I had awoken with—I was tired and even felt a little outside of my comfort zone, I agreed to traipse with Phil to find a hostel. Although he was happy to settle on the first beach-side place that we saw, I wasn't. Maybe I was just feeling like being stubborn; it paid off though. Instead of the overpriced beachside place that they'd recommended in the guide book, we were directed by some local to a house apparently owned by his brother who lived and worked in India. It was clean enough, and he asked for significantly less money than the hotel, so it was a done deal. Also Phil and I could be in separate rooms and (well, mine did at least, not sure about his) at least my bed had a priceless mosquito net.

Of course, there was still plenty of motion from Phil's mouth, only it was becoming more worth listening to as we were talking about ourselves in more depth. As much of an egomaniac as I could shamefully be said to be, I divulged very little about me, as Phil's drab little life was consuming the entire centre stage. It didn't come as any surprise to learn that the man was single and it shouldn't surprise me one bit to learn that he had never had any sexual contact, but this is all speculation that I didn't feel should add anything to our conversation.

Following the long and tiring day travelling, a pretty early night was more than needed. Like a light I went off, though I was awoken before too long by Mr Piggy's inevitable snoring on the other bed was. How could I not have foreseen this? He had the annoying fat face that looked as though it belonged to a person born to stink and snore. This was the worst noise that I had heard in all of my travelling experience. It wasn't even a sound anything close to that of what I'd describe as normal snoring; I can't claim to have ever before really imagined this sound, but Phil sounded like a suffocating vulture. Still, I must have managed to drift off at some point as when the light finally woke me up, it was at about 6:00 A.M.

It was as I was eating feeling and increasingly regenerated and relaxed, that I was reminded of the fact that I desperately needed to rid myself of Phil. Being with the guy long-term would only inhibit me from having the experience that I wanted on this trip. Meeting new people alongside him would only be like having to introduce the poor relation, whilst dreading that any of the people that we meet might assume that we share the same blood.

This thought reminds me that it's actually my mum's—Sandra's—birthday next week and I'll send her some form of card to go with the present that I'll have to buy her for when I get back home. It's a bit of a shame that I can't go to the 'Birthday Meal' that we'd almost certainly have to mark this largely insignificant 48th birthday. This means that she was only 20 when she gave birth to me, and my dad is 60 already. It's never been directly said, but I think the 'surprise' that I've been called is almost synonymous with 'mistake'.

Still, they did the decent old East End ritual of having a shot gun wedding and I did enter a rather loving home. We were never rich, but I never really wanted for anything particularly. The story's almost too trite that it couldn't be made up: Sandra was Keith's secretary…one thing lead to another at an office party and along I came. It was only at a printing press and neither of them were at all high-up, but it ensured that I came into a secure home.

I certainly came about in something of a whirlwind. They apparently had some sort of instant attraction, which was probably provoked by the fact that Mum wanted to find some security and sense of value by a long-time employee at the first firm (Stringer's) where she had recently become a member. To say that Dad just felt an urge to get his leg over wouldn't be in any way unfair (I have never been shielded from this fact) and Mum was apparently a bit of a goer, and that's caused me more pride than shame if truth be told. Although I was far from the richest kid in the playground, without being all sloppy, I always knew that I came from a loving home. Though Dad had the ability to be pretty temperamental and argumentative, it meant that I soon grew a backbone. Retaliation was never something to be discouraged, and although it's not what I'd aspire to, I think it did me more good than harm to have a father that I'd never dare to take for any sort of mug. You can't ever expect fully rely on anybody else, can you? Ironically, this was always beyond my parents.

We never kept any secrets and lies from each other, even given the fact that I forced Mum to have to hold maturity way beyond her years. This caused her to probably miss out on a fair bit of life experience, but she just summed this up her often-repeated phrase that 'it just meant that we grew up together'. This always struck a chord with me and is as heartfelt as it is accurate.

Dad's still plodding along working for the company, which is now based around Canary Wharf, but was on Fleet Street until about a decade ago (though this probably means closer to twenty years), I think. This has made the commute to Highams Park a bit more of a strain for Dad, but the idea of entering into an alternative career path from the job, to which he was posted as just a 15-year-old whippersnapper, has never properly occurred. Never quite was what he's actually wanted, but it's too secure for somebody with his limited remit to throw away. Like so many working-class kids of his generation, the idea of doing a fulfilling job that stretches him—and makes him disproportionately well-off compared to his parents—is the stigma that he's always faced. Yet, just as common is the inferiority complex that means that he could never want to or feel that it was necessary to enter a profession.

Always voted Labour as a young man and perhaps mainly chauvinistically loathed Thatcher significantly for this to continue into Blair, although now I'd say that he'd definitely lean the other way. And I haven't even bothered to ask him what he makes of Corbyn! In fairness, he's never actually admitted to ever voting for anything other than red, but overall, I think that he's just more apathetic and disenfranchised than anything else these days. Though he probably still watches Question Time occasionally. As not to neglect Mum here, I'll just say how having never expressed any real interest in politics, she definitely is not disengaged, and although she's never voiced her definitive party allegiance, she's more left-leaning than Dad if anything now.

All these passing thoughts were an umbrella for my big issue of the day, which was that I desperately needed to politely get rid of this Philip, who was, of course, still sprawled next to me on his increasingly dishevelled looking bed. Like its metaphor for him being within it. Sleeping on any transport had never been a forte of mine, and with it being such a beautifully scorching day, this was certainly far from any opportunity. I didn't even find it particularly presumptuous to conclude that Philip had close to zilch real knowledge or interest in politics.

Still, the thought of my parents stayed lodged in my brain. Travelling without adequate distraction perhaps should always have this effect. It seems only too obvious that this is because as an only child, they were always the consistent people that I'd share my experiences of exploring a different culture with. Friends, cousins with then even aunts and uncles may join us on the odd holiday, but intermittently.

'Family holidays' shall always be seen as a positive addition to my childhood—particularly being the sucker for nostalgia that I have always been—although as I'm sure you guessed, the ventures were a fair few degrees less exotic than my own. Understandably a beach, tasty food and cheap booze was at the highest on the priority list and we never left Europe, except for one trip to the Caribbean's Dominican Republic. The best holidays that I now recall was one year when I was really little in Cornwall and another time in Majorca. Now, whilst my folks may have, in their increased wisdom and boldness, the confidence not to always have to rely on a package, they just cannot fathom many of my holiday choices. Though in fairness, their reaction is less of disdain, and more of a feeling that it's all a bit of a weird decadence. I'm not sure where I got my penchant for travel and the only thing, if I'm being honest, that I could tenuously put it all down to is the age-old and well documented reaction to a need to escape. Not necessarily to explore or even to evade any real inadequacies with my existence, other than believing, with obvious originality, that the grass could always be greener on the other side. Even if only slightly, it had to be better, surely. It's over a decade now since I've been on any proper holiday alongside my parents and I think that we'd now—and as much as we get on—want to strangle each other after a few days in such proximity.

The next time that I could ever envisage going with my parents on any vacation is once I've settled down and somebody else, with maybe even a few children of my own. For quite a number of years now, I have more than halved the age of Sandra, and you may see the inevitability that mum may now be keen to have a grandchild or two. Well, although they'd certainly be far from discouraged, the pragmatism in my parents and even old-school traditionalism means that they'd rather that I remained a bachelor (even a confirmed bachelor going with their theme) than left anybody 'in trouble'. They are decent people.

Divorce is still a bit of a taboo to them both, even if virtually all of their relations had marriages that have long since fallen apart. To be fair, I'm far more anti-marriage than I am anti-divorce. Although part of me does feel that there is something a bit irresponsible about people bringing kids into their home and then allowing it to fall apart and go to rack and ruin. Still, without being a member of either the club that are married or with kids, I can't say that I know enough to remotely trust my opinion here. Clearly, divorce is the best option of many alternatives, though I think that needing to escape 'a loveless home' is quite an indulgent excuse if you've got children. I mean, you made your bed. All that I know is that I just can't foresee ever needing or wanting to have any of my decisions validated or approved of in the way that seems integral to any tedious ceremony.

Phil and I were in the blazing sunshine after I'd done my ablutions. We had an uninspiring breakfast and soon strolled out to what appeared to be in some lay by or coach centre detached from the centre of town. We were soon beside a kitsch looking square with a large green in the middle, a large red church and a municipal building of some description. Foresight hadn't appeared to do me any favours as I continued to be at a loss for an amiable way to separate myself from Phil…there was another beach several miles down the road that was renowned for its turtle sanctuary, as well as the chance to maybe do some surfing. I had thought that I could insist on going surfing and part ways. Only from about the middle of our initial journey onward, I just told myself to 'get a grip'. I hadn't surfed on any occasion post-puberty and compromising yourself to please somebody that you don't even particularly like or respect is probably one of the most tedious British traits that I possess. As I can be mature enough to exploit honesty being the best policy, I merely just said to Phil that: "I'm sure that we're both keen to do lots of our own things on this adventure, shall we collect our bags from the hotel and part ways so that we can do our own thing this afternoon?"

Without massaging my ego, as it just added to my discomfort, Phil looked crestfallen. There were fringing palm trees rather than any olive branches around the plaza, but I rapidly blurted, "Obviously, I think we need a proper send-off, so how about meeting back by the fountain at 8 and we can go for a farewell bite to eat?" If I say so myself, this was a genius solution to resolve the situation, and wearing an expression that I'd most associate with a sea-lion, he looked delighted and promised 'without fail!' to meet me at the said time.

When we did finally arrive at another hostel that I'd selected, it was only just on the verge of 10 A.M. so I just hoped that I'd be able to check in this early. On my own, I just went to the Blue Stripe hostel that looked most appealing to me within my price range. A dorm room may only have been marginally cheaper, though I felt that so close to the beginning of my trip, I still had a few more dorms left in me before I'd need to progress to anything better. Though too much dorm-ing can become a bit tiring (and I hate how that expression makes me sound). The hostel that I'd found did do food, which actually looked incredible and was a great value; there is not much further to say about my stay in this fairly comfortable accommodation near to the centre of town.

It was only after having another small bite to eat at the hotel and a fair few black coffees that I was ready to sort myself out in the room that I'd been given. It was disconcerting as I entered the other room which only had any belongings placed beside one other of the six beds, to find a man a decade or so older than me prancing around stark bollock naked.

I'm not a reserved prude by any stretch and I enjoy being in the buff, yet if the situation was reversed, I'd be a bit nervous that this unnecessary nudity could be interpreted as something a bit more provocative. I mean, letting it all hang out as you get changed can be expected in these circumstances, but this level of exposure in a communal area was just unsightly rudeness. It's all about context, isn't it? If it was a nudist beach—which I've enjoyed being on more than once—it would be fine; in a private room with separate single beds that you're sharing with another male, it's just invasive if it continues for duration. It certainly wasn't as though he had anything to flaunt, although I do grant from my own experience that the size of a flaccid penis is incredibly variable' from a shrivelled concertina to an anaconda, I'm sure we've all been there. But what was the unwanted male nudity on this trip that I was experiencing trying to suggest? Nothing obviously, it was just annoying and unappealing.

It would be more accurate to say that this day involved minimal that was worthy of retention. Exploring the town and drawing up some more clues as to what I wanted to do with the remainder of my travel time from my guidebooks—with a few larger stop offs in between—the time seemed to vanish without my notice.

I felt liberated as I witnessed the verge of dusk approaching, once the sun had gotten to that height where everything begins to almost glisten. The hostel that I had picked out of my guide book seemed to live up to the charm that the guide's description had afforded it. The place was bijou with only 2 small dorms accompanying a handful of private rooms. Being far too premature, from today's experience and the fact that you could tell just by looking that the breakfast the next day should be something worth paying the slight bit extra to have included the next day. Going up to my room on the first floor, the ambience of the guest house automatically put me at even greater ease as it was in a pristine condition with what appeared to be recently painted azure walls with a shiny black dado and a grey marble floor.

There were now only three other bed spaces in my dorm and one of them was of a heartily sixed double, which was taken, leaving me to take my other bits on the bottom bunk of the other bed. After having taken a shower and briefly dried down, I started reading curled up on my bed, glancing on my watch and noticing that it was somehow just passed 4 o'clock, so some hours would have to be passed before going and completing my final errand of the day in order to meet Phil.

Just then, 2 young lads clambered into the room and soon gregariously introduced themselves as 'Pat and Joe'. After half an hour or so of entertaining conversation, we all could feel as if we had quite a bit of knowledge of one another without seeming to go through any of the standardly boring and trite questions. Think that these were a pair around their early twenties, who seemed pretty worldly, with it seeming like Pat was king and Joe was more of the impish jester. Still, we all took a shine to each other and although it feels like a little bit of a shame when you keep meeting Brits, this effect was lessened by their earthily strong Irish accents. This duo were a fine crack and they were talking about how it was almost like me having spent such an amount of time they were almost itching to move on.

I'd thought that they didn't have to deal with our politics, but it turns out that they were actually Northern Irish. Having both been brought up in separate suburbs of Belfast, they'd met whilst both taking some description of English degree at the University of Liverpool (a good few years behind what Helen from my first hostel would have been, but still co-incidental) and now both lived in separate shared houses somewhere around the Finsbury Park area of north London. An area gloriously well-connected transport-wise and fairly priced, with a vibrant—or just edgily downtrodden in non-estate agent speak—atmosphere. This is an area that I'd consider to be my stomping ground, having lived in numerous shared houses around N4 and 8 postal districts for all of my post-university life up until now. They both worked in a school, though were not actually yet fully blown teachers from what I understood. We were too preoccupied enjoying ourselves to much discuss the tedium of what we each did for a living, our levels of education or where exactly we lived. Being Facebook friends was enough to ensure that if we ever wanted to find out any more information, we could ask each other.

Having only just finished the second drink, I said with a sight grimace—I'd given them the low-down on Phil—about how I'd have to go and meet him at the square's fountain to go for dinner and then, hopefully, re-join them at the ivy skirted bar where we were. I'm sure it was not though their vocally despised Catholicism (it is how they had both been born), but far more a shared understanding of decentness, that caused them to understand my position and regrettable need to keep to my arrangement with Phil. Particularly after sinking the second pint, you will be able to appreciate my desire to simply shelve all arrangements that I'd made with Phil, blocking them from my memory—which I was on an increasingly smooth road to achieving—and continue the merriment. Only, I couldn't live with myself and do that so I reluctantly traipsed on the pleasantly picturesque journey to what I'd proclaimed to be the fountain of doom.

As I'd deemed would be more than likely, Phil was, of course, already there. In terms of wanting it to be done and dusted, this was not a particularly bad thing, if it weren't for the unavoidable fact that I soon clocked that he was sporting a pair of lime-green crocs. Jeez, I thought, he doesn't do himself any favours, does he? I mean my Mum's probably got a pair of the visual grenades of her own, but then she is a middle-aged woman now and they're not quite vulgar enough to be lime finishing off a shoddily attired twenty something. Phil's exact age was something that had not been divulged and with my lack of any curiosity, I had no true idea; slightly older than me is how he looked, though I'd be less surprised for him to be younger. Read into that what you will.

My hand was put out in front of him with haste as I could not bear either the awkwardness of having to hug him. I remembered having passed a pleasant looking restaurant courtyard down an alleyway on the walk there and suggested to Phil that we go there. Anticipating that Phil would suggest going for a pint somewhere on the square, I was relieved when he simply agreed and then began to follow on; he must have a healthy appetite, after all. This ordeal was one that, after having tried and tested the waters through all angles, I felt should not go on for a second longer than necessary. Small talk is just long, isn't it, and with Phil, this had been the most relieving element of our conversation, yet even small talk can soon involve having to listen to somebody reeling off a load of lies and advertising opinions that you're really uncomfortable with.

Still, having reached the restaurant, it did live up to my idealised image, as I was able to have some barbecued octopus for starter followed by sea bream on a bed of rice and salad accompanied with a delicious tangy sauce. Predictably, perhaps I fail to be able to recall what he had—think some casserole rings a bell, although I remember thinking that it seemed to act as a culinary representation for him in appearing to be porky and bland—only all that I really wanted was for him and all of our food to disappear as soon as possible.

In fairness though, Phil proved that he could, in fact, be almost fine company, as we had a few laughs about a few mishaps that had occurred to us recently and a few things that we'd both caught on TV. As we had so little that I could find to share with him, it was still pretty stilted conversation, though after a few beers, the juice trustworthily made it all rather less effort. As the main dishes were cleared away and the dessert options were given to us, I made it all too clear that I was 'just too full' to partake. Well, the guy certainly was capable of having a mind of his own as Phil ordered some sort of sugar coated concoction that sounded absolutely disgusting to my ears.

Ensuring that I was constantly plied with enough booze, I continued to make the effort not to clearly appear to rather be somewhere else. In between the dessert order being made and it arriving, Phil broached the subject of our experiences at our former hostels arose and he went on to talk about his experiences with some 'Kayleigh'. Although I didn't bother enquiring, as there's no way that I really had of finding out, I wondered if it was the same Kayleigh as Stephen's object of desire from my hostel on the first night, and, if so, was amazed at the power she seemed to have over pitiable people. Given the journey where Phil and I had met, it seemed more than likely.

Along with it being obvious that there was 'chemistry and that we both fancied one another'. Hmm, I thought, that only looked as though it could be true from one half of this relationship from where I was standing, and the word 'chemistry' shouldn't really be confused with 'lust' from one half of the bargain. Though, of course, I kept schtum as he continued with monotonous, yet animated conversation. Whilst I'm pretty confident that my face remained a blank canvas, the point where he spoke of their parting and the kiss that he'd been going for turned into a hug was where I found it harder to suppress a pitiful internal snigger.

Phil deeply inhaled before treating me to know that, "just as I really made the first move, she said that this guy who she quite liked at the hostel had invited her up to his room to have some drinks at midnight." It sounded as though Kayleigh was being the opposite of any Cinderella that night. This almost confirmed that it was the same girl, and I had a combination of pity and admiration for the stream of desperate guys that she seemed to attract.

Plenty of nothingness about the night after I had departed the first hostel followed, and the brief ongoing between him and Kayleigh sounded more as though he was harassing the poor girl in a besotted way than anything else. Still, dessert had arrived and I could focus on little else than the fact that the time should now be nigh for me to be able to leave this increasingly claustrophobic setting with Phil as my only source of company. It would be getting towards impossible for it not to happen, but thankfully (assisted all too strongly by the natural medicine that I was quaffing), Phil was growing on me, although my estimation of him had not particularly been raised in any real way.

As the bill had arrived, all too inevitably, Phil asked of me what I was planning to do next. Well, I thought, I could lie and say that I had nothing planned as I 'fancied a one-off early one now', but to my constant disservice, I find lying overly difficult, so I just gave him the truth about having met these Irish lads at my hostel and we had agreed to meet in a bar. This benevolence extended as I lowered my arm of friendship with, "and obviously you're more than welcome to join us"; the 'more than welcome' part was certainly a mistruth, though I'd given my message.

Ah, Phil looked like a kid on Christmas morning feasting his eyes on a bulging stocking as he told me 'how delighted' he would be to take up this offer. So, we stumbled down back towards the bar and it was welcome that neither of us particularly felt the need to talk being far too bloated and on the cusp of getting aboard the drinking train.

Almost reassuringly, Pat and Joe did not look as if so much as a muscle had twitched in their appearance, beyond the fact that their faces were appearing slightly more slumped. We all hugged as if to confirm our inebriation and Phil was clearly a bit overwhelmed as, "Yay, you're just in time for round three!" beckoned from Pat's lips.

Joe soon followed with, "What a tremendous pleasure it is to meet you, Phil, we've heard so much about you" and we were all creasing in hysterics whilst Phil's likeness was as self-satisfied as the seal who has now who has just been thrown a fish.

This night was clearly going to get messy from the onset. Still, at least I'd got a good lining with the adage of some of my own fish and I was having the best time in weeks. The company had all been fun and even Phil's shielded idiocy had only contributed to our entertainment, combined with the blessing that he was almost, without any doubt, fully oblivious to any subtle mocking.

Enhancing my delight was Pat's unexpected declaration that, "We've not much touched the gram of blow that we bought yesterday if you two care to join in now?" This was not in any way something that I particularly desired the experience at any point on this trip—it is but a stone's throw from my doorstep back in Peckham—only I'd be lying to say that I ever found this offer anything but appealing. Anyway, I don't like to be rude!

The delight of white powder easily persuaded me to take it on board. Sticking to my ethos that, provided I never actually spend any money on any gear, then partaking of whatever freebies that may come my way can only be a positive thing, I went to the bathroom to take on board a generous line.

It was as I came back to join the revelry of reaching utopia that Phil had to scurry to the bathroom to vomit, perhaps as a subconscious signal of his disapproval for ingesting these Class A substances. The limited respect that I had for the guy would increase somewhat if he had politely refused the offer of joining in with our debauchery. Still, given the amount of mindless ramblings and delusional overconfidence in his plain appearance, I couldn't imagine how unbearable just a few grains of the substance should inevitably make him become.

The bar was gradually emptying, and only armoured with plenty of beer, a couple of bottles of red wine and a significant amount of gin, we were more than ready for this night to long continue, though it was sure to end up in as something of a hazy blur.

Having reached the early hours, we were all still in a pretty vertical state. This was with the exception of Phil, who had hours ago ordered a taxi for and insisted that he get safely to his hostel, even though I couldn't really care less at this point as I was having too much of a fun time. It was then that we were able to let stream off, as we agreed that the time was ripe to go and hit a drinking den in the town.

After a prolonged walk, we arrived on top of the main plaza and were caving that next sip of the elixir of life. Despite being a weekday night, the square was thankfully far from empty, and it looked as though there'd barely be room at all to swing a cat at the weekend. Everywhere on the plaza looked that bit all too family friendly and on the pricier side too, which predictably, we did not fancy. Just a couple of blocks from the fountain where I had met Phil all those hours earlier—which now seemed like a lifetime—we found this low-key nightclub where you could only noticeably see locals.

As obvious Westerners, we automatically attracted a wealth of attention. This was hardly anything other than welcome, beyond feeling the need to check your pockets for your valuables significantly more often than usual and the frequent propositions for some sexual satisfaction. I then gained some insight towards, and I could almost fully appreciate, what must be like for women to fervently feel objectified as they are leached upon in bars and clubs back home.

I didn't recognise any of the music at all, though I cannot say how little this mattered. I liked the sound of it and anything following intermittent trips to the bathroom to do something more exciting than to urinate sounded fantastic, like everything else about myself. It was one of those perfect occasions where I cannot much remember experiencing the direct effects of any drug I had taken. I was just more than happy perched high up on cloud nine.

The rest of the experience in this den is no more than a haze, and I all that I can remember next is stumbling back into our hostel and crashing in our beds, despite the intense light in our room. In many ways, it is only by pure fortune that we made it back to our hostel in one piece; especially considering that we'd spent most of the night going our separate ways, all absorbed by some local's enthusiastic recollection of interesting tales.

We did some of the usual analysis of the night and its goings on as we staggered back to our hostel. I think that as the generally apparent lesser man of the two, Joe was bragging about how he caught a blow-job after being dragged in to a female toilet cubicle. Joe was, soon after having met him, a guy who I would happily walk over hot coals for, only I couldn't help but notice how he had a tendency to exacerbate the truth by offering us an entertaining yarn or five. The truth in whether he'd had oral sex in a toilet cubicle that night couldn't interest me any less.

Still, Joe and Pat were both really sound guys and I trusted them implicitly. It has been said before that I can easily be too trusting and even easily lead. This is complete bollocks. If I do actually want to do something advertised to me, then why not follow suit? As long as my judgement (clouded or unclouded!) always comes first, then I don't care whether or not I seem to be copying other people. As we may have established, I enjoy alcohol, and this infamously causes people to do things that they later regret and make casual mistakes. The fact that we should all be well aware of the effects of this toxin is why I don't have any time for people using it as an excuse for anything. Don't get me wrong, I've made numerous mistakes on alcohol, some more embarrassing than others. Only, as I think that I'm grown up enough to be all too familiar with the numerous alternating effects of alcohol, to me you have to acknowledge every choice you ever make—no matter how inebriated—as solely your own responsibility.

As I was beginning to perk up the following afternoon, after having slept through breakfast (that is that my appetite had resumed and I was confident that I was well beyond having to wretch), I began to fall deeper into the most unproductive drinker's dawn spell; that of self-loathing. Ironically, I was fulfilling the aims that I had set for this trip—having fun with an absence of accountability—although I was feeling a greater degree of hollowness and inadequacy at not exploring the wonders and meeting the people from the country that I was in. As enjoyable company as Joe and Pat were proving to be, I could picture that spending much more time travelling alongside them should ensure prolonged damage to my internal organs and achieve next to nothing. In a nutshell, whilst the litany of binges that I'd be sure to experience with them were great, the overall experiences couldn't encapsulate much beyond having a decent weekend back home. It was a sad thought, but we'd need to part ways.

Pat Halliday and Joe Atkins gave adequate protestation, indulging my ego, when I announced the fact that we'd have to separate. Though I believe that Pat was pretty close to the mark when he wryly announced, "Ah well, I think that we know you well already, so I reckon that you leaving now's probably the kindest thing that you can do for us all!" Along with the majority of things that we had shared with each other on this trip so far, it was merely met with a little laugh and swig of beer. Yes, we were already back on the juice, but none of us were in the mood to actually have anything but a quiet one tonight. All in all, I was mostly just impressed with my epiphany to seek something other than instant gratification so early on the trip. Although it would be sad to wave goodbye to Pat and Joe, it'd be necessary if I wanted to attain anything worthwhile from this break.

The cards soon came out and the time passing until the early hours was enjoyably spent drinking, smoking and putting the world to rights. Although times in each other's company was enjoyable, I think that it was mutually felt—however silently—that it was really a good time to part ways, as me being with them was a bad influence on both parts. As much fun as it was we could easily lead each other astray bringing out our worst qualities in one another.

For some unbeknownst reason, I was actually winning the card games and—as this was the method of gambling that we had resorted to—hadn't had to buy a single drink all night from the beloved bar from the previous evening.

It was ironic and perhaps even typical of me, that upon beginning to actually achieve much of what I'd probably gone on this trip for—fun, possible promiscuity and unaccountability—it was not quite doing the trick. Of course, it was still obviously early days, yet it didn't feel as though my head was on the right road to get into gear, let go and ultimately find that temporary peaceful place. Wherever this place was, I did not know, only I was convinced that my venturing further down into the country that I was in should—psychologically at least—allow me that little bit more detachment from the Smoke.

3. Day 4: Back on the Road

Awaking, I felt surprisingly buoyant and refreshed. It was welcoming to see that Pat and Joe were also consistent in being early risers. Taking a quick shower and even a dry shave, for some reason I still don't quite fathom—on a monotonous side, I do tend to be more of a fan of not using shaving cream—as from my experience, the overconfidence that it offers increases the risk of slicing into your face.

Just before we began to traipse down for the complimentary breakfast, which inevitably was due to consist of some fried egg and fresh bread—which is about perfect for my morning appetite—and a few mugs of Americano. Although it all-round seemed to be the best choice to part ways with these new found mates, our parting would be tinged with a smidgen of sadness and even some renewed exposure. I'd once again be in an environment where there would be no one else to rely on in any way.

A few man-hugs set us on our separate ways. Not being overly tactile, the fact that we embraced so soon after having first met signifies that we're almost certainly going to remain in touch after having parted.

This time, I was going to travel by rail—one of my favourite forms of transport, as much of a square as it may make me sound—to the Francophone sounding 'Galle'. From Thomas the Tank Engine, to having the chance to get aboard the Trans-Siberian Express in the noughties, I've always been attracted to the romanticism of train travel, despite never much wanting to watch Brief Encounter. I'm a sop at the best of times if I'm honest.

Making the most of the chance to use this hostel's—which I can't for the life of me remember the name of now—Wi-Fi facilities, I checked my emails and was relieved to see that there was nothing of any importance to deal with. Perhaps, it says much about the realism of growing up that email is now my first port of call rather than any social media.

Time was on my side, so I did take a quick look on Facebook to keep a vague track of my home life. It's funny that we feel the need to always retain some awareness of what is going on back home, which I find alien to the traditional concept of having a 'holiday'. It's deplorable that we must always be contactable in order to be viewed as accountable. Still, this aspect of Orwellian society has clearly won now and we all march obliviously into it like lambs to the slaughter. If you can't beat them, join them, the growingly apathetic side to me says.

Enough of this tirade, as a more pressing matter arises when I see that I have a message from Phoebe. Instantly, I uplift. Any contact from Phoebe always succeeds in giving me that more glowing gut feeling, although I don't read as much into it as I am about to have the pleasure of doing. The last time that I saw Phoebe was at the Cat and Mutton in London Fields and it was a joyous evening that just resulted in two long-time mates reminiscing and bringing out the best in each other. Talking with pride at how we were always able to drink in the Dove and the pub we were enjoying presently when we were underage. London Fields and Upper Street were our haunts as the almost (in a way that deviates from any classical theorist's definition) contemporary petty bourgeois that we were. Happy days.

This was but two weeks or so before I went travelling. We were having a joyous time and were properly reminded of how well we bounced off of each other. Due to the proximity to my upcoming travels, and out of respect for our emotions and Phoebe's continuing torrid relationship with James, this rendezvous remained purely platonic; complication was just not what either of us needed. The sexual tension was inevitable and if either of us made the first move, you could almost guarantee that it would be reciprocated.

Phoebe and I had, for the first time in our knowing of one another, become pretty expert at just being close friends and nothing more. Our flings had never lasted for more than a fortnight and had painfully (I wince to even think about it) had always been brought to an amicable end by Phoebe. It could be observed that my purpose in Phoebe's life is to validate her ego and sexual prowess when things go wrong in her life, but I am only too aware that this just isn't the case. It's not as though I fail to attract plenty of interest elsewhere, and in fairness, although I am the chaser, Phoebe's reasoning that it's just not 'the right thing to do' to enter a relationship are true enough when we have become involved.

So, I read little into seeing that Phoebe has sent me a message, beyond thinking that it is going to me a funny read. She was winging—which is unlike Phoebe to ever much do—a tad about how much she loathed the treatment she was receiving at the coffee shop where she was based in Chalk Farm. It was handy for her as she lived somewhere around Camden Town and has done so for about the past five years, I've only stayed over there twice and not for ages, and it's been quite some time since we've had one of our properly full-blown and mind-expanding flings. The last time that we even slept together is a whole eighteen months ago, and this barely counts in itself anyway, as it was on the mid-morning of New Year's Day after both having departed separate parties and needing some affection to start the year off. Phoebe's by far the most generous, fulfilling and rewarding lover that I've ever been with.

Initially, I had some slight disappointment that the message didn't appear to be as long as I'd have wished, yet with size obviously isn't everything and the contents of the message highlight this. It read: 'Darrrrrrrren, I've just had to storm out of my job! Also, that James guy that I told you about was such a sneaky and spineless cunt and I'm thinking of coming out to join you for a little bit. I need a break and I've been pretty boring recently, so have the funds to book a flight. The job actually paid quite well actually, clever me quitting it. Can we talk properly sometime soon? Give me a time! XXXXX. Ps. I promise that I'll try and stick to it this time. Pps. I've cut my hair really short!'

This was marvellous news. The elation that I felt was even slightly intensified by the fact that I knew that it was time to get to the station to get aboard my train to Galle, on the Southern tip of the island. I just wouldn't have time to respond to this message until I'd properly thought my response out. This would mean avoiding my all too standard reaction of just hastily sending some words strung-together to Phoebe. It wasn't that we weren't well beyond me ever sounding too desperate or clingy, but making people wait before finding out what you have to say is perhaps practised too often by our generation, though does have a purpose.

What she had done to her hair was also intriguing. In fairness she had reinvented her hair plenty of times before and I was pretty sure that this chameleon would still be super attractive to me bald or grey. It was sure to be something that I was given to find sexy and stylish.

The absence of any signal meant that instead of focusing Phoebe's message contents I could instead just deal with concentrating on getting to the railway station and getting to my next destination.

Chaos is the welcoming backdrop of the station as I end-up having to alter direction at least three times to board my train, so it's with huge relief, some excitement and also a bit of exasperation that I finally find my seat. I'm pleased to see that it's the bottom bunk in a cabin with a big glassed window. This should have been a journey that I was eager to commence, though I'd be lying to say that I felt much beyond the remainder of the agitation that I'd felt navigating my way across the train station; my stomach was still a bit heavy, if you can relate to this dis-settling feeling. These all too lucid bouts of self-deprecation fuelled by nicotine and alcohol give me a feeling of the wind lapsing from my sails.

Matters were not aided as the phenomenon that all too frequently seems to be a bleak reality of aging; a breezy feeling drinkers' dawn intensifies rather than abates as the day lapses through. Particularly in motion. Indeed, a short trip to the train toilets to relieve myself was necessary, though in fairness to myself, the odour exuding from the confined lavatory was enough to provoke a nasty reaction in itself, without being coupled by the effects of last night's ethanol.

Anyway, I did feel much better, and was grateful that I could keep my rucksack to hand rather than have to sacrifice time queuing to dump it in a stow. After scrubbing my mouth and teeth, I was certainly in a better place, although not quite feeing that sociable yet. Nobody that I had seen around me in the cabins around me looked that keen to talk or that desirable to talk with—I couldn't help but journey over my much over trodden memory lane—and Holly was the main feature of it this time.

Reliable, approachable and desirable are some of the first things to say about Holly. Apologies if this comes across as though I am objectifying women, it is the last thing that I'd want; appearing underhand in directly comparing anybody that I know goes far beyond childishness in my book. Holly is conventionally incredibly pretty—the fact that she was what I'd believed to be above my league is what attracted me to her in the first place—I always need a challenge and to push what I'd consider to be above my weight and Holly undoubtedly filled this urge. Her beauty and intellectualism would definitely be considered well above anybody that I'd been properly with at any point of my life and was conventionally my best 'catch' that I'd ever had. This conventionalism is one of the main factors going against Holly.

Never could I describe the continuously on and off partnership that I have with Phoebe in such casual layman's terms. It means much more; to both of us. Beyond the fact that Phoebe was more than hot, she was less a striking picture of orthodox beauty than

Holly. Phoebe gave me the levels of enigma and excitement that could always make the butterflies come back to my stomach with greater intensity, rather than diminishing as the years passed.

Phoebe always retained a mystique, whereas everything was known and predictable about Holly—this is her room, her bed time, the shops she went into, then things she wanted to buy, where her dream place to live was (in Surrey if you don't mind!), how much she wanted to earn by the age of 30, how many kids she wanted and plenty more—it was all so nauseating. The stability and heartfelt affection that Holly gave must seem so ideal to many. This is one of the reasons why I just found that I had to let her go in the end. Clearly, this is not principally out of the goodness of my heart, yet her vast array of qualities were so wasted on me. If you want somebody ever-dependable who loves to inflate your personality—'oh you're so wild' and 'you're just hilarious'—then Holly's the ideal girl for you. This worship just makes me go flaccid to think about. And perhaps it can go both ways, but she struggled around my friends, who all have big personalities and probably are intimidating to those not so willing to just let their hair down. We're all lovely people who just want to have fun, and there are enough of us not to have to bother with people who don't seem to make the want to make some effort. Anything goes, and it's not as though we're at all expecting people to behave in any sort of way or have any particular opinions or musical interests etc., but we have limited time for anybody that just can't hold their own.

As much as it pains me to say, Holly is just boring when push comes to shove. Every part of her life seems to be structured, and she seems to be living against some sort of metaphorical clock. Maybe I should feel a little bit guilty at least for deserting her—however amicably I tried to make this happen—but within a couple of years I could see that she'd want to have children, fairly imminently upon getting married, with some sickeningly expensive honeymoon and a mortgage. Thinking about this too deeply makes me want to faint. It's not even as though I'd have to be a house husband to want to stick my head in an oven, only I think I'd just die of 'natural causes' as a result of the tedium. Principally, I know that as I tend to always believe that 'you make your bed', I'd choose to be stuck this empty shell marriage until the Grim Reaper saves me one day. Due to my lifestyle and the natural tendency of life expectancy, it's not as if I wouldn't be marooned for the rest of my life.

It's not that I have anything against having a family and carrying on within the rat race, only I'd need to be doing it alongside somebody able to not take themselves too seriously. Holly does, and you bet that if ever she was confronted about this, she'd respond with the 'what do you mean? I can let my hair down as good as the next person when I want to'. The suffix to this, personifies lie to Holly; even every aspect of her leisure time has to be managed and this just defeats the object in having any of it in my eyes. Hopefully, Holly's getting further well on her way and achieving her goal of getting to the top of her career as a worthy human rights lawyer. She'd probably be earning about double the amount that I was on now and this was never at all an issue between us in any respect—I'm hardly an alpha-male at all by any measure and as long as I can comfortably fork out my rent with my council tax etc. then I don't much care.—It is just that Holly is far more the ideal consumer, which again she'd vehemently deny. It's not that she's narrow-minded enough to be overly materialistic, only she's impressed by money for money's sake and she does relish owning the 'best' possessions. In this way, I think that I did her a favour by letting her go, as in terms of a trophy, I'm far rustier than the prize possessions that she could set her sights on. I think that I can just go down as that 'eccentric' boyfriend on her list. Our existences just do not complement.

Without trying to guise my finishing with her under any magnanimity, I'm being genuine in saying that I believe, as I even did at the time, that I did her a huge favour by letting her go. This girl that graduated with a first from the University Warwick (her personality sums this place-up in my eyes) a year before I would have graduated (although we hadn't met by this point) and comparing Holly and Phoebe's lives in terms of their looks and intelligence is far too impossible to even bother with. It's as though they come from different storks at opposite ends of the spectrum. They're both admirable people who have their hearts firmly in the right place, but poles apart. Although the former is of the crème de la crème in terms of academia and work ethic, along with not being extremely sheltered, she doesn't seem to have any firm grasp or understanding of...life and how the world is put together. Whilst Phoebe doesn't know her facts so well, or have even a great deal of specific factual knowledge, I always feel that I'm learning fascinating things from her, and she leads me towards new experiences. We're a unit when we're together, only Holly and I will just orbit around one another throughout the week and make passionate love at a couple of intervals. It was usually on specific days and this isn't even a joke.

The irony is that although still it can barely be classed as much more than a fling, Holly's was the longest continuous relationship that I've ever been in, beyond my University girlfriend, Martha, who pretty much consumed our 3 years around Norwich at the UEA before suddenly parting. This was not unexpected as we didn't ever love each other or even seem to like each other much by our closing year of studying. Clearly, it's not as though I'm somebody who's always been in a relationship by any stretch, but Martha does allow me to think that I can understand how you can easily get sucked into it and put up with a long rut down to ease above all else.

Despite having shared so much time with her, Martha has largely been long forgotten and hasn't actually occupied my thoughts, except for the occasional passing flashback, for a number of years. I'm still her friend on social media, but any mutual friends that we had were mainly hers (as my mates are far too much fun for her) and I can't say that I know anything of her whereabouts, marital status or workplace these days. Beyond limiting the amount of fun that I may have had at university, I can't say that I can say anything particularly good or bad came from our relationship and this blandness of recollection can be said to symbolise our relationship. Phoebe was always, in keeping with her character, polite and courteous when we all met and although it was not overly obvious to the outsider, I could always see that she had no real interest in Martha. Phoebe never voiced any opinion of us being together and I think that she always knew that my feelings were never a smidgen compared to our devotion. Never quite understanding why I was with Martha is probably the best way to sum it up. We've all got something of a Machiavellian side tucked well beneath the surface, and part of me believes that Phoebe probably took some delight in witnessing me enduring the relationship that I had with Martha. It further validated the love that I had for her in every respect.

It was as I repeated this realisation for the umpteenth time, that a shudder almost ran straight through me and I was restored to being back in the present with focus on my journey.

The scenery outside the train was beautiful. Whereas a decade ago, I'd have chosen the cheapest third-class cabin, which is half outside, now I could be in my natural habitat as I ventured into the bar carriage. This was indeed where all of the other 'affluent' Westerners were, complete with their holy shirts, sling backs and slacks. They were all old, beyond a group of guys that were depressingly juxtaposed against such varied and exquisite terrain; they looked as though their flight had diverted from the intended destination of Kavos. Avoiding these late-teenage, amoeba-seeming idiots like the plague, I perched down on the one remaining bench seat at the quietest table, opposite a haggard looking man with wispy grey hair. Like me, he was supping his pale ale and it wasn't until three quarters of an hour or so that we even made proper eye contact.

We ended up introducing ourselves and he responded, "Morning, my name's Donald." This was a brisk sentence and I could gain absolutely nothing from this friendly enough voice that sounded like that of a lifelong chain-smoker. There was also something of the European Commissioner Donald Tusk in his appearance, but I did not feel the energy to raise the name similarity to a figure that a) I'm not sure he's be aware of, or b) whether their resemblance went beyond sharing a forename. The next action — which I found to be a bit funny—was slapping a cigarette patch onto his upper left arm; validating or what? Then we entered into some discourse.

Amongst exchanging peasantries, he was rather unsurprisingly ex-military. Not resembling Captain Birdseye, he had been in the army and was admirably transparent in claiming that having retired from service but 2 years past, that he was having tremendous difficulty in adjusting to a life in Civvy Street. This was against the backdrop of a broken marriage after his wife—I forget her name—eloping off with a dude that she'd been having an affair with for no less than 10 years whilst Donald was serving 'queen and country!'

Jeez, I thought, made all of the more dramatic—which aspect I was naturally relishing—by the fact that this happened almost synonymously with his departure from military service. Toppled by the fact that his son, Julian (you have to be more than prepared for this with a choice of this name, I was rather ashamed for not being able to help thinking) also came out as gay, to add some more salt to this congealed trifle. Although Donald didn't strike me as the bigoted sort of homophobe, he'd been in in the forces, and I remembered hearing on *Newsround* in what must have been the mid-1990s, or maybe later, that all sexual orientations had to be included in the military. Even at the time, I remember thinking that it was bizarre that this was happening so late-on, although I guess that homosexuality was still illegal until 1967, so fast in some respects, but going with my 'you made your bed' mentality, you either have to do one or all in my view. Consistency and all of that, and I guess that a lack of this is at the heart of half of the world's problems.

The fact that Donald was complete with an abundance of his own concerns to spout off was just what I felt that I needed; I was able to give my vocal chords and mind a rest and could keep myself a blank canvas. Our meeting became the perfect representation of how train travel is my favourite as it confines you—for better or worse—alongside people who you should never otherwise cross paths with and have any chance to learn about. So, all in all, it provides a window for you to experience personalities that you would otherwise be most unlikely to come into contact with, which seems the perfect construct in my eyes.

As I am found to be delicious by mosquitoes, Donald couldn't help but courteously express some concern for the array of trademarks that these beastly creatures had planted around my skin. As if to be deliberately typecast, Donald came out with: "Och, aye, you don't need to be no dermatologist to see that those creatures have taken some serious interest in your skin, Mate! If any lady's into your body that much, you're one hell of a lucky guy!" I laughed along to this pretty trite old man joke and he kindly offered me some supposedly 'ultra-strong' repellent.

Upon my standardly British response of, "But it's yours, I'll get some stronger stuff at Galle…" After he had assured me that he was jetting off back to Glasgow in just a few days and the 'you'd be doing me a favour really', I had no choice but to accept. It's not that I'd like to think that I was any sort of scrounger or liberty taker, but occasionally being bequeathed things was an added benefit to lengthy train travel. It stands to reason that I try to give out as much as I ever take from people.

After but a couple of hours, we docked within Galle station (Donald had a few more stations which could act as an interchange that he required). That feeling of being completely on your own that can fluctuate between being liberated and feeling a bit scared; it was certainly the former which ruled on this instance. Bolstered still by knowing that I'd soon be actually speaking to Phoebe, once I had got myself sorted in terms of where I was staying.

The cheap place that I plumped for wasn't too far from the station to walk, and due to it being phenomenally inexpensive, relatively clean and seemingly convenient to get around from. I climbed up to the third floor of the soulless concrete block that I was to be sleeping in, wiped the sweat from my forehead and crashed down onto a bed; all of the dorm was free and unoccupied, which perhaps tells all about how sorry the hotel appeared. Especially if Phoebe were soon to come, a dash of solitude was precisely what the doctor had ordered.

Looking at the time, it was relieving to know that with the difference, now would work out as a fitting time to try and arrange to Skype Phoebe. This was a bit of a long shot, as Phoebe is infamously untraceable, but seemed like the best thing to do. Fortunately, the hotel did have a computer with Skype, I had a written record of my user name and password, and Phoebe was online so that I could soon ask her if it was a good time to call on Facebook Chat. Within a couple of minutes, there we were in each other's eye view.

There she was in her white—innocent, I think not—dressing gown as she was lounging in front of the fireplace. This in itself was sufficient imagery of the British décor to make me feel incredibly privileged—although also slightly alienated from my home turf—to be in such tropical surroundings.

Phoebe laughed as she blew me a kiss from the toasty looking setting, sprawled across a white rug on varnished floorboards. We exchanged few pleasantries, as they were always pretty meaningless between two people who know each other inside out. True to form, Phoebe's impulsivity managed to yet again startle me when she soon disclosed that, "I land where you are in three days' time." She IS one of the most intelligent and perceptive people that I've had the pleasure to have met, yet her not being able to recall or even much retain the name of where she was heading shouldn't surprise me in the least.

In some respects, it could even have been called presumptuous and reliant of Phoebe to sporadically book a flight to where she believed (albeit accurately) was the country that I was staying in. For somebody without a great deal of disposable income, she would probably have saved half of the airfare having done enough research. Sometimes, I wish that I could follow this aspect of her raison d'être, but some things just cannot be a reality. I just said that if she gave me a time, I'd come to meet her at the airport. Relieving though it was, she said, "Just drop me where you're staying when I meet and join you at your hotel!"

Responding with, "To be fair, you usually show up eventually…" all was set for Phoebe to be with me in just about two days. Sometimes, life's euphoria is just too good and this was one of those instances.

Phoebe apparently had to rush off to do 'something', but I really couldn't care less what it was, with communication ending on such a high and with such a vast amount of tingly excitable future prospect.

All of the plans that I'd had of the destinations that I had wanted to visit imminently had vanished, in all honesty, as my heart was intent on looking and feeling my best—and most relaxed—when Phoebe arrived. There was also little real thinking work to do either. I'd resigned myself to just spending one night in this godforsaken dry hell hole and then returning to where I had parted ways with Donald earlier on, as this should be easiest place to rendezvous with Phoebe. From the brief bit that I'd read and pictures that I'd seen of the place, this other town looked far larger and this more vibrant. Although in fairness, I obviously had barely even touched down in or seen any of the place where I was staying, so it was rather premature to cast judgement.

A rush of blood to my head that had inevitably succeeded the exchange with Phoebe, and a shower followed by a brief nap seemed the best remedy to settle down on earth again. This was successful as I went out like a log and awoke little over an hour later after my nap following a shower, feeling completely regenerated and recharged. Now, I felt ready to go and start to explore the town by dusk and everything outside of the hostel's windows looked far more appealing than it had done by daylight.

Getting out on the highly congested road with its uneven pavement, hordes of stray cats and dogs once again made me wonder whether having invested in a rabies vaccination may have been the wisest decision to make. Although I fork out a wealth of money for tablets to hopefully combat the numerous strands of malaria—half tantamount to the resourcefulness of mosquitoes! In many ways, the antimalarial medications are little more than delaying the impact of the disease anyway. Although malaria seems rather ubiquitous and as I've certainly never volunteered to work alongside beasty canines before, I've always felt that I can use my common sense to avoid ending up scratching myself with foam resonating from my mouth. In instances like these, I question my instinct and wonder whether I should not have just gone to some renowned quality resort in Europe with some mates, had a holiday fling and be done with all of the tribulations of an adventure. Luckily, this insane thought has the duration of but a millisecond.

Engaging in any paths so trodden should bore me no end; I mean I'm not saying there is something majorly exclusive about the forms of traveling that I enjoy, but I relish any exploring. So, whilst I was under my spell of a little nervousness, and with no real familiarity with the barely lit streets that I was treading, I was in my element. Everybody around, whether old or young looked pretty ropy, though seemed content. My elated mood probably had more to do with this than anything else. From ragged toddlers, to elders with curvatures of the spine and hairs growing out of places that I wouldn't have imagined that they could, everybody looked like they were serving a purpose in the animated.

Although I was clearly an outsider, I was included within this backdrop with propositions of 'weed, coc-ca, skunk…' at least thrice. I failed to detect any real hangouts and although many of the people that I was passing were clearly inebriated to some extent, this seemed more than likely to be done of street corners or from their own basic homes. After about half an hour of walking, and praying that my sense of direction had not let me down here—as weak as it was, I at least had remembered to place a hotel card in my wallet, so I could always get some tuck-tuck or even taxi cab—I stumbled into 'Ritzy's'.

It is extremely rare for me to be able to recall the names of many—even the best—bars that I have frequented whilst on my travels. This bar was an exception. Despite having flickering and only half lit-up gaudy flashing red and yellow lights surrounding its name, this was one of the droopiest and dim looking drinking holes that I ever had the displeasure of entering. But, I'd again by lying to say that part of me wasn't celebrating having discovered something so authentically off of anybody in the world's beaten track. Even the greeting that I got given by the weedy male bartender (with a cigarette in one hand and a drink in the other) contributed to making me feel like some member of a Mafia. The dis-ease that I felt in thinking that I was the only outsider that this place had seen in at least a couple of decades cannot even properly be communicated. Just imagine an elephant in the room.

The barman in fact looked relieved when I merely asked for a deck of cigarettes and a bottle of beer. This was swiftly given to me and I went to the small veranda outside and settled down. The beer, in keeping with the venue that I was in, was not one that I had ever sampled before and was almost startlingly smoothly delicious tasting. After four of five swigs, nature called for my cigarette to be lit. 'Oh shit' I felt as my stomach sank realising that my lighter, even after the best possible coaxing, was going to stubbornly refuse to perform a spark.

The triad of what seemed to be family members at the adjacent table appeared rather abrasive and hostile to just my presence alone, so asking them 'if I could borrow a lighter' didn't seem that it would be a wise move. Instead, I traipsed back inside and half a large bottle of beer didn't seem like it should be enough to make me feel largely welcome and at-home by the clientele of Ritzy's. Responding to my ill-serving black lighter, a man with a colossally sized nose, many grey specks in his hair and a bizarrely ill-matched odour of Ovaltine, signalled to me that he had some matches. We struck up our cigarettes. Notably, he was puffing the full-strength red version of the blue cigarettes that I had chosen and I don't really care if this caused him to believe that I was too much of a pansy.

Anyway, this bloke seemed pleasant enough and I volunteered him for us both to buy a beer. Happily, he accepted and we took them outside together. This guy was actually a great crack. Long a widower, unfortunately, with three children and eight grandchildren already, he had clearly experienced a fair bit of life. We briefly touched on sport, politics (he had been a communist party member) and even religion. The two no-go areas were covered and we had had no reason to quarrel. It was probably helped in this instance that we tended to agree on all of these fundamental larger questions of life, but I was proud of the way that this mysterious evening was turning. Paying for Mufasa's (I couldn't retain his actual name, but it sounded similar enough to the Lion King character for me to choose this way of remembering it, loathing the fact that this may appear casually racist) drinks all night was something that I felt was more fair than patronising. He didn't protest and to have his company was enough privilege. We had smoked through my fresh new packet of cigarettes and drank enough to be way beyond sobriety—for me at least—and I considered this an apt call to make tracks to my hostel.

Standing up and leaning across to shake hands and bid Mufasa adieu, he offered me the chance to go around a few corners and see his workshop. He'd told me that he was a stone carver and taking a look at his work seemed like a worthy thing to do, although it was now well into the early hours. Once again—I can but blame my Britishness—I am ashamed at feeling that my imbued cynicism made me feel obliged to believe that I'd be asked to pay the guy some money for something that I didn't really want in the first place, and guilt-tripped if I refused. But this never occurred, as with pride, his story began with 'this trade's been in the family for over 100 years…' And went on to show me that he possessed a UNESCO certificate and pictures of several apparent celebrities (that I was not familiar with) drinking hot drinks around his studio.

As much as I was tremendously impressed by his family's franchise, sadly my highlight of the visit was still being offered some local grappa-type liquor. This was so delicious that only a misanthrope could not appreciate the offer. I saw a piece on the news quite recently before leaving England, exploring the extent to which our culture can almost make you feel like a leper if you choose not to use alcohol. However tenuously, I just thought that this tendency of being expected to drink unless you state otherwise was a worldwide phenomenon, but then I just thought what a fool I was for thinking this as the entirety of my contact with this man had revolved around drinking copious amounts.

Admittedly, I could be said to have quite a penchant for drama in itself. Perhaps this is why I am forced to ask myself how I can feel that is something particularly lacking in this anecdote, as it does not contain any drama whatsoever. Gratuitously, I took advantage of being offered a second liquor—though monetarily my vulgarly commercialised mind reminded myself that he'd still be in arrears given the amount of drinks that I'd previously bought—and then felt overdue to hit the hay. There is nothing more that should be said about that night beyond the fact that I performed my all too long accustomed to trick of falling down a kerbside a spraining my ankle. Beyond muttering a few expletives, there luckily this time wasn't any prolonged consequence to this, and with there not being anybody around to rightfully cackle a little at my stumble, I just had to laugh a little to myself at my own ridiculousness.

The part in between this little buckling episode and waking up and inserting the bottle of water that is always sleeping beside my bedside has to be counted as a perk to my gradually growing maturity. For all of the praises that I've sung about the drinks—and beyond the trick of it being the last alcoholic drink that I consumed, with its taste still in my mouth, I can't solitarily blame it for my misfortune—I felt more hungover than had done in months or even years.

And I'd ideally wanted to depart to meet Phoebe sometime this morning. It still being before 8 o'clock, I could easily still do this, technically. Although I felt as though I was at death's door, complete with a sandpapered mouth, and would certainly have to skip breakfast beyond some black coffee (even after having to re-clean my teeth several times, if you know what that means), it was clear that this self-induced discomfort would have to be endured.

The logical thing to do was to navigate my way to the bus station again and try and find some light at the end of my tunnel for all of my suffering, assuming that I didn't drop dead and have to be carted off along the way. *Might as well try,* I thought.

For whatever reason, I traipsed all of the way to the bus station. Perhaps I believed that the less-than-fresh air should do me a world of healing. It's true to say that I certainly felt better by the time that I arrived, though I think that this was more due to buying some more cigarettes and chain smoking which I've found can either kill or cure hangovers. Luckily they were performing the latter function. Or so it seemed. What they were doing to my insides was nobody's business but that of my non-existent hypothetical maker.

There was the usual pandemonium when I arrived at the bus station at long last; a sweaty sauna where nobody actually seemed to have much idea why they were there. Some of the most destitute sights can be witnessed at train stations and this was no real exception. Beyond the limbless and scantily clothed, I'll leave these various harrowing sights to your imagination.

Although as a rule, jumping into the shower is the first thing that I do after a heavy night on the sauce, the fact that I had abstained from doing so this time must help to prove the trope that everything happens for a reason. Without degrading myself any more with the niche glamour of this situation any more than necessary, suffice to say that there wasn't a dry patch left upon my skin.

Throughout the rest of my journey to meet Phoebe, I pray that she…does a few things actually; the first is that she keeps to her whim of joining me; then that she is indeed booked onto the correct flights and connections; and finally that she actually gets aboard all of these journeys. There is no real reason why I should expect anything less than this actually occurring. Only—and I'm aware how patronising I could be sounding—after all of these years, meeting Phoebe abroad when we are both alone and otherwise uncommitted is almost supernatural. Indeed, I am rather ashamed of the extent to which I have been realising my dependence on Phoebe, and the extent to which our happiness together surpasses all else in my desires.

Whilst she, of course, may not be to everybody's taste, I find Phoebe so immersive. As I find myself once again in the midst of my utterly uncontrollable infatuation, I take some solace in the fact that, where she may have once been the one calling all of the shots in our relationship, we are now firm equals in terms of our dependence and devotion to each other. It is no longer the classic pattern of the chaser and the chased.

Unless you were exceptionally attractive as a guy, you'd usually have to assert yourself and fend off competition to end up with your match-mate. In fairness, it was just as I had finished sixth-form and entered university that I found that I had my healthy pickings of reciprocation in terms of girls that I found attractive; why I settled down with Martha straight away upon entering the UEA remains beyond me. Still, as some mindless ditty from the era of my teen-hood stated: 'shudda wudda a cudda are the last words of a fool'.

Going along with much of what I've been saying, Phoebe has always been swamped by some man who I have always deemed to be beneath her. I'd say that this was largely down to jealousy and delusional alpha-male pride and, naturally, I've always deemed her to be doing herself a disservice by wasting any of her time on them. As I've said, the pair of us have ended up being platonic friends for the vast majority of our adult lives, and I'd like to think that I've always put on a front of being mostly amicable with the string of her supposed lovers. Granted, even though it sounds like an egotistical misinterpretation, it often felt as though Phoebe was having to apologise for these buffoons (in fairness, they were all right-ish on paper) and was almost embarrassed by being connected to them. So I interpreted anyway.

Whilst I generally tend to shun thoughts concerning Phoebe's old flames, I'm swamped by thinking of a couple of the most recent dalliances. The guy before last, Frank was our age exactly (quite a rarity as they classically have a few more years of maturity) and Jesus Christ, did he think a lot of himself and his supposed intellectual prowess. Without being overly base or petty, you only need a smidgen of pop-psychology, to recognise what a sign of insecurity this displays. Though in fairness, at least this guy was of genuine intelligence on paper; though the degree in Classics that he had from Oxford didn't seem to have provided him with much interest in life or anybody in it.

It was Harry that she was dating before him, and her news that they had separated just colliding with my split from Martha still remains positive old news in my mind. The only times that we had met before, I actually really got along with Harry. Perhaps the fact that he was already nearly middle aged and already had been married and had children made me automatically regard him as less of a contemporary threat. I'm still delighted that they split after a short relationship, as it did confirm, as I had wistfully expected, that her being with him was just a passing phase.

Whether it is because I am weak or not, and whether it is of a matter of any interest, I am the only stable guy in Phoebe's life. People may have, in jest, suggested that I hold this status because I was boringly dependable and at her beck and call. This is obviously an impression that I should immediately refute.

Maybe this was true once upon a time, although as we've both grown-up together, I hardly think this to be true any longer. It's not like we haven't both been in enough separate relationships—her admittedly more frequently than I have—not to feel as though I ever give off the impression of my world revolving around Phoebe. Whatever preoccupations that I have kept within the walls of my mind are surely of nobody's business but my own.

As I am celebrating it being under an hour until I am due to arrive at my point of call, my eye catches the sight of these two women a few rows in front of me. I instantly thought that they looked as though they were primary school dinner ladies. Ones having boarded the wrong flight for a 'giwl's 'oliday' to Torrimelinos or some alternative Spanish costa. This is indeed an eccentric (flattering myself maybe in not just labelling myself as plain weird) viewpoint, but there is a definite dinner lady type—or mealtime supervisor as they're probably called officially—throughout British society. It is my label for those women—call me sexist if you like—who always appear drab, have voices that could curdle milk and tend to imbue a negative opinion on just about every aspect of modern society. They've always got something wrong with them; be it sciatica, a varicose vein or somebody taking them 'for a ride'. Of course, they're always apparently 'not the type to ever complain' as they're grafters eternally harking back to elements of their past lifestyle that almost certainly never existed. They're largely harmless perhaps, but they do not contribute anything of much worth and sap the life out of you when they're around. Perhaps endorsers of Brexit, without really having much idea what they were voting for, sums up my crass description of this breed.

It does make a change to witness a pair of these types without a Daily Mail or some red-top flapping out of their back pocket or handbag. As much of a snob as I may be, they encapsulate what's wrong with so-called broken Britain, as they genuinely feel that we, as Brits, are superior to everybody else.

Everything about their little lives can seem to be sorted out by talking to the right person. Like, I don't know, talking to say Paul about cars 'because he knows about cars' or talking to Sheila about baking because 'she knows about baking'. It could make for a fitting comedy sketch actually; that is just the idea that there is such thing as gospel knowledge on a subject that you'd better not ever dare to try and supersede.

Oh, upon listening to them more closely, I notice that they're not from my home at all. We're not in quite close enough proximity for me to properly gauge a great deal of their mutterings, but I'm pretty sure that they're of German stock. That or possibly Dutch or Belgian. It's often been said that inhabitants of these northern European countries are the most similar to Brits abroad, and while on package holidays (which my parents still rely on to a large extent) generally separate themselves in terms of country of origin. This is usually by placing their towels at the opposite ends of the beach—there is quite a Germanic stereotype here apparently. From what I've heard anyway.

The remainder of my journey continues to be just as uneventful, along with the slight burden of there never having been a seat available throughout my entire journey on this sketchy looking old train. It never ceases to surprise me just how trains in many countries almost literally just sail through farmland and landfill sites. At least it keeps in real, I suppose and the various wafts that inevitably pass up along your nostrils can only enhance your travelling experience.

On the positive side, contrary to the assumption that hangovers intensify with age, I am feeling above 95% restored—or there about—as the train is slowing down into the station that I believe is almost certainly my point of call. Having been so certain on numerous occasions before, only to find myself exposed as entirely wrong, I've limited trust in my judgement to ever be particularly confident of ending up anywhere.

We are going slowly enough for me to recognise the station from when I passed through alongside ex-military Donald. Without reverting too much to my tendency to use flowery language, there was something incredibly sedate and tranquil about docking into this major terminus in the blazing sunshine. I've no idea whether you can relate to that feeling of knowingly experiencing almost chronic *déjà vu.*

Clamouring off of the train, I was instantly slapped back into reality by the hustle and bustle of the station, ambushed by people trying to flog a relentless quantity of old toot, almost obliging me to stay at numerous hotels and generally just begging. This cluster of three increases in unpleasantness as it progresses. Still, I had whilst glancing through my travel guide and desperately trying to hold my centre of gravity, I had already selected the hostel slash hotel where I think it'd be most preferable to meet Phoebe.

Although it was fairly small (only about 20 rooms), advertised as being in a quiet area, it seemed to be central enough. Mirissa, being a small coastal town, had some museums and a scattering of historical sites, it seemed as though people would say how it 'could be covered within a couple of days'.

This a pet hate of mine when it comes to travellers' talk. This idea that you can tick a place off for the sake of boasting that you have been to it, at the expense of actually gaining any true vision and feeling for different places. I recognise that this has the potential to sound just as corny and delusional as what I've been scathing towards, only my real issue is that it almost sounds as though people are travelling for the sake of completing a checklist. Rather than actually having the ability to explore and appreciate being away from home. As opposed to celebrating difference, it's almost as if they're trying to compete with themselves about how well they can come away from home whilst keeping well in sight of their comfort zone. Yet again, I may just be talking out of my arse here as I could be accused of doing the exact same thing.

It seemed a bit overly ambitious for me to traipse to the opposite side of the town where the hostel appeared to be located. Having planned to simply catch a bus—which were supposedly only once every 15 minutes—the taxi driver touting around the station area was victorious. I accepted his offer of a ride because my head finally seemed to have recovered, yet I didn't want to be thrown back by too much stress or exertion, along with simple plain idleness, which is always all too easy to be exploited.

The journey was only 10 minutes or so along fast roads, which exposed to me just how sufficient an unnecessary stress walking would have been.

Having said this, there were several occasions aboard this white cab that my life felt on the line. With this macho attitude, the quip of 'I'm not in any rush!' always proves largely ineffective and all I can say after these hair-raising taxi rides is, 'well, they always seem to get me there in one piece'. Call me lucky, but the fact that I've never so much as been in one road traffic accident in all of my years spent back home makes this seem like a pretty poor reassuring advice. A disproportionately large amount of road traffic accidents do occur and I was just relieved to get to my destination of hotel in one piece; though to say that I didn't enjoy any of the adrenalin kick at times would be a lie.

When I clambered into the *Peacock Palace,* its appearance only enhanced my desire to book into the private double that I had reserved on Hostel World. It was marginally more expensive than my standard places to stay, only for a pretty small and low-key rest house, it managed to appear to be rather majestic. It was painted in a colour that I think should be described as turquois, though this is not a colour that I would be confident enough to recognise. The reasoning behind the alliterative name is immediately clear as I instantly clap eyes on at least a triad of peacocks; they are beautiful creatures, though my mind immediately focuses on the apparent absence of any peahens.

My key is for room 104, which is on the first tiled floor and reached by walking around the veranda. I suppose that I had displayed some decadence in so far as I had automatically reserved a private room with just one double bed. This could be deemed to be a tad forward, only given the history that Phoebe and I had, there was simply no reason that we should not both be fully comfortable to frugally reduce the cost by just booking one bed; whether to be used platonically or not.

Perhaps it would have made more sense to my wallet for me to spend this first night in Phoebe's absence in a dorm, but this seemed to be too great a risk in my eyes. Double rooms may easily become occupied and I was not faithful enough in trusting that it would remain vacant—even if I reserved it—unless I possessed it. This is ashamedly petty and barely an issue worth writing about. If anything, I resented the fact that I was seemingly setting myself up for failure by trying to assure the optimum perfection in the situation I was creating. Though at the same time, I simply could not bear to see this opportunity slip through my fingers.

The room was a decent size, and with its terracotta floor and the shiny satin metallic coloured king sized pristine bottle green duvet, there was something of a cross in the way that the room appeared to my absurdly far-fetched imagination. For whatever reason, I conjured that its appearance was in between that of a bedroom in a Kasbah and a Parisian knocking shop. Believe me, having never visited either location, I have an absence of knowledge of what either abode should in truth resemble; probably something similar to where I was parked.

De-clobbering myself and after quickly sprucing up in, for once, MY private bathroom, it seemed only too necessary for me to go and have a little explore of the locality—although reserving all of the couple of open-houses that interested me, along with the palatial building and gardens, for when Phoebe and I could explore them together.

By the time that it was approaching dusk and having moseyed around a couple of the large town's main squares before landing upon a bustling undercover mixed market. Given that it was now so late in the day by general bazaar standards, the fact that it was so packed to the rafters was testament to the variation of goods that they vended and clear quality of the bargains on offer.

I take it for granted that you walk around this type of environment with your hands glued to the insides of your pockets, although overall, it seemed like a welcoming sort of place. There was an array of tasty looking street style foods on offer as I glanced around the colourful market and I was pretty famished. Even the sight of the scrawny looking birds in cages was not sufficient detraction for me not to purchase some gloriously marinated chicken bap. The taste of it captured what travelling is all about.

Full-blown darkness had descended by the time that I walked back to the *Peacock Palace*, and as always, the absence of any natural light took me by surprise. A water was also much needed. Some may consider tap water to be safe, though in all fairness, I disliked the idea of having dysentery or such like and decided against risking drink. It's a catch 22, as whilst I resent paying for something that I've been used to coming out of a tap for free, the pros still far outweigh the cons in terms of buying bottled water (where it is visual that the seal has never already been broken). Excuse one of the most boring middle class conundrums ever.

It was still fairly early evening, and I was happy to hear that there seemed to be quite a lively atmosphere within the hostel when I eventually returned, having had to turn myself around and walk the opposite way at least twice.

After having returned to my room to spruce myself up a little and re-deodorise after changing into my lonesome mauve cotton shirt, I grabbed myself Alan Sillitoe's book, which I had almost finished, and went to join the masses and get some much-desired beer. It is thankfully well lit and I am in my element getting gradually more inebriated and even rolling some cigarettes as the hotel was miraculously selling *American Spirit* rolling tobacco and a small packet containing the rest of the equipment for pittance.

Knowing that Phoebe was due to arrive tomorrow, and having the rare feeling, for me, of being completely without the need to be in anybody else's company, I was completely content in my isolation and revelling against the backdrop of white noise from other travellers.

As I'd been immersed in several chapters of this angry young man of 1950s Nottingham's dalliances, I was more than ready for another beer along with perhaps some company. A picture-perfect crew was now all that occupied the rest of the courtyard's table, and though they were easy to make eye contact with as I went to replenish my drink, I couldn't find a great deal there beyond some hard work.

There were about 6 bodies in total making up this mixed nationality and sexed group. Although they were all more than friendly on the eye, they clearly deemed their posse as exclusive. These sort of people were generally deplored by Phoebe and myself. Despite being beautiful externally, their seeming hollowness collectively was a trait that we both found extremely ugly.

Individually, I am sure that there were several amongst this swarm who had some interesting conversation and real passions in life beyond the superficiality that they exuded. You may understandably deem me to be forming this conclusion rather rashly and judgementally; I hadn't even properly yet met them. I'd have to ask you in doing this, though, to be subject to overhearing around an hour of their mindless trite and bland conversation. Their tiresomeness was all the more confirmed as I entered into chatting with a few of them, but I did decide to go and change into my swim shorts, as a dip by darkness is always one life's pleasures in my view; made all the better by the prefix 'skinny' though not in a hotel or surrounded this cliquey company in any measure.

When we were still sixth formers and had barely known each other for any real length of time—when Phoebe still couldn't legally drink—it was after encountering a couple of girls several years older than us that we had we foundered the term 'ya-yas' for this sort of breed. As much as I like to think of this as our prerequisite to the current 'rah' term, my late old Nan's definition of those possessing 'more money than sense' is just as accurate. They're as phoney as they are spoilt and Craig was the one English guy who fell into this character.

Reverting to being tastelessly judgemental and pigeon holing, his name certainly didn't fit the bill of what I'd be expecting from this sort of sheltered and spoiled specimen. True, he was as cushiony sheltered—obviously believing he knew it all—as the next man, but upon being introduced to him—through somebody other than himself of course—I was immediately slightly taken aback by his name. *Henry, Tarquin, Hugo* et al. shouldn't have surprised me in the least. Although I was lucky enough never to fall victim to his direct condescension, it didn't take much observation to tell that he was clinging on to some delusional prowess of some unbeknownst grandeur.

Whether it was a mask for insecurities and/or failures, it is beyond my care or business to think what his haughtiness attempted to guise, though immediately came that aged question that I sadly now use all too often to validate myself: 'I was never like that, was I!?'

Craig was strikingly one of the most conceited and amphibious young creatures that I've ever had the experience of meeting. As always with these types in my experience, it is difficult to actually describe what you find so antagonising about them; everybody else seeming to gel with them so well gives you the air of feeling like a leper for thinking any differently. Still, everybody's got a limit and this Craig was pushing mine.

He was of the sort that you seem to be ensured are 'really nice, once you get to know them'. Given how I am convinced that everybody within humanity must have some more pleasant side, the fact that some people seem to put on some front—for whatever reason—unfortunately means that they're anything but nice in my book.

Everything about him could widely be defined as inoffensive. He was a pretty good looking guy I suppose, with pale and plain features and mousy brown hair. To be fair, a hipster is something that I could ashamedly be classified as, although I feel that actually being from the Smoke can at least give me the edge over these deliberately styled fashionistas that have swarmed in from the provinces. Also, I've dressed in that style for in excess of a decade now, so I don't understand how I can be said to be a follower.

Scared that may sound a tad aloof and condescending to people not from London, but I'm sure that this contemporary version of the yuppie can thrive in every town. It's not anything per se other than a lack of ever having being faced with any responsibility, consciousness or anything aside from their over indulged little backgrounds. Of course, I'm not claiming to be enormously different in this respect, only my family have never been meek, and our finances ensured that I could always (at least try to) fend for myself and have independence and experiences from a young age.

All too quickly in front of Craig, I've come to loathe myself for holding some of these judgements, but the cynic in me is imbuing that they are merely bleak realities. Without sounding akin to that all too crassly common defence of apparently derogatory statements—'I'm not being...I've got... friends'—I do have may close friends that would clearly fall into the old school definition of total *prat*. But provided that they don't carry too much satisfaction or vanity, they're more than fine; it's just with anybody who audaciously dares to lord it above anybody else that my patience wears thin.

It's similar—however tenuously—to the way that the poorest in society that may always be the first to flaunt any display of wealth though their clothing or choice of more affordable luxury. Well, although he was filthy rich, there were tendencies of this overcompensation in the fact that, whilst Craig had more limited grey matter, as I said, he apparently knew the answer to just about everything.

Believe me, I really could not give less of a shit about anybody's intellectual prowess or any various certificate from anywhere in itself; only when an obnoxious manner is coupled with an apparent lack of experience it's a different matter.

Without ranting for too long about the one person who occupied a most minor portion of my travels, the fact that I still feel the need to let off some steam about something so irrelevant just shows that even the most easy-going people have their limits. This may sound smug, sanctimonious or whatever else, but I've been told (often less than complimentarily that 'if you [I] get any more laid back, you'll fall off of the end of the world), but unfortunately, everybody's got their breaking point haven't they?

Often in the least likely places, as well. There was absolutely nothing about Craig that I could provide as any justification for my loathing of him; the fact that my dislike could be this intense towards somebody I barely knew was enough of a shocker to myself. In some vague attempt to justify how I had so rapidly come to the viewpoint that he was some abomination, I'll just say that he could be seen to epitomise everything that I most despise.

At 27, this list isn't too long, although people who seem to believe that they are in any way pre-destined to be above the rest of us ranks highly up there. Life has a nasty habit of all too frequently giving mould of people exactly what they want. These people do not even belong to a specific type, as I see it, beyond having a capacity to take plenty of credit without having any real credentials of their own.

Masking their own insecurities is perhaps too obvious an excuse for why people behave in this way. It was from a few of the facts that I learned from Izzy—who seemed more than all right despite seemingly belonging to this collective—which only bolstered my preconceptions about this sort of person. Not only had Craig graduated from some nothing university that I can't even recall now in a made-up seeming degree, but had migrated to London from his birth land of Hampshire. I would never use these factors to cast judgement on anybody, but when faced with somebody of the sort lording it above you, I think I think you have every right to beg the question of what places them onto their perch.

Along with the indistinctive sound of his voice, Craig was clearly no exception to the expectation that this sort of person would be dull. It is not even that I think Craig's sort could wound my ego in any way, but I tend to believe that at least sounding interested—whether feigned or not—in the person that you are talking with is a vital trait. Craig could not by any measure perform this.

Envisaging the worst-case scenario tends to be a defensive mechanism of my own, and the prospect of Craig succeeding in charming Phoebe and eventually having his way with her was a prospect far too grim for me to even imagine. Logically, there is no way whatsoever that I could see this event occurring. True enough, Phoebe is no stranger to capturing (or falling unlucky victim to) an upstarted toy-boy, only Craig was so nondescript that I couldn't imagine Phoebe having any attraction to him. Although I still became extraordinarily beset with the idea—it sometimes feels as though these things can happen just to slap me over the face—Phoebe and Craig getting together just isn't something that I wanted to give too much thought. After several lagers, the thought became all too consuming a prospect.

Enough about all of this anyway. This uneventful night drew to a close sometime soon after the clocks struck midnight and I was relieved to be in just my own company. In spite of not having consumed a great deal of drink, I began to feel a little queasy as I headed back to my room in great anticipation of Phoebe's arrival the next day.

All too often when I am conscious that any monumental event is about to occur—experiences such as sitting my finals in a hall at the UEA and losing my virginity at a house party all of those years ago stick as poignant examples—I have a habit of clamming up. Rest assured, in both of these events I soldiered on successfully, although not without feeling on the cusp of something awkward and deglamourising; a ghastly episode of diarrhoea and/or projectile vomiting have both existed as fears.

On the other side, there is still that feeling of intense ecstasy knowing that I am almost certain to be united with Phoebe yet again in just a day's time. On the darker side of this night's moon (which thankfully does not come complete with being able to hear Pink Floyd from any orifice) is my sudden, although fairly consistent in her absence, doubt that Phoebe feels for me to anything like the intensity that I feel for her. Still, these feelings usually subside instantly upon being reunited, and I have a peaceful night's sleep accompanied by the prospect of some beautiful excitements in my stomach outweighing the coupling of some slight apprehensions.

4. Day 7: On the Cusp

As an all too common experience of my ever all too fast increasing years of adulthood—especially if I've gone to bed less than sober—I stir halfway through my sleep and can't refrain from glancing at my phone somewhere around 4 A.M. The pattern from here is consistently as follows: upon coming to, I rapidly find it impossible to get my head back down until I have consumed some gulps of water, which, in my growing wisdom, I am increasingly keeping beside my bed. Then, I scrunch my eyes back together and retire with the aim of fast being asleep, trying not to think of anything and falling into another realm of consciousness. Tossing and turning repeatedly is my next move before realising that I've been in this situation for quite a long time and, synonymously, I feel that I should probably go to have a wee. I am eventually forced to get up and stagger to the toilet, which when you're backpacking usually involves having to jog your memory concerning where it is. On this occasion, it had the benefit of being easy to locate as I was enjoying the luxury of enjoying a private room, though this advantage did not work on this time.

It's certainly not an uncommon stigma that once you've had a few drinks too many, you conk out yet fail to get any proper sleep, especially true when you've got a day of some importance lined up ahead. All too predictably, I was already feeling a bit tired and irritable, as much as I was looking forward to meeting Phoebe, which should be sometime around late afternoon if everything ran according to plan. Napping was hopefully a prospect for early afternoon, though given the proximity to Phoebe's arrival, I knew already that it was largely out of the question.

Instead, I just downed plenty of the black coffees that came free with breakfast, which were thankfully of the most decent variety. It was still barely half past eight in the morning and Phoebe wasn't due to land until later, and with the time involved in collecting baggage, going through security and exiting the airport, her checking-into the hotel any time before dark would be optimistic.

Until then, I was now wondering what I should do with myself. Always needing to be kept busy, and with reading something that I like to sandwich between events, rather that devote time to in itself, I'd need to find something to consume time with. Clothes shopping is certainly not something that I enjoy, along with hardly being able to afford anything whilst travelling, and although exploring any proper market is something that I relish, it is an activity that I'd like to reserve for when Phoebe arrives. This was also true of two of the few museums that I could see listed in the guide, although there was a maritime museum that I wouldn't mind taking a gander at, which was unlikely to be of any interest to Phoebe. Although I could easily live with never having seen anything that I imagined that it had to offer, I was intrigued by the fact that it was situated at least a couple of hours on the road to be beside the sea!

It was as I was taking the scenic route—largely as I didn't direct myself well—to this museum that I noticed on my phone a message from Phoebe that had been sent an hour or so ago; as I can almost go for full days without checking my phone, this was fortuitous. Only in so far as it confirmed that Phoebe had boarded her plane for the first little hop of her flight from London City Airport to Amsterdam Schiphol, where she should then be bound to reach her destination. It was also lucky that she had managed to wangle a flight—which was to be taking off on time—that only had a two-hour layover. There was absolutely nothing for me to do other than wait. Impatiently doing so was all too inevitable.

I was hoping that Sri Lanka's rich maritime history would be a main focus of the museum. Instead, what was displayed through little beyond writing on placards, was a limited account of the technology of sea fare, which I have barely any understanding of, or curiosity about. This failed in helping to distract me temporarily from Phoebe's imminent arrival and the place didn't occupy my mind for much beyond fifteen minutes or so, with the information offered being little more than the visual equivalent of white noise.

In these instances, I automatically become tetchy and am noticeably (to myself at least) overtired and frustrated that I do not know quite how I am going to kill the upcoming several hours. I aptly realise that I'm not much in the way of being able to just relax when I'm in such a state of anticipation, and I left my book back at the Peacock Palace; not that I'm in any sort of mood to absorb any literature anyway.

Stepping out onto the blindingly bright dusty road outside, I finally feel positive in realising that it's one of those rare occurrences in life where you can rejoice in having absolutely no commitments beyond the anticipation of being reunited with the person you love.

Several yards in from of me, there was one of those men appearing so haggard that you assume that they are ageless, and he was staring at me across the road for such a length of time that he appeared to be giving me the eye. Certainly without offering so much as a sultry stare, he was on my back. Not literally, you understand, only in terms of asking me questions, which didn't make so much as any sense in terms of the word ordering or even half of the syllables themselves.

I walked warily beside him, nodding along to his questions. I'm still not quite sure why I was feeling a bit uneasy—part of me probably thought that Murphy's Law could ensure that, just as my dreams were about to come true, I would drop dead or be murdered—I knew how ridiculous and paranoid I was being. I walked beside this man without any direction or purpose for about ten minutes when he blurted out, "I'm going to die really soon." There's not much response that you can give to this is there? Several things were swimming through my mind such as whether this was going to be some sort of scam to get me to donate money to supposedly help his soon to be bereaved family, and what was supposedly going to kill him?

As it turned out, to my relief, he didn't so much as ask me for anything, beyond whether I'd 'like to share some this' before propagating some sweaty pastry-seeming item in front of my eyes. Out of politeness, and so as not to offend, I accepted some of the food object, and it was actually fairly tasty. It was salty (which induces automatic thirstiness in me) and to my surprise contained some mystery minced meat, which I reckon was probably beef, though it wouldn't surprise me to learn that it was goat or even pork or lamb (it was so bland in itself that I couldn't tell). Feeling obliged to repay the gesture in some way, all that I had found was on me was luckily containing a half full packet of cigarettes accompanied by a working lighter.

Regardless of what little silly aspersions you may cast on offering somebody gravely ill a cigarette, it was most graciously accepted and appreciated. As we continued to talk in incredibly basic half-sentences, I seemed to gain enough confidence and familiarity with the guy to beg a question that may be deemed audacious to ask of somebody that you've just offered a cigarette to; "So what is I that you have wrong with you…not cancer?"

Even at the time of the inquiry, the last two words of this sentence felt a little inappropriate and forward of me to ask; I was in the process encouraging him to smoke, after all. Although it was met with no response. He rambled on as we smoked through our cigarettes in muffled dialogue that I could barely understand it transpired that, "No, I've not been to a doctor and I feel quite fine, I just know that I am about to die." *Christ, is this some prophesy,* I thought, *or is he 'about to commit suicide'?* It turned out to be neither thing. The only reasoning I got was: "I've lived long. My time's up, I just know!"

I found this incredibly bizarre and even a little creepy. Liberating too, perhaps in some ways. Still, each to their own, I thought as we shook hands and parted; I frequently still get the passing thought of whether he's popped his clogs; more likely, I think, he's still the same as he's been for the last, and probably will be for about the next, thirty or so years! Inconsistent with my usual habit, ingrained by my dad, of always asking for names, this was never done with this gentlemen; to be fair, he never asked for mine either. It remains a fair regularity during moments of vacancy of mind for me to feel some twinge of concern for his wellbeing or how he may have died, without wanting to be overly morbid.

As I eventually reach the small parade on which the Peacock Palace is situated, I feel positively rejuvenated and refreshed. So much so that the first action that I take once back into the foyer of the guesthouse is to go any order a large fruit smoothie, go upstairs to my room and fetch my book and read my book in front of the pool; pleasantly oblivious to the fact that several hours pass before I so much as even notice. It is most out of character for me to feel so relaxed awaiting such a momentous occurrence as Phoebe's arrival. It soon seems rude of me not to go and take advantage of for once staying in a hotel that actually has its own private pool, and after a quick change into my swim-shorts, I am soon plunging my head under water and passing time by reverting to my childhood competition of seeing just how many lengths of the pool I can complete with my head under water. Perhaps I'm seeking to validate that the carbon monoxide and tar in cigarettes has far from undermined my lung capacity yet. Two and a little bit lengths is the most that I can manage, though as I have no real idea of how many metres long the pool is; still, kept my brain out of any mischief for a while.

Drying myself off, which is an incredibly illogical move as I realise that much of the waiting time has thankfully passed, I soon, after confirming that I have surpassed my reading limit for the day, go upstairs and take a shower and even a shave. Shaving is not in itself something that I ever much—if at all—do whilst travelling. Although I've no real idea whether Phoebe should favour any of my rather meagre and albeit pretty wispy stubble, the operation of shaving symbolises something else. Beyond wanting to look sharp and well turned out, Phoebe has already more than confirmed that she finds a shaven face on me more attractive and I do not wish to jeopardise any chances that I may have. Freshening up and basting myself in a few squirts of aftershave is always psychologically invigorating for me anyway, though I'm well aware of how ridiculous it is for me to assume that these trivial factors could have any ability to undermine my chances.

I suppose it's just one of those situations in life where you are forcing yourself into an appearance of healthy balance; in this case, showing that I do care, without implying that you've gone to any real special effort. Perhaps it is sadly as predisposed and predictable as it sounds, but you want to feel as comfortable as you can in every situation, don't you?

In the end, I went for my pair of light brown linen trousers…I'd say they're that colour rather than beige, accompanied by the only shirt that I have brought with me on this trip. It is white with some black stitched embroidery for anybody that should care at all. Of course, the killer adage to this ensemble is my increasingly tarnished black leather sandals. It's not that I ever give any thought to much of what I wear! Cleaned teeth complement the levels of hygiene that could be propagated by my wearing of my one pair of lucky and yet-to-be-worn red and black striped underpants.

Strapping on my black analogue wristwatch, it was but an hour until I could expect to be presented with Phoebe. As I sat on the terrace in front of the hotel, I began to have slight concern that overexcitement was dawning upon me as I had my first swig of the large bottle beer that I had ordered and lit only my umpteenth cigarette of the day thus far. The drink was regrettably at its end before too long at all; 'pace yourself' is something that I immediately realised that would be overly challenging during the entire episode of Phoebe's arrival.

As I was fulfilling my pledge to restrain myself from drinking any more liquor, my arse became a new discomfort, as I have this all too regular occurrence on hard chairs where my rear end starts itching vigorously. Of course, it starts off mild, then reaches a level whereby I just cannot get comfortable for love nor money; especially as neither are offered to me in any way, shape or form in this instance. This is not a pressing problem, though just annoying as it is the sort of thing that I'd expect to occur if I was still wearing my swim-shorts and hadn't washed, rather than once I had showered and changed. Not being the most flattering thing to go around talking about, I'm just curious as to whether other people get faced with this same frustrating discomfort, as it is just not the sort of issue that you waste your breath broadcasting.

Checking the time for the billionth time so far, it was already at an hour where Phoebe could be arriving; although not always the most punctual person, she was reliable when needed, so I wasn't that concerned, yet it would be an increasing struggle for her to walk in and to find me an engrossed in my book and casual as I could have hoped. Fetching another bottle—just small this time, mind—of beer, to use as a prop, I saw the silhouette of what could be of Phoebe.

Ha, of course, this wasn't the women that I was awaiting by any stretch; from the brief glimpse that I could take of her, she looked at least a few decades older than us and had the opposite end to Phoebe's dark brunette hair on any colour spectrum. Along with a little laugh, I took another small gulp of my beer before taking leave for the gents. Upon returning to the table, I felt forced to acknowledge the fact that I was feeling increasingly anxious at the prospect that I may be about to have to face—unfortunately not for the first ever time in my life, though not for at least a generation—the prospect of being stood-up. Not only was this unseemly, as Phoebe had never done such a thing before, but my unease also began to fluctuate between feelings of slight concern that she may, in fact, be in some harm or difficulty. I knew it reeked of the irrationality, which any time kept waiting can easily induce in me, and it was only just around half an hour after Phoebe's earliest possible arrival time.

Then, out of nowhere (although not exactly true as they were too lodging at this hotel), upon to the sun-kissed front patio of the hotel appeared—not Phoebe as if it were something out of Hollywood—but Craig and part of his clique.

This was far from the ideal company for awaiting Phoebe's arrival, yet I was soon relived to see that Craig's appearance beckoned almost simultaneously the actual, long-anticipated event.

She was unfailingly as delectable as I could ever have envisaged, without being overly corny and typecast. The one profound change, which would certainly take some adjusting to, was the fact that her what could be called 'gypsy-ish' charm had taken a slashing—though I'm sure in a far more dignified and professional way—and she had gotten short hair. Vulgarising the style is something that I shan't do by attempting to offer my inevitably inaccurate definition, though suffice it to say that it definitely suited Phoebe.

Within seconds, we had caught eyes and with a beaming smile, she dumped her rucksack by her side and half-ran to meet me. Upon meeting, we embraced tightly for an indefinite seeming eternity. Upon detangling ourselves from one another, as was always the case after such impassioned instances, it surprised me to note that absolutely everybody else within my vision was oblivious to this tremendous reunion having occurred. There is absolutely no reason why the rest of the world should have any awareness or caring for the event of Phoebe and me meeting for the first time in ages, it's just that classic feeling of finding it hard to restore yourself to normality after something so enamouring has occurred.

"So, here I am at last!" announced Phoebe in her ankle length, what looked like a full length satin blue rara (are they called maxis?) skirt and tight fitting white short-sleeved blouse. Whatever she was wearing exacerbated her ring thin waist. This was complimented by her subtly rouged lips and silver bangles around one of her wrists.

As ever when meeting this lady, I become so smitten in all honesty, that I have rather limited idea of sequencing exactly what went on, and it soon all becomes a blur. Fittingly, I become entirely unaware of what is occurring around any close proximity to us. After endless overflowing quantities of catching up concerning people and things that, without wishing to feign or boast of our exclusivity, would all be rather meaningless to anybody outside of our one-to-one vision. For the most part, it was just us laughing and me feeling a sense of utter comfort, understanding and peace that I have never felt even remotely close to experiencing in the company of anybody else.

Darkness was already upon us when I noticed that Craig and his entourage had departed from the hotel without my notice. This was only healthy development. "Ah Phoebs, we've missed the clan of River Island Mannequins that were here when you arrived…"

"Hmh, who do you mean, the sleazy like action-men guys and the plastic like girls at the next table?"

Well, I could not have asked for any better or even more fitting response even if I'd paid somebody to offer it. Despite being unprovoked in any way, I'd grown to loathe Craig and all that they represented for unjust and unfounded reasons.

"Yep, they're the ones, that douchebag looking blond guy is called Craig and there's an Adrian and Hugo on the male side. The girls are called Lucinda, Rosa and I think Jasmine or something like that from what I remember".

"Oh, they just all looked dull!" returned Phoebe with a breath of laughter.

Again, it was almost as though she could have been paid to offer me these words as they were exactly the type of thing that I had longed to hear. Any cynic—with which I may strongly identify, only am not comfortable to associate myself with—could effortlessly (as most elements of scoffing are in my little opinion) infer that she must be wanting something.

Aside from being crass and assuming, beyond her collection of small flaws such as that every human must have, I have never seen anything to suggest that Phoebe has a consciously manipulative bone in her body.

Some of the numerous anecdotes we had shared and laughed through with each other throughout the past; it's fair to say that several of the tales can be at each other's expense, but never nastily. The ridiculousness of our lives and existences is a significant part of the crux to much of our humour and own Zen for life.

Discussing each other's past relationships and our current romantic status just never entered into our conversation. Even when it was something just between the pair of us, it was something never talked about, always just self-revealingly evident rather than something ever discussed. This was the way that I wanted it to stay. When we were together, we were, without wanting to come across as deliberately arrogant, almost like an exclusive pair that did not need to be troubled or limited by the goings on of other people.

Whilst we may have the natural disposition to have automatic reservations or even instant unfounded dislike towards whoever each other may be seeing, I'd always like to think that we'd never allowed this matter to spill over into any of our conversation. So, it is only then by *sheer coincidence* that I've believed that everybody else whom Phoebe has been involved with to be an absolute piss-taking fool—so far beneath even me, let alone herself.

Without wanting to go into much detail concerning Phoebe's past relationships or even conquests, given the status of some of the people that she's had short flings with, it's fair to say that they involve an eclectic mixture of people. From a lover called Lewis, who was around 10 years her senior when I first ever properly knew her and developed my attraction. This guy, I suppose, was all right, but it's rather beyond my ethics how he ever thought that a man in his late twenties sleeping with a girl in her mid-late teens can ever not be seen as an abuse of responsibility. Of course, once the flattery and seeming sophistication of a teenage girl going out with a man in his mid-twenties wore off, she soon saw sense and ditched this one.

Whilst he was always pleasant enough to me and not really deserving to be labelled a complete 'loser', he definitely always struck me as a lost person, with an abundance of the Peter Pan syndrome; which, without delving into pop-psychology, seemed to stem from an unpleasant childhood. Although there was nothing whatsoever technically illegal about any of his actions with Phoebe, it always resonated to me as being something a bit seedy and underhanded.

Having absolutely no idea what this Lewis is doing now and without wanting to come across as too cold or uncaring, I really couldn't care less. Also, whether I'd even recognise him in the cold light of day is questionable, having not seen him for coming up to a decade. Amir is probably the only one that I could see myself becoming genuine mates with, or even to extend the arm of friendship towards, even with Phoebe being completely disconnected from the scenario. Still, I wasn't disappointed when their two-year or so relationship—long by her standards—came to an end over his permanent dedication to his job within the financial sector (a realm well negatively juxtaposed to Phoebe's and own interests!) a few years back.

Perhaps, it is testament to our both aging at what mutually feels to be too great a pace, that whereas older men may once have been a slight preference to Phoebe, younger upstarts apparently now have their own appeal. Although this is one crass generalisation based only on her last boyfriend; that James thing.

Although I never knew him well enough, or indeed know enough of him to be at all accurate with his age or many other facets of his personality, to me, he can best be described as 'the man who knows everything'. Aside from being an incredibly vulgar trait and a subconscious guise to cover the wealth of insecurities that I know he must have, nobody likes a know it all, do they? It shouldn't make any difference, but it is a quite salient characteristic when there is nothing in any of their credentials to back this up in any way whatsoever. It's not an uncommon characteristic and in most, I can forgive, but not when it comes from a clearly intellectually challenged person.

There are, unfortunately, always young men who have always had everything done for them in life and are brought up to be complete dweebs.

In many ways, he is the most dangerous breed of person to suck you in and act as a leech off of you, as with any of life's takers, James is guaranteed always to remain the oblivious victim towards any criticisms you may have of his character. So in this way he is needy, although overall, he is also a sharp guy who is savvy in exploiting any generosity or good nature displayed towards him and then disguising it under expectation and ingratitude. Phoebe's kind nature could be shamelessly exploited; as do I, she cares and feels guilty succeeding any confrontation, and this is a quality that James rapidly tapped into.

The year or so that she had spent in a relationship with James led me to observe the gradual erosion of Phoebe's assertiveness and tremendous trust in her judgement. Within less than a couple of months dating, James had become a lodger at Phoebe's apartment. Small credit's where small credit's due, he did contribute some meagre rent, but only a miniscule amount of the property's market value. Of this fact he was utterly unappreciative, always seeming to be pushing the boundaries of how much he could take the piss out of staying in the flat; spoilt brat that he is.

Predictably, he was the epitome of self-sophistication and worldliness in his blinkered grey eyes. The reality was that his balls had barely dropped and he possessed limited exposure to, let alone knowledge of, a great deal of the real world; let alone a life in adulthood. Granted that life's a learning curve for us all, but I like to think that I never actually put on the guise of knowing everything when a second-class degree from what would have to be classified as a polytechnic (I'd be surprised if he had a clue what that meant) is all I've got to show for it. Without being a snob, this fact means nothing about a person in itself, though when somebody with this lords it above you, then it does beg the question.

Only he knew everything and could almost make you feel like the subject of his condescension whenever our paths would cross. Still, I've enough confidence to know that, as with Phoebe, the world shall eventually catch-up and see that, beneath his affirmative and knowledgeable exterior, is a frightened and insecure individual who is lacking a great deal of—if any—true depth. Like I could really give a stuff about whatever somebody's supposed credentials are in life; it's like with exclamations such as 'oh yeah, he's super intelligent with an IQ sky-high'. I just think *and this is relevant to anything because...* There is no measure that I have of a person beyond their consistent decentness anyway.

Of course, there exists a slyness to this, as whatever situation of Phoebe's that he turned around, he'd succeed in employing the most basic reverse psychology to any issue and make Phoebe feel like it was entirely her own fault rather than a consequence of his actions.

Largely, he neither knew nor understood the concept of responsibility. It may seem extreme and even unnecessary for me to lay such fierce venom onto somebody that I barely know and have no personal grievance against—beyond his taking Phoebe for granted—but he corrosively transformed her and that I'll never forgive. Phoebe is such a positive and bright spark, that to see her crippled under his overriding is a classic case of passive domestic violence. Even our friends and any relatives would say that I was exaggerating and being unfair with this demonising label, but although James didn't abuse her physically, there was sufficient emotional blackmail to warrant my label of a 'toad' to him when I am talking to Phoebe. Cocky, conceited and cowardly would be an alliterative cluster of three that I'd choose to accurately sum-up this James guy. Once you get to a certain age and are forced to look back in to the mirror, you realise that other people are actually far more aware of your insincerities and inadequacies than it would ever pay you to confront. 'Ultimately, Mate, nobody in truth likes you' is what I'd love to say to him. Of course, he exudes the persona of a man about town who automatically knows everything; but think a male caricature of 'fit, but you know it' being reversed into 'so thick, but you don't know it'.

The instinctive predisposition to automatically veer away from anybody else that Phoebe's sharing a bed with is something that I almost determinedly make a point of overlooking when I come into any contact with them. If I bumped into Amir these days, I'd more than happily accompany him to go to a local boozer and we'd put the world to rights! Whereas, despite succeeding as good as always in being a peace-loving person, I'd just want to punch James hard in the face.

Of course, due to receiving obvious indulgences and a preponderance of self-importance, with James comes an arrogance, propped-up by conceit, that would make him revel in the knowledge that I had vested so much time and energy into my dislike of him. If I were to cross James again, say on the Kingsland Road, I could almost guarantee that I'd be snubbed as if I was some breed of Untermensch unworthy of his time or company. This may be true, given my possible reactions to him, and if we were to make eye contact, it should almost certainly guarantee the souring of any relationship that we should ever have. Souring is a good word, as I have to admit that I do feel bitter towards his existence; all of his notions of superiority just need to be pressed upon and squeezed out of him. Sometimes, when I've been travelling on my own, I just find that I have an unhealthy amount of time to ruminate thoughts, which can often be unproductive and even shameful when it is Phoebe, of all people, acting as my catalyst to unlock all of this pent-up hatred.

But as with the *Mastermind* slogan, I've started, so I might as well finish. It is so hard for even me to comprehend how I have so much chagrin towards somebody who I shall almost certainly never see again, and who is no longer an active part in the existence of anybody that I know or care for. As I tend to enjoy being a calm and even, dare I say it, rational person, it could be deemed quite an accomplishment that somebody has gotten under my skin to this extent; especially as I barely know him. He'll always be all right though. That I can guarantee. One of those people.

Since arriving to London from some 'Shire within the recent past, James has got some trendy job in Shoreditch, working for some media-based company doing something that sounds most cutting edge. In reality, you know that it involves being near the bottom of a large pile and having next to no influence on anything. Everyone's got to start somewhere, in fairness, though you know that many of these newly transformed hipsters have absolutely nothing to say or even think for themselves. Being something of a weirdo ever since I can remember with my tastes, and always operating as something of an outsider, along with the fact that—as irrelevant and even arrogant as it may seem—I've always lived in London, I feel relieved of being overly tarnished with this label. I've always felt like more of an observer than real part of the crowd.

Anyway, there's certainly now been enough said upon the weasel like to call it quits and move back to the joy in my situation at being with Phoebe. James' aloofness and self-centredness has been well noted in my eyes, although I do not actually think him too much beyond the personification of a perfect prat.

It's noted that I'm overcome with this reignited hatred for James directly after my reunion with Phoebe. As much as it may expose my insecurities in my relationship with Phoebe, I'd say that the thought of him ever sampling her splendour is something that I find appalling.

It's a rarity for me to eat at any sort of hotel restaurant when I am travelling. I'm usually desperate to escape paying for overpriced, average food, surrounded by other travellers, and I welcome any extra exploration. Phoebe's always been of the same mind-set, and we have stumbled upon many a gem. Although with her coming off a tiring long-haul flight, and so desperately craving to catch up, where we actually are is secondary.

I decide that I am going to be decadent and order some scallops and prawns for us to share to start, and then lapse into an abrupt return to globalisation and tomato salad to follow. Phoebe follows suit, and between us we have one seafood pizza and one vegetarian pizza, accompanied by a bottle of white wine. All positive spirits and even elation that I possess for this situation quickly return. Although not in keeping with Sri Lankan cuisine, we all crave a pizza once in a while, and I'd only seen such few being even offered and had not had one since commencing this trip. The hotel also had a noticeable large pizza oven, which made me all the more likely to salivate. Of course, this is metaphorical, though Phoebe is the sort of lover that any accidental drooling should have to be met by animated laughter as opposed to any real distaste.

It is as the starter of a generous portion of garlic and chilli prawns arrives, and we've barely finished our beers along with starting make way on our sauvignon Blanc, that I catch the first furtive glance coming across the table from Phoebe. Aside from a smile that I prayed at the time did not appear to be too smug, we rapidly resumed into our frivolity as we soon cleared the rounded black ceramic plate of the prawns.

"Ha, my breath reeks of garlic, so you won't want to be going anywhere near to me tonight!" sniggered Phoebe in an incredibly offhand and throwaway manner. Any critiques could have shown that Phoebe was using pretty obvious reverse psychology, and in fact was well aware of longing lust; but this would be incredibly over-analytical bullshit.

“Well, we’ve both been eating it so I doubt that your breath will smell…any different to how it usually does,” came my response.

Succeeding this, there was that defining moment when our positions and our body language could quite easily have led to tongues being exchanged. This never happened, and even at the time, I was relieved of it; if this sort of thing was going to take place, it shouldn’t occur so soon, and we still had loads more chatter to cover. Once we did, the pizza would take a clear second place and I was desperate to enjoy every mouthful of food, as the prawns had only worked as the perfect appetisers. As stupid as it sounds, Phoebe needed to give nothing more than enticement for now.

The pizzas took an awful long time to arrive and given the pace at which they could be created and cooked, this was beginning to feel ridiculous. To Phoebe, I simply offered that, “It’s so clearly because we’re the most attractive people at their restaurant and the hotel feels the need to keep us here for as long as possible.” Clearly in jest.

A quick, “Fuck off, Darren!” was briskly emitted from Phoebe’s lips. We were both laughing and enjoying each other’s company until the food came, which seemed all too rapid, as though I’d forgotten that I was hungry. This is a feat that only Phoebe could successfully achieve.

As the food arrived, we hastily ordered another bottle of vino, as the previous was long drained. We continued on piste with our selection of house sauvignon, and the all food—even the large salad—soon disappeared. The waiter came over to issue the bill (adding such extra charges to the hotel charge was a dangerous slope to fall down in my experience), and afforded us a complimentary nightcap-seeming drink of a brandy-like sprit. It went down nicely, despite managing to burn my throat in a way that I’d expect of paint stripper.

After our spluttering finished, we began to get ready for the night ahead, which merely involved stumbling into a kitsch-looking bar. Handily, this was located just around the corner, and although I say that we went inside, one of the best things about being in the tropics is that you can comfortably ever sit in just a shirt outside come rain or shine. Another bottle of wine—red this time—was soon half way down and we had as much endless energy and tales that we were finding increasingly hilarious to share (many of which were at our expense). At this point a baseball cap wearing, fat and greying middle-aged man entered the bar. More of the buttons on his electric orange coloured Hawaiian shirt were undone than fastened, and suffice to say that that the salmon coloured cotton shorts that accompanied them were way too short to provide any observer with much solace. Although I have no idea of this man's name, or many more observations upon his character, his booming movements and voice spoke for themselves, and his rotund figure was decorated with several unsightly tattoos which were, of course, accompanied by several gold medallions. He gave off a burp of a high volume, which I don't think he even noticed.

This was the sort of instance that Phoebe and I lived for. That's people who unwittingly resembled what a caricature. To top it all, he was American and though he was gone in a flash, he'll leave a lasting impression in my mind as one of those sorts of dowdy mythical creatures. Why they leave such an imprint on your memories is beyond me; probably just because it was something that I found funny whilst having such a fun time.

This man was, as far as we could tell, unaccompanied and simply minding his own business, and I'd be astonished if he'd taken note of our presence at all. Regardless of our fixation upon one another, I'm still surprised that we managed to miss such a delightful spectacle for such a duration of time. Fittingly, once we had caught sight of his departure from the venue, we were in sufficient inebriation to be instantaneously in hysterics. Nothing extraordinary, or even outside of normality, had occurred, but in many ways, that was the beauty of the abundance of laughing that Phoebe and I shared.

After we had calmed down enough to engage in any sort of conversation, being most matter of fact, Phoebe stated that, "I really feel like a cigarette." Ever since I had known her, she rarely smoked, but was partial to have a cigarette on the odd occasion. Unlike me, she seldom rolled any tobacco back in the UK if not assembling a spliff. As I nodded towards the more than half-empty packet of fags lying in front of us (I'd misplaced my baccy somewhere), she asserted that, "Ha, that's not going to last us that long is it! They sell them behind the bar…" As she floated towards the bar, I feel an overwhelming ripple in my gut of sheer admiration and downright affection for the lady.

"These were all that I could get I'm afraid," Phoebe shrugs as she bangs down a 20 deck of Marlboro Lights onto the table.

"Ha, I think the fact that they're Marlboro Lights as opposed to Marlborough Gold is confirmation that they're fakes," I quip, only to surprisingly be corrected by Phoebe with her adding that,

"Well, they can probably still use that title outside of the EU though." It's unlike Phoebe to say such things, not at all because she's in any way unengaged or stupid, but just because this is the sort of almost pedantic detail that I'd never have thought her to have sufficient interest in to notice. It is also in many ways the sort of thing that I'd anticipate hearing from a point-scoring half-wit; coming from Phoebe it was merely an impressive little fact to add to my canon.

For some ridiculous reason, after the bottle of wine has emptied, Phoebe returns from the bar with a fresh bottle of rose wine and two large glasses filled with double brandies. "Well, well, well, better get down to business!" was my main thought followed by, "Thank you for whatever wine this is, and are you trying to get me drunk!?" as I glance towards the brown spirit in front of us. This just proves that sometimes, unguarded drunken statements that you would by no means utter whilst sober are often the best sort of things to say, as within seconds, and I can't recall how it in fact started, we had each other's tongues glued into our throats. With drunkards' coordination, this process was almost certainly quite sloppy as well; relief is the main thought that I recall, riding above all else.

After an intense first round, we were soon having an in-depth political discussion about the Brexit campaign. This revolved around the increasingly desperate British Government's investment in pamphlets instructing us all upon how to cast our votes in referenda. We not only concluded—as with the vast majority of our political thoughts, we were unanimous in individual agreement, as opposed to being juxtaposed in any way—that the whole thing was a farce. There is more than one name amongst the Cabinet who is staking their political career on encouraging us all to leave the European Union. The prospect of Boris Johnson eventually running for leadership of the Tory party should disaster strike and force us to leave EU was, at that time, leaving me with some lucid hellish nightmares. Oh, how little I knew.

Often, when Phoebe and I are spending time in a bar, we incorporate any fellow people around into our chats of all ages, statures and walks of life. Due to there not being anybody around that struck our fancy to talk to on this occasion, we were merely becoming aware that we were both drunk, on the border of being compos mentis and in any sort of control of our faculties. Perhaps, it is in a large part to the increased sensibility of age—complete with its reduced confidence in your knowledge—that we were now drinking at a snail's pace. Not to mention that directing a wine glass to your lips even becoming increasingly more strenuous effort.

Smoking and kissing were now the only toxins that we were consuming as we remained in an increasingly vacant bar. All of the smoking—we consumed the entire pack that Phoebe had bought, with only one or two grappa type drinks in between—and displays of affection did their trick in so far as convincing me that I was now fully back on form.

All that I can recall from the remainder of our joyous evening is the sound of the crickets, or whatever they were, by the side of the road seeming to be particularly loud. The remainder of the night is a particular haze of mine. It only consisted of us stumbling back into our hotel room and going to sleep after what can't have been a particularly long length of time.

The next morning, all evidence present confirms my suspicions that sex (I'd call it lovemaking, though we can't have been in any state to do that properly) had definitely occurred, and this only enhanced my mood to what feels like an unprecedented state of glory. The only real graphic memory that I've been left with rearose during my drinker's dawn and that is that of Phoebe sticking her finger up my bum. This act had never been practised before or occurred since; my grimace unaccompanied by a smile at the time must have achieved its aim. I do remember the 'so we're back in the game now' feeling.

Feeling as though I was a concertina as I attempted to de-coil myself the next morning, I tried to push the fact that I'd managed to jolt my neck out of place during the night to the back of my mind and forget the dull ache. Largely, this was surpassed by the strong feeling that my brain had evaporated inside of my head, leaving only disorientated remnants of satisfaction to singe inside. There was a dried-up feeling in the channel of my throat, which I'm sure you can imagine if you've ever passed excessive smoke and liquor through your mouth over the course of an evening. Having smoked definitely intensifies the feeling of discomfort the next morning; kill or cure is the general rule, in so far as placating the several dry and chesty coughs that were being emitted from my mouth. On this day, the thought of a cigarette was so repulsive that I simply chose to crash my head once again down on the pillow after taking a few swigs of water from the bottle, which I had strategically placed within arm's reach.

Overriding my discomfort, though, was the smug resounding feeling of immense gratification.

This was without question the longest, if not the only, proper lie-in that I had taken so far during this holiday. Phoebe too was generally a rather early riser, although she still appeared to be completely sparko, with the added excuse that she had also completed a lengthy aeroplane journey during the previous day. As she lay there looking so peaceful, along with noting that she had managed to remove all of her make-up and earrings somewhere along the line, I was naturally wondering about her reaction to last night's events. Hoping that it was the same for Phoebe, I just felt so at one with myself.

Returning from the toilet for the umpteenth time, I noticed that Phoebe had moved into a slightly different position, although was still not making any further sound. Getting out of the increasingly stuffy room was not my major priority, and as the eventual prerequisite to curing just about any hangover (though dawn had passed by several hours since), I needed to go to use the bathroom again. I needed some lengthy time washing and generally just freshening myself up. This took a fair while given the slow processing of my thoughts; and regardless of the general standard of the hotel that this was, the water supply didn't amount to much beyond a tepid dribbling stream.

Upon my return to the bedroom, it was within a matter of seconds that I began to feel as unclean as I had done before attempting to purge myself with water. My feeling of dirtiness was intensified not by the night of blissful passion, but more by the growing musty odour of the room, which we now seemed to be sharing with numerous aphids and mosquitoes.

Phoebe had now stirred and predictably with lots of feigned or genuine chagrin enquired as to, "Ah, why do I always end up feeling like this after a rendezvous with you Darren!" This was almost rhetorical and before stretching and rolling over she cooed that she 'had the most wonderful time though'.

5. Day 9: Bobbing Along

This leads on to potentially the happiest time of my life that I can recall. Certainly, the most freeing and fun in my recent short little history.

Taking the most welcome excuse to go and grab some supplies from a local shop and guarantee that our hotel booking would enable us to stay at the Peacock Palace; we certainly weren't in a state to do much beyond dipping in the pool this afternoon. Increasingly, this hotel was pearl of fortune and stability in my eyes.

Approaching midday and having flicked through several pages of my unopened book (Orwell's Animal Farm), which I was reading not just to appease my conscience as a Politics student for never having read the novel, but as the perfect opportunity to grab some time on my own.

"Right, I'm just going to go and fetch some food and water, Holly…I mean Phoebe, do you want anything?"

This was one of those Freudian slips that I'd fail to be able to say whether it was deliberate jest or completely accidental. There's nothing more to be read into it though; Phoebe is somebody who I adore in every way. I've little feeling for Holly, other than thinking of her as no more than a welcome distraction; I'll always wish her well in everything that she does though.

After a slight delay, Phoebe just grumbles that she'd 'actually really just fancy a plain cheese sandwich!' Laughing as she exhales, which is amongst the litany of things that I love her for.

"Err, well you'd better go down and find one then hadn't you!"

"Fine then," was how she responded as we laughed each other cheerio and had a warming kiss as I departed the room. This continued affection was just the sign that I needed that all was well on track for us to be lovers. The only obstacle is that, as we're always so engrossed in each other's company, we live for the moment and just never tackle any of the poignant issues concerning our status. The ideal moment to address this question always manages to just slip through my fingers. It feels as though it'd be adding an unnecessary complication to a blissful situation.

It's not as though the pair of us have not been through any real hardship of life together either. This unfortunately involves a wide range of things. These range from being in Phoebe's presence as I learned that my Mum had breast cancer—from which she is fortunately well on the road to recovery since, and that was…shit around 6 years ago!—to Phoebe once being sexually assaulted on the way home from meeting me. Granted, these may well be trivial things in comparison to any intense hardship, but beyond this we've certainly been exposed to vulnerability and I think that we're both well aware of how lucky we are in life. Overall, I think this proves that we are naturally amongst each other's first ports of call when faced by any crisis.

The stroll in search of a shop to buy the few bits was just the respite that I needed from the intensity of the wonderful situation that I had found myself caught up in. Being towards the real heat of the day, it was certainly a far from comfortable mission, yet nothing at all mattered in life to me at this time; if you could raise yourself to imagining life above cloud nine, that is where I'd be.

Walking past a solitary market stall, I was able to purchase a couple of apples and being a sucker for nostalgia, I was forced to also buy a handful of greengages as they strangely evoke my nan standing beside her massive fruit bowl. It probably wasn't so large, but rather that I was so small. The memory almost certainly dates to when I was less than 5 or so years old, and I feel that many of my recollections at this age evoke a more vivid imprint than anything I could conjure from scenery that I'd more recently witnessed.

A few patties, along with some crisps and obviously fruit, completed my paltry offerings as I returned back to the Peacock Palace. As I approached the door to the hotel, I felt myself taking on that senseless, disbelieving disposition that overwhelms me when I'm getting what I want; has the perfection of this situation all been the remnants of a delusion?

As I entered our room on the first floor, part of me was preparing to find that it would empty; I mean, as much as I love her and am rationally able to convince myself that all of last night's action took place, things always seem destined to take a turn in the exact opposite direction to what they should, don't they?

Imagining the worst case scenario—like I always find that it's best to do if you want to be inflated rather than disappointed—it even looked as though it could be true. After my milliseconds of genuine concern, Phoebe came out of the bathroom (yeah, I'd been stupid) with a white and green hotel towel draped around herself.

"See, that I couldn't track down any gastronomic treats, so these basic supplies shall have to do!"

Phoebe's smile and hastily rapid response simply consisted of: "You managed to get a few beers though, didn't you?"

"Oh shit, how did I manage to overlook something so fundamental…?" Was my slightly agitated thought pattern, which was soon followed by a wry digging myself out of this hole.

"Can't you be relied upon for anything!?" She retaliated with the jest that she was: "only protecting you from the social disgrace of being seen with a smelly and ill-kempt hussy who lived in sin with you" and even for Phoebe, I thought that this was particularly self-deprecating.

Saying this, my response was merely that: "I obviously put up with enough, being seen out with you in the first place!"

Whereas this could have the potential to be rather uncouth, if not just plain nasty, the fact that I consider Phoebe to be significantly out of my league in the first place means that this sort of remark could not give even a smidgen of offence.

Within seconds, the picnic was forgotten as we were passionately kissing. The only sound words that I recall being emitted from my mouth that actually formed words were, "You smell a burning forest…of mango trees, Phoebe. I love it!"

We were soon rolling around on the bed, and before much time had elapsed, my clothes had all been removed and Phoebe's towel had found its way to the floor. If making love can ever be defined, then this felt as though it was. The only thing that makes me question this is the fact that I was consciously aware of this at the time. The entire passionate episode can't have lasted for longer than quarter of an hour or so before I had to tell a seemingly enlivened Phoebe that: "Well, that was a badly timed shower for you then, wasn't it!" Feeling energised rather than worn out by our romantic tryst, it wasn't long before we were taking a joint shower and scrubbing each other's backs; if you know what I mean.

We had now entered one of those junctures in my life that was just a permanent state of splendid surrealism. Eventually, we did go and assemble our little picnic—to use the term in an incredibly generous sense—and go to the roof terrace a few flights of stairs above, which is, again, to use a term generously; it consisted of nothing beyond terracotta tiles. It's fortunate that we both love a bit of sun worship, as there was now a clear sky. Still, we'd both creamed up, and Phoebe had brought some cream coloured cloth, which I guessed was some sort of sarong, to sit and place our food upon.

This was one of those days—which I'm relieved to be able to say is a real rarity—where we just didn't have any need to even leave the hotel. I may have taken the short jaunt to fetch some uninspiring food, but Phoebe hadn't done anything. The remainder of the afternoon was passed both reading and supping a few bottles of beer by the hotel pool. We splashed around in the pool and then entered into a completion—which seemed to last forever—of seeing how many of the pool's short lengths that we could manage to swim underwater. When this soon became too much hard work, it was simplified into just timing (in the form of us counting, rather than using a stopwatch, so there was nothing technical about this tremendously serious completion) how long we could hold our breath underwater. We sure know how to live.

Although we had exerted the decadence of ordering plenty of hotel beers—although certainly not flowing with standards back home—we hadn't spent much that day, so I purchased two decks of Lucky Strikes—my first knowing pollution of my lungs to complement the doubtless level of pollution in the considerably sized town where we were staying—red for me and blue for Phoebe. Accuse me of being patriarchal here if you like, but I just know that as an inconsistent—containing just manufactured tobacco anyway—smoker back home, this is what she'd almost certainly prefer. That first exhalation after doing anything joyous is always the icing on the cake of life; doing well, exercising, hearing good news etc. and losing out upon this if I ever had children or any dependents or had poorer health, it is not a joy that I look forward to sacrificing. Perhaps one day, I'll just get bored of the taste, but that feeling of acute asphyxiation being cured by a relieving exhalation is not one that I look forward to permanently leaving behind. Still, life must all about compromise.

It was soon turning into one of those intervals where every person in the world beyond each other becomes at first clouded and then completely irrelevant. It was a wonderful day. Beyond the orbit of devotion that you're thinking within, nobody or anything else at all matters. Still, neither of us are people to vegetate, so it was agreed upon that we'd have to actually do something different tomorrow.

We'd been more than content, but after darkness fell in the form of a breathtakingly beautiful sunset, my stomach began to rumble. Although, it was sheltered to such a confined space, our day had been most active in several alternative ways, so it could certainly be claimed that we had justifiably worked up a healthy appetite. As we re-entered the hotel, I noticed a pamphlet advertising an incredibly cheap sounding Chinese buffet. To see another country's spin on this renowned cuisine was something that interested me, although it certainly makes me guilty of feeding into the inexorable levels of globalisation. Undoubtedly, I'd plump for a curry any day of the week, when given the choice, though the e-numbers in cheap Chinese food—as this certainly was—did have their appeal to my rumbling stomach.

Gargantuan quantities of food were consumed. This was largely induced by my mammoth appetite, though Phoebe's dainty lips could certainly put away their fair share. It was here that our privacy was invaded by none other than Duncan. Although this contemporary of ours (though probably with at least a couple of years taken off) had barged along uninvited to fill one of the two pastel green fixed seats around our table, he did seem harmless.

This said, if I were in any way responsible for his wellbeing, I'd not have a great deal of confidence in his doing anything whatsoever unsupervised. All that I remember finding out about him was that he too was an only child—which made complete sense—who, having recently graduated from the University of the West of England in a Nutrition degree, was living and working back home in Reading, helping out with his father's picture framing business. The disclosure that his Duncan's degree revolved around diet, and that he had a most big boned—to use the term generously—physique, certainly induced a need to supress a snigger. A twinkle in the eye from Phoebe as we deliberately avoided falling into eye contact assured me that she had also needed to conquer some decorum at this time!

Along with clearly being bright-eyed and bushy-tailed, this guy had a propensity to reel of one meaningless anecdote soon followed by the next. We were slightly flattered that he was taking the trouble to feed us with such elaborate tales, with the clear desire to defeat his insecurities and fall into our friendship. Not only did this bolster my unabashedly large ego, but it meant that he always seemed to feel the need to buy us more beers. Naturally, I offered him beer in return, but after that new cans came at such a fierce pace that I happily shut up and supped up.

Comparisons were all too easily drawn between him and a long time mate of mine from back home. Due in part, though not solely, to his relentless fabrications, Josh falls nowhere near the inner circle of my most intimate little home friendship group. Granted, I like the guy and would always defend him against any criticism, but he's a chronic bull-shitter.

A personal favourite of mine dates to the mid-2000s, sometime when we were in sixth form at Highams Park. We were mostly eighteen-year-olds and I think that the majority of us had actually, or at least claimed to have, lost our virginity at some point in the not so distant past, or would within the non-too distant future. Predictably, not wanting to be left out, Josh needed some input into these conversations. And oh no, he couldn't just contribute, he had to exceed us all in some way. It's priceless that not only did he have to have his cherry popped by somebody glamorous in her early twenties, but he did it as part of a threesome. Oh yes a female,

female and male ménage a trois with two exquisitely beautiful, yet conveniently nameless females. And this yarn gets better.

This action hilariously took place after we'd all been out at some DJ set at the once-great Plastic People on Shoreditch's Curtain Road. We'd lost Josh whilst making our way home, which, given the ease at which he can form part of the background, is not the greatest surprise. Anyhow, supposedly the action took place back down Catherine Wheel alley whilst the rest of us were aboard an N26 bus back home. If you're not aware of this little backstreet, it's a small passage that leads off directly opposite Liverpool Street Station. Given the size of Josh and the width of this alleyway, this extra details provides extra challenge to the tale's minimal credibility.

It is one of the numerous snippets of Josh's elaborated history—such as his dad's red Porsche, which they were always driving too fast for any of us to ever see them, and his holiday to Thailand's Koi Samui (according to his parents they rotated between Blackpool, to visit some relative, and the Canary Islands), to name but a couple of examples—that is now completely overlooked. In fairness to the poor guy, the invention of such adventures has largely ceased as I think that he has reassuringly grown comfortable in that we've always accepted that his dad, Kevin, is a primary school caretaker and his mum, Annabel, is a home-help provider. Although they're both most worthy and respectable jobs, our growing awareness has long informed us that the luxuries Josh boasts about would be almost completely unobtainable. Although they're without doubt the type to do scratch cards, nobody gets so consistently lucky that these exploits are anything but an impossibility.

It was just this type of situation that we had ended up in with Duncan. Harking all of the way back to the beginning of this trip, I was amusing myself in imagining what an unbearably awkward situation it would have been to observe Stephen from that first hostel, competing with Duncan in terms of who could share the most elaborate experience. Whatever the pair would choose to recount, it would inevitably be some complete fiction. The two would either bounce off each other to their mutual delight, or, as Phoebe believed, they'd be each other's nemesis. Perhaps because they are so alike, they'd instantly see right through one another and be forced to confront the reality of their existence. Still, whatever people have to do to combat loneliness and gain approval I suppose.

Phoebe and I were happy enough to entertain him; I think that the way in which you react to such situations indicates a lot about your temperament. Holly, for example, would have dealt with the situation in her overly serious way, and her ample degree of amicableness might have even led her to suggest that we travelled together for a bit. God forbid. Whereas a slime ball such as James would probably have manipulated the situation so that he could bask in Duncan's inevitable showering of compliments and ensure that he has a wealth of drinks bought, whilst behaving openly condescendingly towards the poor guy.

Phoebe's an absolute exception in her ability not to cast judgement on character and to be warm and genuinely inquisitive, even when talking to even the most hard-work people. Duncan without doubt fell into this category. He lacked even the most basic socialisation in the game of conversation—such as reciprocating the questions asked to you and finding anything close to mutual topic of interest to discuss—and was only content talking about himself. We all must have to tolerate this at times, and with some people, it is actually more than bearable as they have enough fiery chatter; be it so-called banter or deeper stuff. Duncan described absolutely nothing of any worth, though we were forced to learn a great deal about him; none of which I can now remember. I think that Phoebe dropped in something about us all being from London as Duncan lived somewhere far like Uxbridge (right at the end of the Piccadilly line) or something. Obviously he never bothered to enquire anything whatsoever about where we were from, and the conversation soon trickled on to his mindless topics of conversation.

The chicken sates that we had been served for starters were accompanied by two tasty sauces that included the generic yet worthy peanut sauce and some unusual smooth green concoction that, nice as it was, gave me no clues as to what it actually consisted of. This was definitely the highlight of the meal as the quality of further dishes brought towards us was substandard to say the least. Duncan insisted that it was all 'delicious' and even 'the best food that I've eaten in ages'. This depicts more about Duncan's character and sheltered life—without sounding too snobbish—than anything else. Much like Duncan, they certainly were dry and hard work to digest. What a boring metaphor.

The main prerequisite of entertaining Duncan's company seemed simply to be an ability to keep up a sufficient level of smiling and bemused nodding. Conveniently, he seemed more than happy to gobble up whatever food was within his Cyclops-like eyesight. Several more beers had been ordered, and I had insisted on paying for some digestive, largely because Duncan had kindly refused our—or I should say Phoebe's—offering of hard cash as our payment for the meal. Although he did this in a chivalrous way, I didn't feel that a great deal could be read into it. Our nightcaps soon arrived. Phoebe had opted for an amaretto and I fancied a whiskey; Duncan chose a Malibu and coke. Each to their own is all that I thought. It was only when he decided to lay his hand on and stroked up Phoebe's thigh that an atmosphere of real discomfort descended.

This incident was understandably meant to go unnoticed to me, and I only detected it when Phoebe caught my eye mid-way through Duncan's unprecedented and uncomfortable action. Hopefully, without sounding overly arrogant, I was mostly astonished that Duncan had the temerity to not only take the liberty in what could be loosely described as sexually harassing Phoebe, but also in daring to believe that he'd ever even stand a chance. In truth, the guy clearly couldn't handle his drink all that well, and I do not think that he had any real vision of the situation's aftermath, let alone believed that Phoebe would reciprocate in any way.

In the typically British way, nobody appeared to acknowledge the situation, and we were luckily afforded some distraction as the drinks were brought over. Phoebe and I rapidly downed ours; predictably Duncan soon followed suit.

'Didn't you get some more cigarettes today, Darren… I really fancy one now actually, shall we go outside?'

'Well we've not asked for the bill yet have we, but here's the money for those last drinks, Duncan (I left a rough estimation, which I knew was bound to exceed their charge if anything) and we're both really tired, so I think that we'll scoot back to hotel and smoke on the way.'

'Sounds good!' Phoebe quickly responded.

Duncan predictably looked deflated, and whereas I might expect him to display some sign of shame in acknowledging how inappropriate he had been in displaying affection towards Phoebe, his brow merely tightened, and if anything he looked detectably angry.

'But the night's only just began hasn't it guys! I know that you say that you're both tired, but couldn't we maybe just go for a quick drink on the way back to our hotels!?'

With this response I was of two minds. Not at all over whether to take him up on this suggestion, as Duncan was somebody I'd never want to have to endure again for a second longer than necessary, but merely over whether I felt mainly anger or pity. Even after the whiskey, it's not as though I ever felt the need to be violent.

I was simply agitated that he had failed to realise that he was in any way in the wrong for his lusty action and relentless lecherous stares. The sympathetic side of me couldn't help but feel responsible for the lack of accountability that he felt for his actions, which was confirmed by the lack of worthlessness it appeared that he now felt…

Although I overlooked it at the time when he suggested we go for *another* nightcap, it is instantly noticeable now that, although I didn't believe him to be at all a conscious schemer, he was guilty here of the classic tactic of blaming us for a situation not going as he'd wanted. And although getting rid of Duncan's tedious company was a most welcome development—we genuinely were pretty whacked—the thought of making the relatively short walk back to our hotel was a welcome relief.

We slept together again—quickly this time—that night. The adverb here was the operative word, yet this holiday was regardless turning into one of the most regular experiences of sex that I'd ever had. It could be observed that this most recent occurrence was largely Phoebe's attempt—as it is fair to say that she was often the principal instigator in our little liaisons—to validate ourselves against the unwantedly forward invasion of Duncan. As with many of my attempted insights, I may have been reading far too much into the fact that, once again, we just fancied having a shag.

On the morning of the next day we failed to make any disappearance from bed. No further action took place, and although we were clearly decompensating for a wealth of lost sleep, we also recognised that we were being sucked into that vicious trap of ghastly slumber. Neither of us had any direct call to venture outside of the room, as we weren't hungry and still had two more than half full bottles of water, yet we also wanted to avoid letting time pass us by without doing anything of worth.

By midday we had changed into swim gear, which included a red polka dot swimming costume of Phoebe's that I had not yet seen, and me wearing my pink swim shorts that I really would need to make sure were washed somewhere soon. Although passing time in the shade of a eucalyptus tree next to a pool in blazing sunshine reading our books may be the ideal holiday for many people back home, it certainly did not much suit us as something worthy to do for beyond a couple of days. Eventually we wandered to the adjacent beach; we were both suckers for sand and sea.

The by-now uninspiring large town had limited appeal to spend much, if any, more of our time in. Instead, during this day I raced through no less than five meaty chapters of my book, slurped more delicious beer that I doubted would stand much stead within the polluted environs of London and embarrassingly succeeded in getting my back sunburned. This was despite believing that I had been adequately careful with sunscreen, but then I suppose that the delusional 'got to go red to go brown' mentality did exist tucked away somewhere deep down within my conscience. After all, we did hail from what was shamefully once part of Essex, before greater London came to its rescue. Teddy Sheringham was born in Highams Park, if it's of any interest, though as my Dad ensured that I was conditioned into being a Hammers fan, so I never had to endure Spurs' tremendous fall from being the twentieth century's first—and I believe only ever, up until that point—double winners in 1961. Encapsulations of events that have occurred on your home turf always seem slightly delusional, if not bizarrely armed with more poignancy, when you're in some far-flung corner of the world.

This is the paradox that I find myself in whilst I am as detached from my reality space. It's also why I find travel so effective in getting a fresh perspective on things, as you are aware that the vast majority of any issues that you departed with shall still exist once you return, yet their potential solution is more vivid and far less challenging. The presence of any close friend is always magical as you take the blinkers off in terms of any delusions that you may fabricate about your life, but to me it's a reassuring reminder that your life is not empty.

With much longitude, the daylight is beginning to pass, this time without even venturing much outside of our hotel. For whatever reason, I can't help but feel guilty and even ashamed of myself when such feats are achieved. We agreed that it'll be best at this stage—after such a lazy day and with us becoming so irreverently used to exploiting creature comforts—to pass this evening on a coach to our next point of call.

We select the more remote coastal resort of Kirinda as our next destination. Thankfully this shall be new territory for me, as this is miles away from my first point of call. It also appears in all of the literature that I have read to be more remote and unspoilt than the previous resort; which in fairness was still organic feeling and beautiful enough to make me feel excited at how this could possibly be outdone. I assumed that it would be more peaceful and less lively, and this was set to be exactly what the doctor ordered; especially with the reiteration that I had indeed fallen into feeling uncontrollably mushy and loved up.

6. Day 12: Beach Bar 2

Ideally we'd have been able to do a night's bus and saved on a night's accommodation, but as the only buses left twice a day, at 6 in the morning and 6 in the evening, this was just not an option.

The events occurring in between dusk falling and waking up the next day, ready to jump back on the road, do not contain anything all that worthy to account. Other than perhaps the fact that we had some more sex and, particularly given Duncan's nasty advances, we were more than overdue to get out of the town where we were.

What I can presume was down principally to my lack of a healthy recharge, the next day commenced with some of the most unamicable interactions that Phoebe and I had ever had. This does merely extend to several crossed words, and could be laughed over more than quickly, only it involved my waking her up at 5.15am. Physically prompting somebody to get out of bed is never something that I feel comfortable doing, and it certainly had the feared effect, as Phoebe's grouchiness all too effectively proved as she stretched herself out on the bed.

'Ah, piss off, Darren!' This was succeeded by a look of scorn.

To avoid a prolonged and hostile silence, which was just not in the vocabulary of when Phoebe and I were together, I quickly told her the time and reiterated that the bus we wanted to catch left from the other side of the block in just under an hour.

"Well I thought that you were messing around when you said that was the sort of time we were planning on leaving last night?"

"No, that is the bus that I meant. You know that there only appears to be another one running today anyway, and I wanted to find somewhere to stay and charge into the sea whilst we can still enjoy a good couple of hours on the beach!"

I believed this response to healthily balanced charm and assertion, and it must have succeeded in having the desired effect as Phoebe was jumping into the shower, whilst she still appeared to be carrying the hump. Deciding that I was clean enough not to need to bother with a full on wash, I cleaned my teeth using the green basin and sink that revealed the room had not always been en-suite. Fascinating as this is, I quickly threw on my travelling uniform of my short-sleeved white shirt and overly short, if anything, denim cut-offs. A classic situation of finding yourself having to cut things higher than anticipated to even them up, always shoddily in my case.

Within seconds upon exiting the hotel, I bought several pieces of fruit for breakfast and some cheese and tomato sandwiches for the journey, which, although they were the only variety on offer, are probably what I'd have chosen anyway. They were mostly courtesy of the fact that I'd found a scrunched up £10 note, which somehow had made it into my shorts' right back pocket, which I never usually use. Happy days, I thought. The next trip was to a bank in the direction of the bus stop from which we would depart later. The ATM thankfully was working, as otherwise I'd have felt pretty screwed, with the only currency left in our room being about $70 and a tenner in sterling. It was after I got back into the hotel to settle up and, if anything, I was relieved that, after expecting the worst-case scenario, having a tab hadn't managed to bankrupt me at this early stage of my holiday.

Entering back into our room, it was a relief to see that Phoebe's shower appeared to have purged her of any morning angst that she'd awoken with.

"You've probably got time to jump in the shower now…"

Which I only returned with the fact that "you know that I can't shower against a clock, so I'll just wait until we've been in the sea I think"

"Pa, it's me that'll have to put up with your stench on this inevitably overheated journey!?" Phoebe quipped, which if anything confirmed the restoration of our form.

"You know that the smell of my e-MASCULINITY turns you right on!"

Deservedly Phoebe did not dignify this pettily ridiculous remark with any response as she seemed to take an age packing the remainder of her belongings into her rucksack. Meanwhile I took myself out onto the communal balcony to eat a banana, and although it was unusual for me so early in the morning, I was really craving a smoke.

Climbing up the stairs to the hotel's highest roof terrace, I was pleased to note upon my arrival that I had remembered to bring our half full bottle of water, only for my stomach to sink as I rummaged around my pockets for a lighter. Being like buses, I either seemed to have plenty dotted around my pockets, or I find myself desperately wishing that I had the ability to conjure fire.

It was as I was traipsing back down the stairs in order to retrieve my lighter (that I was thankfully certain still contained a fair amount of gas) that I was startled and almost sure that I had performed some double take. This was as old Cas-aan-dra complete in her drapes of seaweed. Mike was there as well, but we exchanged no more than a couple of words at this meeting, and I fail to recall anything about him other than that he blended perfectly into Cassandra's background appeared to be increasingly hen-pecked, as I could only imagine she liked him best. So much so, clearly, that he'd easily been coaxed into extending 'their vacation of a lifetime', beyond the return flight that they were soon due to be on after I first met them.

Cassandra's attire was my biggest surprise of our exchange, if I'm honest as I thought that her visually polluting seaweed… dress I suppose, though I really don't know what you'd call it, was certainly on display. Though perhaps this was not such a surprise considering we were in a coastal region. Just my luck.

It is only when travelling that you can establish familiarity and even friendship with people who you would never otherwise in a million years cross paths with. Yet this is within the narrow remit of knowing that you're most unlikely to ever see them again and that you have so little interests to share in your *real lives*. Stating the obvious I suppose, but you can only ever afford to treat strangers so earnestly for a brief time.

It can be something of a strain, even whilst you are all travellers, to be coerced into having some sort of conversation with people who you would not otherwise, yet this also gives a snapshot of what it must be like to be some sort of nomad. As pretentiously bourgeois that sounds. Admittedly the workplace also offers a load of od-bods being forced to get along, only you all at least get your income from the same source and normally share some similar goals.

Some good friends of mine from back home—like our cantankerous Charlie in particular—hail that 'all you see when you are travelling is other like-minded, middle-class and upwardly mobile white people, and you all go for an orgy of supposedly enhancing yourself. LIKE YOU DAZ'. Charlie in particular merely goes around from one dead-end menial job to the next, which would be absolutely fine if he wasn't so het up on a self-ascribed working class inferiority complex. This is all endorsed by his huge, yet vulnerable, little ego. Especially as he is as often as not on the dole, which surely discredits him from this label? To demonise anybody for being middle class must in itself suggest that it takes one to know one.

As a soft leftie, I'd blame the increased lack of any soul in society and the absence of social conscience on Thatcher.

Still, the social decay and denigration of all sense of justice in British society was shelved to the back of my mind as I took on a right wing short-sightedness, self-satisfaction and instant gratification in eagerly anticipating our next destination. In all of the literature that I had seen of the place, it was hailed as a remotely adventurous destination, with the quality of the coast and ambience of the scenery supposedly surpassing anything that I would have experienced so far on this trip. Without further cheapening myself, the numerous pop-up bars and the established intimate drinking dens that I had seen in travel guides and pamphlets scattered round so far on this trip ensured that I was more than a little excited.

Deep down, I had some slight concern that in completing my adventure alongside Phoebe, I was not travelling in the solitary and independence-affirming manner in which I would have planned. In itself. Having Phoebe sharing this experience with me not only increased the comfort emotionally—and you could say physically—but it was also carving a new benchmark of perfection whilst travelling, which I had not so far experienced. Simultaneously, as I was celebrating my fulfilment on this trip, I contemplated the fact that, as our former Prime Minister once stated, I had 'never had it this good' (Macmillan, H. 1957). This me suspicious that my fortunes may mirror the demise of this Tory tit. I know next to nothing about the geezer, in fairness, though the political party that allowed him 6 years as Prime Minister during the bumbling post-war consensus overly relied on the fallacy a trickle-down theory of wealth; the rich can get richer in other words.

As many of my inconsequential thoughts may indicate, I love a tenuous link, and I am linking this (albeit vaguely) with my own experience in stating how I am never allowed to have it this good, and I'm convinced that my harmony will have to burn out pretty soon.

In other words, the tranquillity of my clear horizon will soon become overcast. What was predominantly niggling me was concern that any other travel trip that I should choose to take by myself in the future would automatically be inferior compared to this famous little adventure that I was enjoying.

Whilst it did make me feel more like my mum than anything else, 'get a grip, Darren!' was the main message that I forced myself to take on board at this point. Undermining and then jeopardising my current state of enjoyment, there was my own inadequacy complex where I just couldn't bring myself to believe that people such as myself could be allowed to be this happy. Carpe diem and all of that—without sounding like too much more of a prat than I do usually (as my chronic state of self-deprecation returns) I should just focus on enjoying myself and make the most of my overly brief detachment from my job in the charity sector, which is rewarding to the minor and infuriating to the major. But life cannot never be that consistently kind can it?

Granted, I've been more than a little fortunate in never really coming aboard any hard times. Whilst east London's Clapton was my initial residence before it became gentrified in any way, and I entered into a less than prepared and provisioned world for a wee nipper, I knew that I was always well loved; without wishing to appear too much overly sentimental.

As well-cared-for and protected as I was within the comfort of my own home, the fact that you alone had to fend for yourself and fight all of your own battles single-handed, whilst also making sure that you metaphorically tidied up your own mess, was always well ingrained. It was only as I reached the age of nine, in preparation for my transition to secondary school, that my parents, wisely in hindsight, decided to depart the chaos of a Clapton life for more salubrious suburbia.

Although I much resented this at the time, and my parents could both validate that I am no follower and almost certainly shouldn't have ever been coughed up in gangland, life would undoubtedly have been more of a challenge had we remained in Clapton. Personable as I have always tried to be, and although I always had some mates, my destiny to always feel as though I was something of an outsider was spawned as early on at Clapton's much larger than average Daubeney Primary School.

I completed a bit of my last year of primary school around Highams Park's Oakhill Primary School before undertaking my secondary education at Heathcote Secondary School within the same area. This is where I obviously first crossed paths with Phoebe, though containing a swarm of pubescents, I didn't actually meet her (I'd say be introduced, though that would be an alien concept to pupils at our school) until I was 16 or 17. Happy days, my love of nostalgia could lead me to say, though of course they were far from this in reality. As a charming and outwardly confident girl, Phoebe obviously attracted a great deal of attention from a range of guys with the same ambition—to get laid—than I did as the pretty zit-faced, more academic guy. We'd find it hilarious, I'm sure, to go on to Myspace or MSN messenger (if you're old enough to recall this early modern social media) and delve into the archives of our friendship.

The crux of the matter is that we both feel detached from identifying with any particular niche in itself and always feel slightly on the edge. Phoebe spent her formative years living around De Beauvoir (the posher the name sounds, the rougher the place in my experience) Town in Hackney although I'm told that her parents had enough similar foresight as mine to get her moved towards their native E4 postcode before she even would have even commenced primary school. So although she would have arguably appeared more settled in our neck of the woods, the fact that we always feel as though we're on the edge of everything is at the forefront of our mutual understanding of life.

In keeping with my neurosis at ever missing something that I'd booked to travel on, we arrived at the small coach station with ample time left. This results in me lighting up and propagating Phoebe with a cigarette, which she accepts. If people stopped filling their lungs to pass time, cigarette companies would be significantly worse off, though in as much of a smug boast as it sounds, it is a rarity for either of us to smoke at such an early hour in the day, if at all before nightfall. Still, when in Rome, and although this time without having to receive Cassandra's condescension, I vividly recall feeling some profound sense of shame in tying myself to the chain of nicotine so early in the day.

With its tinted windows, our maroon 15 or so seater minibus looked the biz. It had an abundance of leg room and a TV screen, and it satisfied me that it had definitely been worth paying the extra bit of money for, even if we were tied to more limited options for departure times. Of course it would hardly have been the end of the world if we'd missed our bus (though we'd already paid and got our tickets, so I'd be sure to be a gnarly mood for several hours at least) as there were plenty of other ways to get to our beach destination, though they'd involve changing buses a third of the way in. This was something that we both really did not need.

The minibus' ambience was enhanced by the fact that there were several scrawny chickens on board, in cages that the RSPCA certainly wouldn't condone. I was mildly entertained also by the collaborative prayers that just about every passenger aside from Phoebe and myself seemed to be uttering. I felt slightly guilty for the second time this morning (like the want for cigarettes, this emotion seems to have a nasty habit of gripping over me in a chain), this time for failing to understand a word of what the fellow passengers were saying in their native tongue. Perhaps this is the emotion that religions and capitalism so fiercely manipulate; guilt and fear are intrinsically linked. There was not a single thing about this situation that should make me feel any more ashamed than the usual amount.

The sense that I was experiencing of a lack of self-worth, was an understandable scapegoat for the fact that this country's roads had a notorious death record, and I justifiably did not feel at all safe at the hands of this particular dreadlocked driver. It was probably an urge to eat away my underlying fear that caused me to purchase a kebab off of one of the street sellers who walked onto the bus. For the equivalent of about 5 pence sterling, I was being offered half a dozen or so vaguely appetising looking pieces of marinated…what looked like some white meat? This could be a poignant example of fear making us engage in all sorts of irrational behaviour. Admittedly it is a tenuous link to voting behaviour, but I can and I will use the example of me buying an incredibly risky-looking meat skewer in an instance of desperation as a metaphor for the potential appeal of some extremist voting behaviour. If you've got absolutely no idea what I'm talking about here, then I apologise. Profusely.

The nutrition—to use the term loosely—tastes fine, to use the operative expression, though my motion sickness is coming over. I am feeling as angry at myself as anything else. Although I am all too well aware that motion sickness is a psychological, it is certainly an unfortunately a frequent occurrence, only significantly worsened by being at the back of the bus. I glance to the front of the bus where Phoebe is sat reading *Down and Out in Paris and London*, which she has borrowed off of me, and which I have read numerous times and always take alongside me for comfort when I travel. Phoebe knows full well that I can never read whilst on the road. Audaciously she is engrossed in my book as I struggle not to have a bilious attack. See, this is the other thing that panic and fear succeeds in: creating irrational bitterness and resentment towards everybody else. In other words, I'm becoming a bigot. Only briefly, mind.

It is from about this juncture of the journey that I am plagued by a causal fear that I may have to erupt everywhere. I illogically, yet unavoidably, wish that we'd opted for the marginally cheaper option of breaking the journey up and having to change buses. Going for that age-old trick of focusing on some stationary object upon the horizon, as usual, had absolutely no effect. The beautiful scenery at all times proved to be of absolutely no distraction, but finally, after a couple of long and painful hours, we reach our destination, and to say that I feel relief is an understatement.

Whether we've arrived in the much fantasied beach resort that we had planned or taken a detour and ended up in Southend is purely secondary, if irrelevant, compared to the fact that I can instantaneously stop suffering from the fixable woe of motion sickness. It does take me a fair while to come back to my senses as we wait in the basking heat for an abominable duration of time to collect our baggage. Until you completely disembark, I always find it impossible to conjure conversation, as the mind always seems elsewhere and all concentration is focused on getting to your final destination. This complaint is another factor that makes me just feel a tad odd, and I can only manage to make my lips curve into a sort of smile when Phoebe exclaims, 'I'm loving this book!'

Nothing is working to conciliate my frustration at the fact that, for no apparent reason, we are not being delivered our baggage for such a lengthy period of time. Phoebe enters into an impassioned rambling about not being able to 'believe that I've not read this before' as she cuddles Orwell's book. This couldn't interest me any less at this moment as I am too preoccupied with why we are standing there in silence waiting for our belongings to be returned as the driver stands in animated conversation with another minibus driver who seems be some long lost comrade of his. As I am becoming too preoccupied with the fact that we are not appearing to be getting anywhere, I take out a cigarette. Although it is all something of a touching reunion, having chain-smoked cigarette number two—with an urgent desire to smoke that I have never before experienced—I am fast approaching the end up my little hissy like tether.

In order to placate the beast of being delayed, I pipe up with a politer way of articulating 'what the fuck's going on with our bags!?' cushioned with a 'good morning' and 'please and thank you' in the native tongue. Well, it turned out to be something along the lines of the fact that the porter (or whatever he was) had simply forgot to return our bags before entering lengthy conversation. The quantity of time that was lost—okay, not exceeding more than a number of minutes—along with the fact that nothing was done to rectify the situation is surely a metaphor for the inadequacy of people as a collective. I wonder, where is the benevolent dictator when you need one?

It is in these instances when I begin to overanalyse and dissect the relationship between the disconnected goings on and the failure of the world to prosper that I most acutely worry about my wellbeing and the sanctity of whatever sense of self I have left to deal with.

‘So we’re going to aim for your beloved Bay of Biscay now then are we DAZ?’

Phoebe had certainly awoken in much higher spirits than I had that morning, as even her affectionate-seeming abbreviation of my name caused me to take some unwarranted offence in this instance.

Replying with the coldly belittling ‘I don’t remember you having any other suggestions’ was, I am relieved to say most out of character. Proudly, I can reflect upon how this was only one of several occasions where I had directed anything towards Phoebe that could be interpreted as passive aggressive and offhand in any way or intent whatsoever.

The wonderment and admiration that I hold towards Phoebe is exemplified in her indifference to this remark, and without retaliating in any way whatsoever or storing it up as ammunition in a Machiavellian fashion (behaviour that I’d ashamedly be likelier to practise), she merely hailed down a rickshaw. We may have opted to walk or catch a bus, but it had miraculously started to shower, and we were within minutes outside of our selected *Bay of Biscay* hostel.

In a corny example of the weather mirroring our sense of security, I did feel as though a weight had been lifted as we approached the whitewashed guesthouse where I had proposed for us to stay for at least the first night. I’d be offering you a mistruth, though, if I were to claim that anything in my guide book’s write up, beyond it being called the *Bay of Biscay*, had enticed me to go gallivanting to this hostel. We were thousands of miles away from the Bay of Biscay in the Atlantic corner between France and Spain, and I found it quite funny that this hostel was advertising itself as a hub for tranquil and relaxed respite when its namesake is notoriously rough and choppy. Although it had no pool or functioning restaurant (you were allowed to bring your own food to eat in the dining area and there was limited room service on offer), the peacocks greeting us looked to exist in splendid health.

My discomfort throughout the journey had long been put behind me, and with at least a dozen banana palm trees in the vicinity, whatever slightly bourgeois-eque tumultuous woes I had been feeling were tucked away well into the periphery of my mind.

I remember just assuming that there would be room at the inn on this occasion, never addressing the likelihood that this wouldn’t be possible. Vulgarly presumptuous and conceited as this may seem, sometimes this attitude of just believing that everything will work for you does seem to work. This is frustrating when you take into account that many people seem to walk around with this invincible take on life, where everything seems to work for them and for no conceivable reason. With any luck they'll gain some level of self-realisation in life to choke on their silver spoon.

Dastardly James has invaded my thoughts again, and the injustice of this pollution frustratingly seemed entirely unnecessary. In particular this thinking is antithetical to our gorgeous backdrop and the glorious state of entering into the most wanted relationship that I could ever imagine, and having a comfortable (if bound to be something that I'd find less than fulfilling) job to walk into next month back home. To my dad's eyes just be a classic example of me worrying for the apparent the sake of it, not being able to find anything better to do. In fairness, he only says it to wind me up, and it certainly succeeds in touching a nerve! Defending myself to him, I'd just say that he is just not competent at lifting the blinkers off of his eyes… Even this is the exact sort of reaction that he want. It's all just harmless banter (does any such thing really exist though?), you could say.

This is a term that I've come to dread. Particularly as it fills me with the apprehension at having to initiate myself into a plethora of people, with whom I'd almost certainly never normally associate myself, when I start my new job next month. The 'game of life' as it could justifiably be called. All of the awkwardness of a group of relatively disconnected people being forced to endure large quantities of the week alongside one another all being guised as *banter*. When in reality I am sure that you know as well as I do that this often consists merely as term to license workplace bullying; 'why can't you just take a bit of harmless bantz!?'

In reality, I'm sure that we can all recognise as well as I do, after spending all of my working life with in the office environment, how banter is just a coping strategy that people use to feel better about their petty existences. Irrespective of whether I'm ever guilty of using this supposed wit, it always seems to cause people to go way beneath the belt, preying on people's vulnerabilities and licensing this under a namesake, whereas in reality they're just causing somebody else discomfort. Like pack animals, the more dominant (and probably also the most insecure) individuals get their moment to be the court jester at somebody else's expense.

Whilst I am conscious that I seem to be painting us out as the most boring and unadventurous Brits abroad, before too long we were sitting within an almost empty beach bar, sipping some sangria-like concoction called something else. It tasted a cross between pinot and aniseed, and I wasn't complaining. As some justification of our all-too-predictable actions, we had trekked a fair number of miles along the varied terrain of a white-sanded beach and cliff tops. It was all a beautiful panorama now under the backdrop of a now almost clear sky and a fertile looking rock face. Of course, prior to our insensible rambling in beachwear and canvas shoes we had been taking a lengthy dip into the salty sea; this wasn't brought to a close by any cramp or our growingly wrinkled fingers, but the abundance of jelly fish that then suddenly appeared alongside us in the ocean.

The fact that we were both covered in a fair few scratches, along with bumps and bruises, only cements my love for Phoebe. Never before have I known any girl—or even bloke for that matter, so as not to appear sexist—who appears so indifferent to what the world makes of her. For sure, she can pull off the glamour as well as anybody if she feels that she wants to do it. And *want* is the operational word here, as everything that Phoebe decides to do is on her terms alone. For example, when we went into the sea in a secluded place earlier, she went topless, not in any attempt to put anybody in understandable awe of her body, but simply because she wanted to be able to put on something dry for our stroll after. Phoebe was the freest spirit that I had ever had the pleasure to meet.

We were half way through our sangria lookalike medicine (and this is as worthy a description as any other that I can muster) when I was again invaded by some urgency to ensure that Phoebe knew exactly how I felt. Quite how I was going to articulate this, or even exactly what I needed to say, was well beyond certainty. It seemed premature to exert my relentless ability to manufacture obstacles in the way of any of life's perfection. Though I had always known well that I was no exception to this: the human condition. Typical of me perhaps, a need to rock the boat.

After waiting for a juncture of some less animated chat—which was never at all common when Phoebe and I were within close quarters—'why can't things always be like this!?'

As the words that came out of my mouth I followed them up with a deliberately exaggerated shrug and breath of laughter. There was then several seconds of complete silence, which would likely have been a bit awkward if amongst any but ourselves. 'Sorry I can't tell who you're impersonating there!' were the words that rebounded out of Phoebe's mouth.

It is fair to say that, as so often in conversation, I felt embarrassed by the inanity of what I had just said and Phoebe certainly played on this echoing my 'why can't things always be like this!?' with greater exaggeration being placed on each of my words for some comic effect.

'Look I know that we're on holiday where the rose tinted specs always come on easily, but I am just having such a great time…'

This fumbling pause of mine was soon followed by faster speech than I would have intended, as it most probably brought out my nerves and made our situation far less comfortable than it would have been before.

'That I just think that we'd both have a much better life if we spent more time together'

What a pitifully pointless thing to say this was. The truth is that I wasn't 100% sure of exactly what I wanted to articulate to Phoebe at this time, or more broadly in life in general. I suppose I wanted Phoebe to be a more constant part of my life, though we were far too close and had too many shared experiences to ask 'will you officially be my girlfriend?' Phoebe would almost certainly despise the patriarchy of if she didn't just assume that I was being ironic and laugh it all off.

Yet the statement I had made showed nothing but cowardice, as it does not directly address anything. But how was I to ask a direct question when I wasn't even sure what I wanted the answer to be? To my dad this would be nothing beyond a classic example of me 'fancying about and over thinking things' rather than actually sorting anything out.

A lack of much potentially awkward pause is pure credit to Phoebe, even though she was clearly just trying to deflect the situation by bringing in some light hearted 'well the tropical sea isn't on my doorstep and but you've gone and been the traitor moving to the south of the river!'

It is true that that Peckham and Camden Town were not the best connected parts of London, but with the Overground it wasn't much hard work to commute between the two necks of the woods. Geographical locations were certainly not the real issue at stake. Neither of us would ever—so we had said to each other anyway—want to complete the absolute farce of getting married, and we were well beyond the phase of dating and even going-out, so you know what's in between; living together, obviously.

'But Phoeb, (as if to solidify the importance of my conversation with the personalisation of a name) I could easily move and you could easily soon move'

Although I had only recently upped sticks from the north of the river for the first time in my life, I could easily sacrifice any potential attachment that I'd forged for Peckham with the sanctity that Phoebe would be with me for all of the time and all of the way.

Whilst I didn't want to cheapen this conversation by talking of money and logistics, co-habiting would be loads cheaper for us both beyond the many 2-for-1 deals of which could easily be taken advantage of. Even beyond my on-going devotion to Phoebe, it was also fast reaching that point in my life where my tolerance for the borderline unkempt and passive aggressive nature of numerous flat-shares was elapsing. When friends and strangers are living in each other's pockets, it inevitably seems to tragically result in creating more new foes than friends. Also, now that my life now only affords me the opportunity to really, properly go out 3 or maximum 4 times per week—discounting the odd bender—as I am reaching the maturity to want a more settled pace of life.

Phoebe and I now both earned decent enough salaries that should afford us a comfortable standard of living (although I deplore the idea of anything being male-controlled, it had to be fair to say that I'd carry home at least a third extra of wages) in a fun flat.

'What on magic carpets…' Phoebe shrugged wryly.

Somewhere between uttering the conception of us living together and now, I had lit a cigarette, which was mirrored by Phoebe. This seemed to symbolise the gravity and intensity of things that we were discussing. It almost feeds into that myth that cigarettes are speeding up the neurons working within your brain and thus making you more intelligent. Take a look towards the average person that you see on the street carrying a fag, though, to tell you all you need to know about that one.

Noticing from my response that this was not a situation that could be skirted for any longer, Phoebe's eventual response that 'I'll give this some thought. No, seriously. But I think that it could jeopardise all that we have'. To me, this statement contained an all-too-predictable swerve towards Phoebe actually divulging how into me she was.

Phoebe's broad and almost cheeky smile was enough ending. There was some ambiguity as to whether she was talking about the potential of us sharing a flat or whether we could feasibly exist as a long-term item. Knowing that Phoebe could understand (who would I be kidding to think that she didn't know already) what I wanted and give it some serious thought—however minimal—was enough for me to go on for now anyway.

7. Day 14: Hopes and Expectations

Something had certainly lifted within me after sharing the potential for us to live full-time together, and I felt more at peace with life than I'd ever managed at any point previously. Although I was perfectly rested, other than the slight concern stemming from my long-term faith in sod's law; so to soon be bitten on the arse by something, I went along with what I've now decided is for the best: bask in the sun for as long as you can. The painful dose of sunburn that may well result was not going to be today's problem, although I was aware that the more sensitive part of my soul could begin to get damaged beyond a skin-deep level.

Waking up after spending the first night with Phoebe this holiday without having sex, I was ironically the happiest that I'd ever been (at least since making the transformation from a less than bright-eyed and bushy-tailed youth and becoming a real adult who was still able to enjoy minimal responsibilities). Though with Phoebe, what I would have previously seen as the bleak potentials of a mortgage, marriage and even children didn't seem quite as frightening. The fear that I'd always had was probably largely entrenched within the fact that all of these things had always seemed so inaccessible to the likes of me; times were a-changing in many respects and so too potentially were my prospects.

We both fell asleep at the earliest that we probably ever had whilst in each other's company after first arriving at the *Bay of Biscay*—though I've no idea what the time was, it was most likely about half past nine—and we were yet to explore much of the area. Phoebe must have much needed this extra bit of rest, but the earliness of going to sleep helped me to perform my classic trick of waking up in the early hours, and the few drinks that I'd taken during the day ensured that I got no more sleep. Luckily my relentless tossing and turning failed to awake sleeping beauty lying beside. God only knows what worth there is for myself in recounting this, but I remember feeling really windy. It's not that the pair of us hadn't heard each other fart more than once before, only flatulence is a pretty grim thing to do when you're sharing a bed with anybody, let alone somebody that you want to think highly of you. Of course we both knew each other far too well for there to exist any pretence of being a deity, and wouldn't care any great deal what we heard of each other's bodily functions, but nobody that you want to have a relationship with should have to hear them. With anybody who claims they don't pass wind from the early stages of relationship once they've reached our age, you can have the confidence that the person is either yet to have much maturity or that they are just never to be trusted. Our bed didn't seem to smell at all by the time that Phoebe awoke, which was a relief.

Once I'd got out of bed, Phoebe almost instantly awoke and after a quick platonic shower, my aggravation at spending several hours in bed being unable to do anything beyond lying down with my eyes closed had relented and my positive attitude had been restored.

We were soon walked a couple of miles in the opposite direction from yesterday to a lively little market, which stank of weed even at the early hour when we were there. I'm sure that picking-up would have been incredibly easy, though neither of us wanted anything beyond a bite to eat and some chai at this time of the morning. It was a fun market with reggae style music blaring out of a loud speaker. The atmosphere was friendly, although it was certainly the sort of instance where you'd want to keep your hands rooted within the bottoms of your pockets, if you know what I mean.

Phoebe bought some vibrantly coloured sarong (I think that's what you'd call it) and then almost straight away, after glancing down at her phone, she seemed uncharacteristically distant after she had looked at a recently received text message. It was so unlikely for either of us to check our phones at all, beyond feeling that they were still inside our pockets, whilst we were out and about, that the rarity of her phone audibly bleeping did spurt my curiosity.

'You all right!?'

'Yeah I'm fine…' Phoebe rapidly almost cagily responded before she quipped that 'actually could we go somewhere with Wi-Fi for a bit?'

It certainly wasn't a place with any hotels around and finding somewhere with any internet reception did to feel a bit like looking for a needle in a haystack. Though perhaps this proves that the world is sometimes moving at a faster pace than I can keep up with, we eventually found a downtrodden and dingy café, with hazel coloured tiles skirting a beaded door and a sign advertising Wi-Fi.

This felt miraculous, though I have to admit that I couldn't see it as good fortune, as I was more than happy to continue moseying around with my head joyfully up in the clouds and not having to face any reality.

'Okay, what's the problem??' I spit out, making a conscious effort to say this without too much short shrift, which I probably failed at achieving, miserably. 'Look it's not really a problem, but I just need to check a few things on Facebook. Now, it shouldn't take long!'

This seemed to be so weird in itself. I was far more likely to fall prey to trivial gossip and other general goings-on, as far as social media was concerned, while Phoebe had never shown any more than a passing interest. It must surely have been something in the text message that she had received that had forced her to want to check so urgently; I mean you could get fucking Facebook access where we were staying if you felt the need, for whatever reason.

The one bottle of Sprite that I had bought to have to suffice for the pair of us was fast running out by the time that Phoebe looked up from her phone, finally attentive enough to fully respond to any question that I could think to ask. Coming back into the zone, she said, 'everything's fine. It's just that I think I could well need to get on a plane back home pretty soon'.

I couldn't see Phoebe's reasoning for being evasive with me (she well knew what I sucker I was for needing to be kept in the loop), and it was so unlike to conceal even the more cringe-worthy details of our lives from one another. Given that she had more than once actually expressed some serious interest in taking up training as a professional counsellor, I'd have expected better from her in terms of fuller communication, or at an expression of some sort of emphatic understanding.

To be fair, Phoebs had a fair collection of passing fads, and the only thing about her that would in any way mirror a counsellor at this instance was the fact that she was sporting some asymmetrical earrings. I'd never seen them before, and aptly they were metallic, almost as if to reflect her current coldness. Though this simple metaphor to be used in a GCSE English exam, in this instance it could be used in real life.

It was almost abhorrent to witness Phoebe behaving in a way that I could only view as callous. Although I'd suffer extreme disappointment to have to wave goodbye to her succeeding our short episode of perfection, I'd have deep concern for any reason that should force her to return to London so abruptly. Phoebe's problem was my problem. Though this is my entire point. I hadn't been allowed to gain any knowledge of the issue that precipitated Phoebe's return to London. I found this alien to our entire relationship, as we had always openly shared all information and realities of our lives—however lurid—with one another, knowing that it was in strictest confidence.

Not only did the fact that Phoebe was being reserved with me 'hurt my feelings' (of which I'd feel emasculated to admit) to a significant extent, but it also was trying the implicit faith that we'd always trusted in one another. For once, it was as though we were inhibiting separate orbits, and as to '90s Mike Leigh film: there is never anything at all healthy to ever be had in secrets and lies.

We'd talk about going to check out some turtle reserve only a couple of miles down the road after having some lunch, only I doubt that either of us were now at all in the mood. If I was being cynical—which does, unfortunately perhaps, always tend to be the trait that comes to me most naturally—I couldn't help but view this as the start of some exposure to bleak reality. Some of my friends (all of the Josh breed, which says it all in my opinion) insisted that by always keeping me on my toes, Phoebe was just taking advantage of me and messing me around. It always struck me as ridiculous, though, to think that Phoebe always had the upper hand, with me just rushing around after her like a love-struck puppy. And this strong belief of mine was down to more than just a figment of my optimistic imagination, surely?

'So, I guess that you want to go back to our hostel to sort out your return ticket in comfort and with all relevant documents that may be needed around us?'

'Yeah, sorry, thanks' Phoebe replied with a bright smile. Of course I still felt some degree of hope that her decision to return home was only a brief phase of madness, and that I could shut my eyes and the entire thing would go away and we could revert to eating, drinking and being merry by the time that darkness fell. Naïve though this is, I wonder if it is for the better or worse. I mean, some people seem to be capable of—which seems delusional to me—always having the confidence that the worst-case scenario shan't happen, and they do seem to get out of jail for free. Within the space of an hour, I had transformed from the most enlivened that I had ever been, to having reached my hubris in experiencing an unhealthy sense of hollowness and a strong conviction in life's worthlessness.

Although I had been more than content been prior to Phoebe's arrival on this trip, I already was fearing for how I'd cope with the remainder of my time without her company. Once you've tried the elixir, it's difficult to go without... Prior to Phoebe's decision to depart, our separation had not at all entered my periphery, and our returning had not even being given much thought. I mean, my direct return flight was only in about 8 or 9 days anyway, and as Phoebe was far from the most frugal person—for better or worse—I'd optimistically thought that she should probably just try and book a flight back on the same day as I was returning. Like walking back home through the wilderness with our hands held (bit much even for me!), I imagined that we'd solidify as some united force.

Instead, although nothing at all had directly altered between us, our worlds had become separate entities within such a brief lapse of time. Although we linked arms, which was rare for us when we walked, there seemed to be something extra symbolic about us traipsing back alone this time and in almost complete silence. The beaming sunshine and breeze seemed directly juxtaposed to our downcast dispositions. Beyond Phoebe glancing at her phone on many occasions during the walk, there is not a great deal more to report, other than that I felt drained, as though I had been walking over at least five times he distance by the time that we returned to the hotel with its welcome A/C and water dispenser.

After we'd returned to our room to rifle through some of our bits, Phoebe went downstairs in the confidence that one of the hotel's couple of PCs should still be free. Not being at all in the mood for exploring or finding company, I merely found my way to the garden area and, although it didn't much appeal to me, I ordered a beer and had my first much-needed cigarette of the day. The stained colour of the filter and the quickness with which it burned out only validated how much it was overdue. Failing miserably to digest any of the seemingly meaningless words that I read, I soon put down my book and was before too long lying on a reclining chair with my eyes closed.

Within a pretty short space of time, Phoebe was entering my vision waving some print-out. 'I've booked my flight! All sorted. It departs in the evening in two days' time. Have to make two bloody stop-offs, but it wasn't too badly priced' she said as she gave me a big fat kiss on the forehead.

Neither of us were ever much ones for any open public displays of affection. It's never even been mentioned, but my instinct tells me that we'd both find this sort of thing to signify an overt covering of all of the obvious cracks in your relationship, all the while executing some potential possessiveness.

As I glanced at the price of Phoebe's return flight, I saw that it was almost the same cost as my return ticket, and taking account of the fact that she'd booked her flight here barely a week ago, I dreaded to even imagine the total cost of her week in the sun. Feeding this into my ego, it was a positive confirmation of how much she'd forked out on this trip to come and join me—I'd never just throw money around in this way—and I did automatically have a twinge of guilt at thinking of her motives in a less than positive, if not just purely selfish, light. I'd miss Phoebe's company so much.

A suspicious mind is far from an attractive one, but I'd be lying if the thought that the text that I'd seen Phoebe reading over at the market may have been from James hadn't crossed my mind. Though what information she could possibly receive, beyond something bad happening to one of her close friends of family, could induce her to come home so rapidly mystified me…

Somebody's death or other tragedy was what I saw as the only viable options for events that she'd feel the need to return for.

Artistic license was all that I really had to go on, not having seen anything of the evil text that Phoebe must have been reading. Another conclusion that fell into my overactive imagination was that perhaps James had some STI and this meant that Phoebe needed to return home to get herself tested. Pft, this was such a morbid thought of mine. Her safety was my prime concern, but what if this meant that she was now victim to some ailment, with him walking away Scott free…The fucker.

Just yesterday I had expressed fears at potentially finding any travelling experience that I should have in the future to be inadequate after having carved out this new epitome of travelling, and now I found that these fears were being realised far more rapidly than I could ever have envisaged. The suffocating feelings that had overcome me after the sudden news of Phoebe's fairly imminent departure were already beginning to relent. Although the fact that Phoebe was due to be vanishing in a puff was still unwelcome, it had already become far easier to digest.

If I didn't fear that it could make me sound like a Tory, I'd just say how I ever attempt to be a pragmatist. In this light, I think that my elation should still be the predominant focus. Not only had Phoebe come to visit me, but everything had been rekindled, and we had done more than our fair share of loving. That did not terminate either, as for the remainder of our time together we even became an overactive couple, almost as if to mollify the fact that we'd soon be going our own ways. It did not even seem pertinent to broach the prospect of us cohabiting at this time; it felt as though Phoebe and I had been pushed back to passing like ships in the night.

We were still thousands of miles away from home, and a holiday romance is a holiday romance after all. Though considering that I believed that Phoebe was still in the clutches of a vindictive creature when I commenced this little adventure, I had little reason to feel overly dejected in the grand scheme of things.

Onwards and upwards. You might beg the question as to how I allowed for Phoebe to go through with booking a flight home so rapidly, based on news she had heard less than an hour ago. Could I not have talked her out of it? Yet I know Phoebe, and if I'd have allowed myself to be swayed naturally by some possessive instinct, it would only have further backfired. We'd have just had long-winded conversations—that would most likely still be going on now—before Phoebe would end up booking a flight back anyway. It would have been nothing but a long detour and would likely have soured the atmosphere. This way was far better as we had remained fully each other's friends and lovers, without the backlog of having to dig any claws in each other, which would all too inevitably occur, even through my resentment becoming harder and harder to keep a lid upon. It is what it is and it was what it was.

8. Day 15: The End of My World Is Nigh

Digesting the traumatic news of Phoebe's decision to depart was made all the easier by the fact that it was so swiftly made definite. It could be packaged and boxed up into a corner of my brain so that I wouldn't have to confront it for now; out of sight, out of mind and all of that shit.

Even by the end of the day in which Phoebe's flight booking became an actual transaction as opposed to an idea, I was back to feeling relaxed with reality. Her dubious reason for suddenly having to return was an issue that was surprisingly easy for me to bury alongside the bleak reality that I'd be on my lonesome again well within the space of just 48 hours. Whilst as much as I often crave company, I can be something of a loner too, so I rarely have any issue with being on my own. Things that I enjoy, such as reading, running and writing, are all things that I have to do on my own.

I can easily hack going to restaurants, pubs and even gigs on my lonesome as well; the cinema's perhaps an exception, though as I feel the need to go next to never, so this is easily avoided. Still, I'm certainly more of a social animal than a recluse, even though I initially came on this trip with the intention of being on my own and would soon be once again be by myself. Although this was more than bearable, it is always harder to return to normality once the forbidden fruit's been more than dangled in front of you, isn't it?

Almost within seconds of the flight booking having been made, we were back upstairs in our room, fiercely shagging. Whether this was compensatory or contractual sex (so romantic, I know) never even entered my mind at the time. Just thoroughly enjoying myself and releasing some intensely pent up emotions was optimum for us both, and how we achieved this was secondary. At least this way was loads of fun.

Whatever the quality of the rhythm is far less important than the fact that it, in my silly little mind, symbolised some continuation of our relationship.

Though saying that, the entire process of the day's events is nothing more than a haze to me now. We both seemed to feel equally alert and up for doing something as soon as this tryst of intensity had ran its course.

'How about we go to that massive white Buddhist temple, dedicated to Queen Viharamahadevi, who lived in the 2nd century BC?'

'Sounds worth it Darren, from what I've read. Let's go see it!'

Far from being convinced that Phoebe had even heard of this site beforehand, I was just happy that we were back onto the track of enjoying ourselves.

We got on board a tuck-tuck and were soon outside of this ruin in the middle of a big roundabout—which looked more like a shrine than a temple, if I'm going to pretend to actually know the distinction between them—and, having rapidly clouded over, the heavens had erupted. We laughed at the rain acting as some sort of metaphor to depict our deeply imbued distaste for anything remotely religious. There were an impressive amount of signboards displaying interesting information, though this far from substituted the lack of wonder that we both felt towards this red stone. The intensity of our joy came instead out of the good old red-top trope of the temple appearing to be a flaccid phallic symbol. It was more of a monument—to some revered figure that I can't remember—than any religious building, although there were plenty of prayer mats. We appeared to be the only ones there, which only made the matter more tiring.

Despite the heavens opening, it still looked pretty amazing and we captured quite a few photos were still given the time to be allowed to be captured by us.

Now being drenched through, due largely to there being a lack of any shelter available, it was as though the weather was catalysing the return of my worst feelings of Phoebe's departure. Luckily, as I was on the cusp of asking for the full reasoning behind Phoebe's decision to leave, a couple of guys who also appeared to be—well were obviously—fellow tourists came up to us.

'So are you here to meet Judd too then?' a thick Irish accent came out interrogating us from a man wearing a t-shirt depicting the evolution of an ape. He didn't look much like the sort who'd much trouble to wear a jacket in a bit of rain, but what I almost instantly found amusing was the question of—given the amount of gruff body hair that he carried—at which stage of the transition he regarded himself to currently represent?

I just shrugged as Phoebe and I both stood there looking perplexed. 'What you're not picking up any class A's from here then?'

'No' was all that I needed to say.

The ironically baby-faced counterpart looked more exasperated than anything, and I was just enjoying hearing an apparent contemporary of ours using a term which to me gave the impression of sitting bored in a way out of its depth school drugs lesson. Though this journey was definitely becoming more interesting.

They never gave you any initiation into how to protect yourself from unnecessary harm if, after all of their scaremongering, you independently made the choice to consume illicit substances. The whole 'don't give in to peer pressure' line is as crass as it is hypocritically futile, as surrendering to convention and aspiring to be a so-called 'functioning' member of society is the wealth of my socialisation at school. Learning how to adapt and fit in to a London Comp. was all about being able to follow and blend in. For them to then to advise you to just 'be an individual' is a complete fallacy as it is within a paper-thin remit of the supposed successes advertised. Life's all about brainwashing yourself after all. You can still have your own conscience, but I think that being selective about which peer pressure you give in to is an invaluable survival skill. People that don't give in to any are unfortunately the biggest losers. You just need peer pressure to influence all of the choice that you make in life, in terms of shaping your opinion. Whether you easily surrender to it or not, so long as you can step back and form an independent opinion of what you make of it, then you must be onto a winner.

‘Ha, so do you reckon this Judd guy’s actually coming?’ Phoebe casually asked, and this being un-rhetorical was part reason that I loved the girl; unassuming and never wanting to lord it above the person that she was talking to in any way. And this was after having made a fair deal of forgettable small talk as dusk was fast approaching. It had transpired that the outwardly dominantly engaging member of this twosome was called Fergus and the counterpart Sean (such almost fictionally stereotypical names only enabled them to easily become ingrained) appeared devoid of any personality. Sean certainly crossed the fine line between shyness and stand-offish behaviour; I mean, I couldn’t even make-out his accent, although he was brought up around Cork on the same street as Fergus. This made sense, as they were not two people that you could imagine instinctively founding a friendship as adults. If you know what I mean.

Sean’s attire memorably consisted of a well-faded Slipknot t-shirt, accompanied by a pair of full-length plain jeans, which seemed to perfectly capture his personality, or lack thereof. There was more than a little bit of sweat present under his arms. Whilst there may be thousands of similarly soulless backpackers traipsing around, as exemplified by running into Mrs Seaweed at our last hotel, in my experience it is never unlikely to bump into each other again once you’ve moved on.

Without wanting to be at all xenophobic, I nationalistically could claim to have more in common with Pat and Joe from the second hostel than I shared with Sean and Fergus. Perhaps provoked by our common purposes in seeking to procure and enjoy the same white powder, I had to ask them whether they’d heard of Pat and Joe. Although I had got their contact details written down in my rucksack, I couldn’t confidently provide their surnames off of the top of my head. ‘Nah mate, I’ve never known of any people called Pat or Joe in my life!’ boomed Fergus. Although this statement was made partly as a joke, it is fair to say that they’d not heard of these guys; I suppose even in the narrower context of backpacking, it would be rather like me being asked whether I’d happened to meet another traveller from, say, Manchester. That’s unlikely enough without there being a border in between. Co-incidences do seem to always be coming in the most unlikely and inconvenient places in life, but this just wasn’t one of them. C’est la vie.

It had about reached the point when I’d begun to wonder what Phoebe and I were actually doing, still being stood there, having this satisfying enough, though pretty meaningless, conversation. Other than being increasingly bored as the clock ticked, I remained hopeful that I take a supply of what was on offer. Phoebe solved this for me with an, 'ah, my clothes are all clinging to me… Are we about ready to go back now?'

'Yeah, I think we've seen all here that we need to! Enjoyed meeting you two…'

Fergus joked—or convincingly feigned surprise—'Oh, I thought that you'd wanted in on our little exchange when it eventually arrives?'

Although it may have been vaguely tempting, I was no longer enthused with the idea of taking a part of what was on offer 'Err, well it doesn't seem like this Judd fella's coming does it…'

Almost as if to compensate for our new friends from the opposite ends of Ireland not knowing each other, a man in all white appeared out of the blue, and in broken English told us that this mythical Judd was not going to show up with the supplies today. This was down to illness I think. There wasn't really any way in which we could remedy the situation, and there was absolutely no reason to shoot the messenger. Why Phoebe got involved I do not know, but an almost sultry sounding (which is not uncommon coming from her, at least in my point of view) 'Thanks for passing the message on for us, but surely he must want for the gear to get to us, and I'm wondering how come you couldn't bring them with you?'

All that I remember being taken aback by was her use of 'us', which insinuated that she was for some reason volunteering to form part of this pact. I mean, given the overall disappointment of the news that Phoebe's departure was occurring almost a week earlier than I had envisaged, indulging a few lines of coke certainly shouldn't go amiss to fully restore my spirits. It's hardly a gateway drug, as it's already well up there in the futile rankings of strength from the archaic 1971 Misuse of Drugs Act, upon which our law still takes precedent, though occasional usage is exactly what we all need to deal with modernity. Anyway, all that we are left with is the message to 'just come up to…' and he gives us a business card of what seemingly is a spice distributer tomorrow at the same time, and ask for Judd or Cornelius.

Apart from finding that he had a name that couldn't be more ill-fitting or hilarious in itself, there was nothing more to really say as this Cornelius skirted off in a manner reminiscent of a member of Hare Krishna. What I found most bizarre is the fact that there had been absolutely no response from anybody; this verbal contract seemed to have been initiated though. The outcome was actually something close to ideal from my perspective.

As we were staying at inns on the opposite sides of town from each other, we decided to do nothing beyond exchanging mobile numbers for tonight. We agreed to meet in the far superior location of the more desolate end of the beach-front, next to a distinctively wonky tree that we could all easily place, and all equipped with our own torchlight. As darkness consistently swept in at an hour well prior to what my body clock was prepared for in such surroundings, it was accorded that we'd all convene at 6pm. Well, this circumstance for Phoebe's last night with us could not have been better ordained; Fergus' benign call that 'there just wasn't any point in us all going' to collect more white powder was well welcomed and I gladly opted to make myself a user, in in more ways than one.

Having taken the journey once in a taxi, we decided to fully walk back. It had certainly been day of mixed emotions and some degree of walking in silence with our arms linked was just what the doctor ordered. It was just as dusk set that Phoebe broke away from my arm.

'Thank you. Thank you so much, Darren'

'What, I've not done anything!' was all that I had to say, although, as always with Phoebe, I thought, though wasn't sure that I knew exactly what she meant.

'Listen, I know what a bitch I am being with my saying that I have to leave this paradise that we have created together. For each other… You need to understand that I'm not going because I want to be with anybody else or be in any other place in the world than with you here. Right now.'

This ending to the sentence only seemed to complicate matters for me, I mean was she only referring to at the moment in preparation for her departure, or did she just want to be with me forever? No point dwelling on these things in the moment, though I fought against my instinct to ask why nothing could ever be simple in this life. For us in particular.

All that I said was something along the lines of, 'you obviously need to go back, and as much as I wish that it could be otherwise, life's a cruel mistress isn't it!' and along with smiling and nodding, this brief exchange seemed to do us both the world of positivity. To me it was enough that Phoebe had acknowledged and was well aware what a spanner in the works that she had placed; she was probably relaxed that I had now accepted her decision and wasn't about to make a snide remark at some interval. For some unexplainable reason, I knew that I was no longer much cared about whatever reason she had for wanting to return.

'Listen, if we're having a… 'Bijou beach party' with the other lads tomorrow night, it would seem wasted, but as a leaving present, how about I treat us to a slap-up meal tonight?'

She had an uncanny ability to read me and to know exactly the sort of thing that I wanted at any given time; she was well accomplished in playing all parts of me as instrument. 'Yeah, well-up for that, but don't go being silly with the bill, we'll go Dutch' after a pause of several seconds of walking the response was 'all right, if that makes you happy, but I'll sneak off to pay sometime whilst you're in the toilet or something!' Within a hundred metres or so 'or I could just pay!' boomed out of my mouth 'no I'll pay' was the response and this exchange kept us amused for several more blocks until she started to put me into a headlock whilst tickling me relentlessly. In defence I slapped her on the back and it didn't take a great deal of pinching each other's bums before our faces were interlocked and we had both opted to do the flamingo stance—ironically of course—and we soon ended up as a pile on the floor in our usual hysterics. It seemed that order had been restored in our relationship.

As we'd been having fun acting as teenagers without the acne or such a wealth of insecurities, time allowed us a chance to get fully intimate with each other to take a shower and get fully spruced up before going out for this last supper.

Showers always seem to be apt locations for epiphany moments to take place. This time the opportunity arose following the intimacy we'd felt during and succeeding the walk back to our hotel room. It wasn't so much revelation as stark truth; I loved Phoebe. This was in herself and not dependent on anything.

Having always been most capable of being soppy and sentimental, convincing myself that I was 'in love' was no strange sensation of mine. I covered myself in an accidental abundance of shampoo and managed to successfully sting my eyes, and it was almost as though this was a representation of the purgative experience I was putting myself through, in so far as I was painfully coming to terms with all the ways in which my worship of Phoebe made me so reliant. She was the only person that I'd ever loved. Although Martha was certainly somebody that I'd convinced myself that I was in love with all those years ago, when I was a naïvely grown-up boy, in all the relationships that I'd had since, I was only ever in love with an idea of the person that I had fabricated. At least

I wanted to be in love though, which is an alien concept to many of my male mates.

With some subconscious determination, I seem to just fit a lover into my ideal of them and turn a blind-eye to the reality that, although we may be mostly compatible, there is something missing. Being in love with an idea becomes exhausting. Whilst I hardly doubt that there are many highly functional marriages based on this principle, Phoebe and I are so lucky in having something more, and I am now so determined to never let that crumble.

Granted, everybody in love—consciously or even unconsciously—believes that they have something, only this devotion that feel for Phoebe is something deeper.

Phoebe had taken her shower before and was now stood in a flowingly loose red and gold short dress that I'd not seen before, looking utterly delectable.

'Which closet did you dig that out of!?' I exclaimed before being casually informed that 'oh I've had this ages, from a trip years ago with our schoolmate friend Kitty, to Thailand. I so nearly didn't bring it, but now feels like it's an occasion!' Feeling incapable of offering anything other than a beaming smile as I clambered into my pair of half-decent linen trousers and now all too well creased, varying textures of white polka dotted short sleeved shirt.

'Yeah, I booked this place (as she pointed at a pamphlet left by the hotel) called the Knofi——whatever that was all about—and the first place that they had available was at 9.30, does it seem all right? They could not do any time before, which must be positive I guess…'

'Wow! You've actually booked somewhere then?'

This was a new experience for me whilst travelling, as it had never seemed necessary at the sort of places that I'd be going to eat, but I certainly found it to be a nice little touch to our upcoming ceremony.

As rhetorical as this question was, it led to a kiss before we marched downstairs to climb into a taxi outside of the hotel. So we headed to the downtown area where this Knofi was; although it would probably be within walking distance, the vibe of the evening had some call for superfluous decadence (as it can only be if done properly) written all over it and I was in the mood to oblige. Without yet having touched a drop of liquor during the day, I had taken on board that happy feeling of mindlessness and indifference to everything. Even when I'm in one of these phases, I know that it can't last forever, but am happy to bask in it whilst it lasts. The on-going angst that us mortals have to suffer needs a bit of the 'nothing really matters in this life' every once in a while don't they?

Feeling like this at all times, though, must make you into a deplorable person, with stoicism towards everything. Possessing this perpetual insensitivity and absence of any concern for things would petrify me, but occasional glimmers of everything being irrelevant feel more than needed.

As we are dropped off outside of this supposed seat of gastronomy, it certainly exudes grandeur, in a way that seems astutely sympathetic to Sri Lankan and Southern Indian cooking. It appears to be an old colonial house that has been converted into a quirkily contemporary eatery and it fits my ideal image, Phoebe tends to hit the nail on without fail.

It is a damn good job that we were booked, as with only several blue checked topped tables dotted around each room, Knofi is intimate restaurant, at which I doubt that many table spaces ever go empty. Often us pair end up half-cut by the time at which it comes to actually eating, and looking at the fine menu, I'm incredibly glad that the first beer that we order is the first drop of alcohol that we've had all day. At least our taste buds would not be too clouded to sample these culinary delights. Mind you, a fair amount of Chablis had passed through our oesophagus' by the time that our Lobster Thermidors arrived and I'm just glad that I'd taken advantage of the mood that I had been in—and my mounting level inebriation—to order the food. And yes, sharing (even with our exuberance of the evening, there were limits!) a huge plate of mussels did mean that we were having fish followed by fish. I never understand why people can be so weird about this. Often all-too-bland chicken followed by all-too bland-chicken is fine though. People are so weird.

Our conversation too was tasty throughout, and it even reached a point sometime in between the mussels in wine and the lobster where we'd reflected upon how much fun we'd had together on this trip and how we'd miss each other 'so much' after parting. Phoebe and I both knew each other way to well and went way too far back to ever be 'going out' together, but before I knew it, the facetious expression of 'so we're exclusive now are we?' left my lips.

Immediately this was covered up with a laugh, which was all too quickly reciprocated. Whilst I do recall being slightly phased to hear a response of, 'but you'll still be out here travelling won't you…' Which, hopefully without being snappy, I instantly responded with, 'But I'm only out here for just over a week without you aren't I!'

'Well that's never stopped you before has it!?' was the expression that came out of Phoebe's mouth followed by a dry laugh. As much as I knew that Phoebe would never deliberately manipulate me, this is exactly what she was seemingly doing, by deflecting the situation around to one of me being most likely to cheat. But then that doesn't even make sense, as we were technically not yet even an official item. As infantile as that sounds in itself.

Jeez Louise, I didn't not know where to take this. Let alone what I was ever fully expecting form this conversation. We were only just on to our new bottle (of rose wine, which Phoebe had selected for some reason), and my reaction time and ability to formulate solutions to situations already seemed to be significantly reduced.

Succeeding a brief little laugh coming out of my mouth, we had resumed some animated conversation. It must have been about something rather futile—which I fail to be able to remember now—but it clearly managed to engross at the time. A trademark of our conversations was always the mutual ability to avert serious situations concerning ourselves, and our ability to overlook imperfections is perhaps how the relationship between Phoebe and I had sustained for so long. All that I wanted was for it to now become firm rather than so flimsy.

As always, I go on to Phoebe's potential defence and reflect on the ways in which enquiring as to the nature of our relationship was testament to my insecurities and carried the danger of undermining of all that we had already established. Perhaps we were both reliant on that lack of solidity for the excitement and passion to remain between us.

Following in, we went on to do the have the full works with a dessert, coffee and digestif. Of course, as well, we evenly split the bill between, though I think that only I put in for the tip, come to mention it. This was all later rounded off by probably the most passionate and longest lasting sex that the pair of us had ever had together.

The next morning I slept solidly through to sunrise. I could not remember the last time that I'd managed to complete an entire sleeping session that was unbroken by a toilet break. Lying in bed and glancing at Phoebe's deeply dormant body lying beside me, this morning was set up to be the calm before the storm, being our last whole day in each other's company… for what would only have to be 10 days or so. From experience, this may well be the case, but it could also just as likely be a matter of months before we clasp eyes on each other again.

Phoebe would be parting this holiday tomorrow, and I did not quite know if this day had anything in store beyond meeting with Fergus and Sean for a session of debauched time in the evening.

There actually a great deal at all for us to do beyond shuffling through our bags to check that we weren't about to accidently nick one of each other's phone chargers or something, which meant that we ended up enjoying a pleasant—if pretty inactive—day on the beach. Couldn't fault Phoebe's logic of doing lots of swimming so that she'd supposedly sleep on the plane. Though given what we were planning to indulge ourselves in, it all seemed a little futile.

Although I was by this point consciously making the most of my last day spent with Phoebe for the most foreseeable, it flew by in a flash. After our second generous helping of street food (always so-far stomach friendly, so we felt that it was worth the risk), we were about ready to go and meet Sean and Fergus on the beach. All that I had left to do was the errand of providing enough beers to last the evening, in return for the other two being responsible for its organisation. I'd definitely got the upper end of this deal; they knew that; I knew that. But you know what: you win some, you lose some!

Despite expecting that complete opposite, they were already ready and raring by the time that we went to the meeting place on the beach. 'PLAYERS!' Fergus screamed enthusiastically as we approached, and we all had a big embrace, before getting down to business.

In a way that automatically made me feel incredibly excited and nervous, Sean waved around a copious amount of white powder. Not much time elapsed before each and every one of us had a fag in one hand, beer in the other and were itching to throw some stuff up our nose. Fergus—speaking for the rest of us—casually reprimanded Sean for being so overt in advertising our wares. Although I'd read that people usually turn a blind-eye towards recreational drug usage where we are, I still feared that you can technically end up facing death for what we are planning on doing. Although this under the circumstances seems like such an empty threat, my overly astute conscience insists on giving me many sharp twinges of guilt relating to dissolute risks that I am about to take. If you die as the result of a self-induced drug overdose, doesn't it beg the question of how much sympathy you should be entitled receive from your friends and loved ones? This is an incredibly morbid and self-indulgent and even nonsensical thought process, given that I'm sure that once you're dead, you're dead anyway, so aside from being narcissistic, this thought doesn't really have much place in my psyche.

But what about my health? Yes, I do exercise to try to exercise actually. Meagre if non-existent compensation for my vices as it may be, at least I try and put some good in. Seeing that I also eat a pretty balanced diet, why should my odd little dabbling be seen as any more of a drain on our society than a fat person enjoying a clotted cream scone!?

Appropriately, any little quandaries that I suffer towards taking a strong drug are—as perhaps all too often—rapidly forgotten as soon as I have done so. Credit where credit's due, we're not that stupid, so armed with a book and torchlight, we each at separate intervals forage about 100 metres or so into wilderness the forest backing the beach and invoke a line or two.

A favourite element of mine of this process is the transition between the pranging apprehension that I take with me into the forest and the exhilarating feeling that is embedded within my stomach as re-join our group in our circle. It's not obligatory, as a tasty cake is a tasty cake, but having a lit cigarette gripped between your fingers after you know what, is magical.

Judging by the sort of people that we all were—bar Sean—it is not as though we appeared to have a great deal of any inhibitions to start off with. After I'd taken a few inhalations of the mystical substance, I was something that... Although I wouldn't call it euphoric, felt more than a bit pleasant. This what I saw as a wonder of the substance. This crowd was an ideal representation of how the usage of this drug only paints out the inadequacies in our society and the longing for the grass to be greener.

As painstaking a label as it is, I am now a middle-class guy serving the charity sector, and I'd like to think possessing an adequately functioning moral compass. Still, what annoys me the most is the double standard in all judgements surrounding the (it no longer needs the prefix of 'sub') culture of drug taking. How is it directly less responsible for harm than someone engaging in extreme sports or sharing my love of street food when you're travelling? Fundamentally, it's just a case of people being obnoxious in demonising the drugs they choose to regard as a taboo lifestyle choice; this requires no real understanding or inquisition into the topic other than to just box it up and arrogantly/ lazily exert an opinion upon it.

Jeez, not that I want to advertise drug use as something that you should choose. I've never been anything more than a casually social drug user, but at the same time I wouldn't have the audacity to tell you not to take them. Just don't expect much. And maybe be aware of the delusions as well as hard truths that the powerful substances you're opting to ingest induce. Once you've been to utopia you'll never quite get back. I realise that I'm sounding a little holier-than-thou in all of this!

This is why cocaine in small and seldom can be such a useful little drug in my view. There is never any pretence that you'll expand your mind or much alter your perception, other than gaining an enhanced degree of confidence and inflated ego. Still, I—deluded as it may be—feel that I am never unaware of the insincerity of my self-belief when my emotions are invaded by stimulant. It ties in, I suppose, to that old inane concept that drugs are only used as a cover for lacking a personality and social confidence, and must compensate for something lacking in yourself. What is the point of ever taking it then, you may ask?

That is a fair question, and one that I do not know the answer to by a long stretch. Only I can't really see a reason not to indulge myself from time to time. Without being too great a hypocrite, the depressant of alcohol is by far my favourite drug and also the substance that I feel is the most potent in making me completely unable to control any part of my physicality or emotions. So, I've no plans to halt my relationship with drugs using the narrow—yet incredibly ignorant and conformist—view that illegal drugs are any more than something that alters the way that our body behaves. As does tea, as does coffee and as does Paracetamol, etcetera.

Ha, and this is perhaps noticeable, I find both the demonization and celebration of drug culture more than a bit annoying. I'd recommend looking into Professor David Nutt's argument that we legalise all substances before you instinctively condemn my viewpoint and call me naïve, or even callous. It's surely all about how capable you are of being as responsible as possible with the drugs that you use.

Anyway, once my internal dialogue (that would I believe have been a rant if I wasn't now so enjoying myself) had relented, I was having a ball with our crowd back on the beach. Beyond sand appearing to soon be within just about every orifice of my body, it was one of the most comforting experiences that I've ever had in my life. We all loved one another in these moments, around our circle of intimacy.

From my experience, social drug users tend to fall into one of either two categories: boring or edgy. Hopefully people would consider that I fall more into the latter camp. Still, I'm beyond the age of much caring what anybody else thinks and although I'm a million miles away from being any hedonist, I can't see that I owe a great deal more to society through my odd bit of fun. It's not like I don't work full time, always vote, pay all of my taxes, read (this is most important) and respect everybody and treat people as I'd like to be treated myself #self-justification.

It's not like I'm so bright-eyed and bushy-tailed anymore. It's just that I'm getting increasingly peeved at having to accommodate people who continue to have some moral panic over how I choose to occupy my leisure time. The most negative repercussions that arise through drug use are surely the exploitation of people arising from their illegality, and therefore the wealth of corruption that surrounds drug usage?

I feel something like a self-righteous adolescent in writing all of this—and all of my rhetorical questions seem to do nothing more than expose my insecurities—but I would rather be seen as naïve than be one of those people who fail to grasp that some deviance is required for society to progress. A society that fails to ever evolve must stagnate and crumble? Objecting to this fact inadvertently implies that you wish that there had been no suffragette movement, no end to back-street abortions, no end to 'bugger' being written on inmates' doors… Christ, I need somebody with far more knowledge than I possess—especially when slouched on that beach—to articulate this properly and less colloquially, but this is the best that I can manage. As we're all sprawled out across the sand, I was plagued by the thought that we'd let our ancestors down; is this what people went over trenches for?

The character Mark Corrigan voiced a similar sort of argument when at some drug-fuelled club night in a Peep Show episode, and to me it worked to shine some light on the idea that our decadence is only practised by people like us, who don't know they're born. This is exactly why, out of respect for their memory, we are entitled to take on the onus that our ancestors afforded us and cherish their legacy. Freedom was a root cause of past battles, and the concept of recreational drug use would be so anachronistic and alien to our forefathers that it barely even qualifies as an argument against any supposed hedonism. After our ancestors endured an eternal fight against being freezing and hungry, I'd say that affording ourselves a bit of enjoyment while we have the opportunity is something that we must now have some duty to perform; being twisted seems fine without the prefix of being bitter alongside.

Anybody who dismisses my argument on the simple grounds that these issues are disconnected entirely from drug-taking need their head tested. This is so impertinent to the argument. I've got ample respect for British law, but anybody believing that unquestioned obedience benefits us all either has too idle a mind or is just praying for a benevolent dictatorship to sweep us all under… Confidence that we have a right to question everything must be needed to escape an inferiority complex? You could perhaps accuse me of arrogance, but given how much I detest all traces of this quality, I'd argue that I am in fact acting from the complete opposite of any pride. This is what I see many of the anti-drugs brigade basking themselves in, as they're all croissant-eating, quinoa-digesting fools; but then, so are many of the drug users. On both ends of the spectrum I can assure you that there are fantastic teachers, social workers, milkmen, lawyers… And any other job that you can think of on either end of the spectrum.

What is worse, though is the way in which drugs can armour drab people with an air of exclusivity. Granted, there is the age-old argument that 'people need to feel like they're rebelling' and drugs provide a workable backdrop to this, although we can easily get taken in by gateway drugs. This is such mindless bollocks. Media image clearly has one of the most vital roles to play—i.e. I'd never touch heroin or crack due to the deadly ways in which they are portrayed (and injecting yourself seems like a level way too far up for me!). Yes, going with this argument could be a fallacy that shows just how susceptible I am to propaganda. And for anybody deeming that my reaction to illicit substances must be a consequence of having received too liberal an education on drugs, then let me assure you that I had wanted to experiment with drugs since I first ever heard of what they were. The most accurate comparison I can draw is to my liking to eat snails or frog's legs when I go to a French restaurant. Nonetheless, drugs, beyond alcohol and cigarettes (which I just love), aren't really what they're cracked up to be; but when you're being given the chance, might as well. I'll leave you to enjoy your own food choices (or lack of) if you let me enjoy mine in peace.

Anyway, after having detailed thoughts along this spiel, I think that it is time to resume my reality. 'Hey, why've you been going like a leper all by yourself' winces Fergus as I take my place in the centre of the little circle that we have formed. 'Just enjoying a little bit of me time mate!' and we all laugh before adding that I was 'feeling overwhelmed by this select company'. Whether I'm being serious or shamelessly sarcastic is beyond the point, as well as beyond my true knowledge. Whether the sun or white stuff expires first is certainly something of a chicken and egg question. We're all incredibly burned-out, but we have created a positive Zen and we still thrive upon it. We're all snuggled in a happy ball on the beach, and it throws me off of keel to remember suddenly that Phoebe will be flying out of the country on this same day. This reminder is just not what I need.

9. Day 18: The Aftermath

The fun and frivolity fades gradually, along with the group willpower to do anything other than fall asleep. We had all ended up just bouncing around to the music coming out of Fergus' speakers, and disco had seemed to be the vibe as we revelled aimlessly to some camp-ness, like Ottawan's 'Hands-Up', Chic's 'I Want Your Love' and Sister Sledge's 'Lost in Music'. It still wasn't too long before remaining it any way vertical had proven far too momentous a challenge for us all.

Surrounded by scrunched up bodies, I realise that whilst I was on the cusp of drooling and long overdue in getting my head down. With the level of over-tiredness that I was experiencing, the only real viable option was to force myself to lie with my eyed scrunched together.

It is during one of the increasingly lengthy lulls of rested silence that Sean quips (and it would be him too) that he 'needed to take a dump soon!', and I distinctly remember thinking 'charmed I'm sure' along with some repulsion. This isn't particularly due to any chivalry that Phoebe was present, but more down to the fact that this sort of toilet talk is always as grimy as it is unnecessary. It was pretty safe to conclude that after this sort of all-nighter, we'd all be feeling pretty much the same way, but why did people feel the need to announce it? In front of an audience especially…

Any seasoned traveller can bank on the experience of shitting yourself, but it is definitely a low point, and it is beyond me how anybody can ever feel it at all apt to announce their clearly beloved bowel movements.

Phoebe and I take this as an appropriate juncture to take our leave of this group. And hopefully grab a lengthy nap back at our hotel. The state that we were both clearly in made us incredulous that she'd be aboard a jet engine and making her way back in just under 12 hours' time. Indeed, when we finally (it wasn't actually that great a distance, but felt like an incredibly long and winding road at the time) entered our room, it did not take long for us to complete our ablutions, have deep glugs of bottled water and get our heads down.

The napping lasted an incredibly long time—this in itself was an accomplishment that I felt to be worth celebrating—so that when I eventually stirred and unlocked myself from Phoebe's embrace, for a number of seconds I had no idea where I was or even who I was with. It was with a much-needed level of comfort, in spite of the degree of heat that had increasingly enveloped our room, that I became aware of where I was and who I was snuggling alongside. If a snapshot of that feeling could be encrypted, the quantity of positive energy would make me into a deity.

When Phoebe eventually stirred, I think that we ended up just smiling at one another for a significant duration. Having both slurped a number more glugs of water, and validating that we both felt absolutely fine, it wasn't a great deal of time before we were kissing, which with increased passion led to making out. And it wasn't long before we were making the most of our final bit of fun of this miniature adventure.

Well, it did seem like it was something that we both needed to commemorate, and the remaining time in which it could take place was incredibly limited. Also, as we were yet to have showered, it would be annoying—especially for Phoebe who'd soon be aboard a plane—to have to take another wash. And she'd probably want to wash her hair as well, (although I'll never understand how a shower constitutes a proper shower without doing so) which would mean a far lengthier ordeal. It was getting on to late afternoon by the time that we were looking spritely and ready to face the big wide world again.

Prior to doing so, though, we needed to undertake the monotonous task of ensuring that all of our belongings were kept completely separate. There was more than one instance in the past when I'd ended up being separated from my phone charger or malaria tablets (although that wasn't a precaution worth taking now in Sri Lanka). As a next step, I volunteered to call to make sure that a taxi would arrive to take Phoebe to the airport. Almost pathetically, this bitterly ironic gesture attempted to communicate that there was no hard feeling caused by her decision to depart.

Not having eaten anything beyond a few staling paprika flavoured crisps that had been lying about our room for ages, it was time to grab ourselves something to eat before we'd have to wave each other farewell. We checked out of the hotel. Although I'd still be staying in the beach town for another night or two, I was going to join Fergus and Sean in the dorm room of their decent-enough sounding hostel on the other side of town. It seemed to make economic and social sense, if I want to help myself to sound like the biggest square that exists.

In a café just up the road, we gorged ourselves on a couple of rolls (can't remember, if I ever could identify, what was inside of either) and had a few cakes each. With some more crisps. We were certainly by this point beginning to feel the repercussions of the excesses of the previous day, and I don't recall that we actually said anything to each other. Normally we could never properly shut-up when we were in each other's company, but this is only because we'd usually have a wealth of worthy things—about any and everything—to share with one another. Here we had said all that we could find say, and it really did not feel as though there was any need for us to utter anything else.

Time was creeping by, and it was getting to around the perfect time for Phoebe to be getting our taxi, which we'd booked from the *Bay of Biscay*.

As always with these moments, the time at which we parted remains nothing more than a blur in slow-motion, if that makes any sense. We merely squeezed each other and the car with Phoebe aboard seemed to disappear within a blink. There was little that was particularly emotional about our farewell.

Despite the pair of us having long witnessed each other within our most destitute and vulnerable states of minds, both of us were more than capable of exerting impassiveness when we felt this was required. This is an invaluable in my mind. It's not like we can't validate the strength of our feelings towards one another without crumbling as helpless emotional wrecks within each other's presence, is it?

Besides, despite Phoebe's departure being unprecedentedly sudden overall, there was nothing unexpected about the course of events by the time that she was leaving. For this reason there was nothing at all surprising about my feeling being something closer to indifference as opposed to heartbreak.

In spite of my usual inconsistency in giving to beggars, perhaps it was my confused state of mind in the aftermath of Phoebe's departure that led me to give far more generously than I would normally. Clearly I was trying to compensate something, if indeed this was just reduced to feeling that there was some value left to my existence. At least I could still have some purpose, however instantly gratified and surface-level.

The realisation occurs to me that I am potentially just in desperate want of several stiff drinks to get back on board with the final week or so of my travelling, and to adjust to the come-down of being on my own once more. Instead though, I am grateful that I opt for my other favourite form of digestion at transitional instances: going for a run.

This is of course after I have checked into my new hostel with the trite name of *Coconut Lagoon*. The grounds (though it really wasn't that grand by a long stretch!) actually went onto the beach. It even had hammocks. How could there be anything lacking from my life…

It was actually a relief that Fergus and Sean were otherwise engaged somewhere, as I was far from ready to face anybody else's company at the time. I certainly did not feel 'on form' on any level. Within no time, though, I was as ready and raring as I could be in this mind-set to go for a jog.

I am an expert in mulling things over, yet working up a significant sweat soon defeats the processing of any percolating thoughts beyond the focus of keeping motivated. This is exactly what I needed.

Just before embarking on my minor little exertion, I failed to resist temptation and glanced down at my iPhone to see that I had, as predicted, received a wealth of emails since I had last checked my inbox. As I feared, the bulk of them were either from subscriptions that I could have sworn I'd unsubscribed from, but then there was to my surprise an email from my infamous auntie Daphne.

She was from my father's side and his senior by a little over 5 years. My paternal grandmother had died in the early years of my father's adolescence, leaving him to be raised by my sternly stoic grandfather. Daphne stepped in and had apparently nurtured him as a child, as the relationship that he'd always had with my growingly cantankerous granddad—he never again remarried, and although he died when I was seventeen or eighteen, going to his funeral was the first contact that my immediate family had with him in years—was always fraught to say the least.

Daphne was not even present at my granddad's his send-off, as she'd believed him to be too much a 'sad and bitter old fart', to even bother. If my memory serves me correctly, she was in Thailand with her latest 'toy-boy' lover (sure that he'd have been at least 50 at the time) anyway. Don't think that I'd ever met this old flame, as he wasn't around for long enough, and she'd admirably never succumbed to any of the many marriage requests she'd had over the years. Especially as Daphne's entire life seemed to lead from one failed venture to the next with the string of no-hopers, at least she could always leave these trysts as casually as she had entered into them.

A juice spa, florist, lingerie, soap and jewellery businesses had all rapidly gone under, and this was just within my lifetime. There was a running pattern though. Although she may sound like the independent woman who is always doing her own thing, the reality is that she is continually propped along by some waster of a bloke, who soon becomes a distant memory when their business fails. Daphne's whims soon move forward, though my dad would always stress the fact that they just involve 'one failure followed by the next disaster!' Although this is always said with a touch of gest, I know that it involves plenty of deeper underlying feelings.

To as large an extent as Daphne and my dad are capable of always being civil and even jovial at face value, there is part of my dad that resents her freedom and sees her lack of responsibility as something of a hedonistic decadence, drifting around from one crisis to the next. As the only relative that I'd ever dream of smoking alongside—be it a spliff or tobacco—I've always had a close relationship with Daphne, though there may be some truth in my dad's condemnation of her lifestyle choices, she always appears to be happy and never burdens anybody else. In many ways, I feel that my Dad just suffers from frustration in looking at the carefree free-spirit that Daphne embodies.

It is almost as though the pair have undergone an exchange of responsibility—that between Daphne having to care for my Dad as a teenager, and Dad having to support a wife and son fully reliant on him, with Daphne gallivanting from one failed experiment to the next. She always seemed to have plenty of fun, being the goer that she was. The relationship that she'd always had with me mirrored more that of an eccentric old blower than that of an auntie, and give or take whatever flaws that she had, Daphne was probably the relative that I'd trust to confide in the most, and I felt most at ease in her company.

Anyway, the long and the short of it was that she was, by miraculous coincidence, about to end up in the exact same part of the world as I was in. I do find this fitting, as years ago, it was Daphne who had originally instilled the idea of visiting this part of the world, where she'd been numerous times over the years.

Off I then planned to journey to the island's famous second city of Kandy, where I'd hopefully have the success of performing the miracle of locating Buddha's mystical tooth!

Meeting Daphne would mark some stark transition in my trip. I welcomed seeing a familiar face during my last week or so of travel, which was otherwise destined to be something of a slog from which extracting any enjoyment was bound to be effortful. The flame had only become stronger in the candle—which I'd never been able to successfully extinguish—that I had burning for Phoebe. Whether this was related to fantasy or reality is the main question. The idea that any of your troubles leave you when you try to escape for pastures yonder is nothing beyond a comforting myth.

In classic Daphne form, she had suggested that we meet in Kandy in the middle of the island in just two days' time. Only it wasn't really a suggestion, as she'd already booked her hotel and was only staying in the town for a couple of nights while passing through the country on her detoured journey back to England. On a side, this means that she'd have completely missed all of the unnecessary Brexit furore.

Whilst I'm definite that she'd have vehemently deplored Brexit—she's not the sort of person possessing enough foresight to make arrangements to get a postal vote or vote by proxy—she's just as much to blame for its initial triumph as all of those people with enough patriotic audacity to 'vote leave'. Still, this is one of the few things better left unsaid when I meet her the day after tomorrow.

Simply refusing Daphne's offer to meet up would of course have been completely acceptable and there'd have been no ill-feeling. Yet having the chance to meet a relative who you rarely see whilst travelling was enough of a novelty for me to make an effort. Perhaps it is an all too common occurrence that Daphne fails to consider how other people can't always fit their plans around her lifestyle, but I don't intend to expose this in any way. This was simply an example of one of those increasingly rare instances in life where it really felt as though the sun was shining at us all in the right way.

Welcoming Daphne's presence could not be any more contrary to whatever pretext that I had possessed in setting off on this trip. I had never envisaged seeing an OAP, yet neither was the ambiguity of having a brief rekindling with Phoebe.

All too easily, I could most likely have just drifted happily alongside Fergus and Sean for the remainder of my trip; this would pass by in a flash. Our triad would probably all have enough fun, see many an interesting sight and inevitably inhale or snort our adequate share of mood and wellbeing enhancers. Yet this was just not what I have set out on this trip for, or anything that I much wanted anymore. Without going as far as to say that it shouldn't enhance the state of things on the odd occasion, it was far from a state of being that I wanted to regularly revisit, as I now felt that there just must be something more to this life.

For too long since graduating with my Politics degree from the UEA, I'd felt ever more aware of just how little I knew about anything in this life. For a long enough time I'd felt that I had attained as much adulthood to easily spend my life with an overall absence of responsibilities; now though, needing something more is probably the best—if all too vague—way of defining my current state of being. Still, I was shy of making any of the compromises required to obtain this 'something more' and was far from ready to break away from my all too casual approach to just about every facet of life. It's not as though my existence was in any way that bad; *I worked reasonably* hard and played *reasonably* hard and this didn't create much void in itself. There was the unavoidable feeling that all of us inhabitants of a capitalist society possess: the feeling of inadequacy; enough is never sufficient.

This bleak thought of the failing redundancy of everything in life somehow lifted my stomach at this time, and without anything other than my dorm key in the pocket of my vile lime green jogging shorts, I embarked on a jog at a pace that would be impossible to maintain. The feeling of burning out was exactly what I needed, whether as a metaphor for myself or to purge the fervent and piercing thoughts from my brain.

The sense of despair that begins to brew in my mind as I set out upon this jaunt gradually fades, and exercise triumphs as the best remedy for the loneliness of this long distance runner. It is only as I begin to reach the end of the beach that my struggle to maintain a pace against the sand exposes the reality that I have not done any exercise amongst my substance abuse for far too many moons. Still, I just keep on going, and although the suffering is relentless, it soon allows for at least some solace once I stop choosing to hurt myself.

In spite of my little workout meaning that I did not have sufficient energy or concentration left to focus on a great deal, the reality did poignantly dawn on me that Phoebe was a large factor in my growingly painful discomfort. If I'd have made the minimal effort in sticking with the reliably dependable Holly, or even Martha from UEA, at least I'd have something more to show for my open-ended and worthless little life. A life without any commitments has its expiry date in my eyes, and largely this point for me had long been reached. Ever chasing Phoebe was more down to the intensive quality of the times that we shared when things were going well than any real conviction that we would ever be together. Surely, though, the times that we had spent with each other on this trip had proven that my fixation on Phoebe was no longer a quest for the non-existent pot of gold at the end of the rainbow? It had been dangled closer than it had ever been before, and you can't spend your life—or at least after the end of your twenties—chasing after a dream that you cannot identify.

The life that I could have with Phoebe was now more than tangible, at least to the extent that we both knew all too well that it could not all be idyllic or forever harmonious; we were far too honest with one another. Only we both knew—or maybe it was just I—that we could feasibly give it the best of all stabs. The domestic drudgery of marriage to either Holly or Martha was already more than visible before it even began. Already I could predict that they, along with other mates, could just raise their eyes at how Phoebe supposedly could still apparently play me like a fiddle. The truth is that these poor conventionally repressed creatures had just never experienced anything like my helping of the Holy Grail.

Going through the pain threshold achieved the goal of keeping my mind vacant, and I kept on running—or at least galloping around—for the best part of an hour. The run certainly succeeded. After I'd showered down, it was a pleasure to be able to take a beer into the hostel's communal drinking area, where I was given the impression that Fergus and Sean had been enjoying themselves. Though having said this, they were certainly still more than compos mentis to have some proper chat. It was the perfect sort of evening all in all.

The three of us slinked out to a small eastern style tavern type of place (if you can picture it from this description based on a patchy memory, I'm more than a little impressed) just several buildings up from the hostel. We had become royally sloshed on the large carafes of cheap red vino. This with our tasty yet incredibly inauthentic pasta dishes was all that I think any of us wanted out of life in this moment.

10. Day 20: Rest Bite

Fergus, Sean and I parted fondly the next morning, even though were all united in paying the price for our excesses. The night before last was still the one where our bodies were most wounded, though this was not at all alleviated by some copious consumption of the vin-rouge last night. As quaffable as it may have being (to less than particular plebs at least), it certainly put more than a couple of hairs on your chest.

After our farewell, it dawned on me that I was actually conscious of their absence. Granted, I'd probably never make the effort to journey over the Irish Sea to cross paths with Sean again (even if I no longer felt that even his company would go amiss), though there was something about the bond that Fergus and I had created during our night of excesses that automatically made us feel like close comrades. Knowing that they'd both seen me in my most idyllic state alongside the person that I'd like to share the rest of my life with seemed to sooth the friendship that we'd founded.

A fun day of travel would have to be tolerated. As annoyed as I was to have long finished my Sillitoe novel, I did not feel in the mood to devote myself to any new material. This was almost like a melodramatic personification of my current state. I had enough close friends, enemies (regrettably), money (as inadequate as it could easily be seen), health (as much as I seemed to be doing my best to make it corrupt) and the person that I wanted to be with for the remainder of my naturals. If everybody moved in this situation as I wanted them to, I'd be left without a single complaint.

I just sat looking out of the window on this coach as it began to drizzle, which if you could capture, was a perfect emblem for my mood in this state. Downcast and drab. All that I had any real yearning to do was to go the a local boozer—the more basic and even run-down, the better—and just sit and drink beer in front of a magazine or newspaper, certainly nothing that required too much thought or concentration. No quantity of travel whatsoever should heal the void cast upon me by Phoebe's departure.

In Phoebe's presence I could have stayed on the road forever. Life alongside her was just a grand adventure of exploration that I just didn't want to ever limit. Without her, I was left with nothing but a feeling of apathy towards everything in my life. It wasn't anything like a depressed feeling. Whilst I've never had an official diagnosis of being blue, and I'm sure that I've been through spells where I would probably have qualified for some medication, it's never been something that I'd feel at all comfortable receiving. I'd like to think that this was less out of delusional pride, but more out of paranoia over what I'd turn to if I ever still saw death as the best option. Sorry to be so bleak!

Because however many months it may have taken, I've always worked through the spell and come towards a more healthy attitude, where the thought of suicide never enters into my mind-set. Still, this is more confirmation of the fact that I've never been depressed (beyond what must just be part of being human). If you've never experienced extreme lows, how can you ever feel the real, prolonged, heightened highs? Attitude has to be everything, but society now seems to increasingly advertise that there must be some medication that you should take if you are not always be happy or at least fulfilled.

In a fiercely competitive, capitalist world, without even mentioning our reliance upon technology that we do not even understand, this idea has to be a complete charade and all port of the rhetoric that consumerism creates. The reality must be that in the UK, we've all got it far better than we could ever have imagined. We can afford to be depressed against the backdrop of everybody else's supposed success. Not so long ago, when much of our lives were consumed on keeping fed and warm, happiness must have been far less of a concern. I mean, I can't imagine that there was any such thing as the feeling of *depression* for one of the thousands of serfs on a feudal estate, with their shit life involving bare survival.

I'm far from trying, let alone wanting, to suggest that anybody is ever necessarily at all at fault for their own despair. Close mates of mine that have been prescribed these manufactured pills, which seem to do nothing more than dumb-down their sensitivity to mood and just made seem zombielike. From the people that I know, anti-depressants just seem to be like a chain that it's hard to disconnect from. Obviously whatever works for you, but if I'm honest, I'd just be scared of always having to turn to this crutch as soon as life started becoming hard, with the bar for what you consider necessary to get back to normal gradually getting raised. This is nothing of any real knowledge or value; what do I know? Horses for courses I guess, whatever works for you.

As I'm stuck on this long bus ride, I can't help but feel numb with indifference towards life, along with a growing feeling of travel sickness. It is as I try to practise the old remedy of 'focusing on something dormant way out on the horizon', yet this seemed to further augment my nausea.

All am I am left with is that old atheist's feeling that I have been selected by something to have the piss taken out of for some unbeknownst reason. Just having to exist as me leaves me with a feeling of self-deprecation.

Downhearted would be no accurate picture of my mental state. Emptiness may be what I feel, though I'm certainly a good few furlongs off from my most meagre of emotions. There is no real trace of my bio-rhythms being much involved here. Unlike any real downcast state, I know exactly how this could be remedied: Phoebe wouldn't have left me feeling lost and dejected.

Though in fairness, if she were still out here with me, we'd probably now be aboard the same sort of coach as I'd ended up on now.

Daphne had actually met Phoebe once or twice in the past. First it was when she was just a 'friend' from school at my 18th birthday celebration (Daphne seemed to read Phoebe far better than I did at this time) with my family and some close friends, and another time it was, quite weirdly, just the three of us at the Flask in Highgate. In this instance I'd agreed to meet Daphne, as she was about in London and I'd not seen her in over a year, and sporadically—as it always was with both of them actually—we'd arranged for Phoebe to join us, as she and I were in the midst of one of our flings.

Daphne and Phoebe had always gotten along so well. They were kindred spirits of some kind, and although they were clearly from different ages, they'd always managed to share a lot of laughter. Thinking of this led to a sudden yearning that Phoebe were beside me on this coach, on the way to meet Daphne together. The silver lining may be that wishing for Phoebe's suddenly eruption out of thin air worked to abate my motion sickness.

Eventually we reached our stopover point in the city of Ella, where we had an hour or so to go and stretch our legs and have a look at the place's magnificent waterfall. Waterfalls to me always smell so fresh. The sun was shining by now and I got a few decent snaps. Naturally, I managed to get lost on the way back to my bus, and the panic was only intensified by the fact that my luggage was in the hold. Though I actually arrived back there within about quarter of an hour of the bus's further departure. Typically, the bus was running late, and this just meant that I had to sit for longer drenched in my own sweat and scratching my uncomfortable itchy arse. A violin's what I felt that I needed.

Other than feeling some more irrevocable moodiness, all went successfully in the remaining few hours' journey to Kandy, and when I disembarked, I was relieved to finally be free of the rickety, vomit-inducing coach. The cheap B&B that I had set my sights on didn't appear to be far from where the coach left us (as it stated in my guidebook, actually, but you know, seeing is believing).

The hostel, which I think was called *The Other Foot* (or something like that), seemed to do exactly what was indicated on the tin that was my ever-tried, tested and trusted *Rough Guide* #plug. Upon greeting a friendly receptionist, without much contemplation, I asked for my own room. It was lucky that they did actually only have single room spaces, and it wasn't even much pricier than a dorm space at many other hostels. Daphne was to be staying at a more expensive **** hotel not too great a distance away, and even though we were not to be staying in the same hotel, something about Daphne's presence conjured the sentiment of being on a family holiday. Probably because she was family. Even though holidays alongside my parents had not been luxurious, they were a level beyond backpacking and afforded more refinement than my more shoestring travelling.

With a few pieces of fruit and packets of crisps, I had a really pleasant afternoon. There was something about being within a day of meet somebody who'd almost certainly changed my nappy as a baby that strangely afforded me some sense of assurance. I had a stroll around Kandy's lakes, and was even happy that the weather was overcast. Almost as a pathetic list ticker, I set off for the place where Buddha's tooth supposedly existed; if I'm honest, I just wished to get it over and done with really.

Of course there was no tooth to be found, but the place was interesting. Of course I'm not sufficiently stupid to be a religious man, but if I had to pick faith, Buddhism's definitely what I'd choose. Unlike what I've read about the others, it actually seems fair and based upon being the best person that you can, without so much threat of how you may be punished for your lifestyle, and without the patriarchal rhetoric of making everybody live in guilt. Devotion should be based on appreciating life and getting the best that all of us can; this seems mutual, rather than paying any undue homage to the ridiculous notion of there existing any superior being.

All I know for definite is that, in whatever ways it may or may not reveal itself, I am not one iota more devoted to Phoebe than she is to me, and our time together during this trip has certainly helped to reveal that; she is no Oscar-winning actress after all.

There was some enhanced pleasure as my stomach was all settled bang to rights during my exploration of this beautiful old town. It was obvious why Daphne had this down as amongst her favourite places in the entire world. I don't know quite what it was about gulping a beer and smoking my first cigarette of the day, but as I sparked-up, I felt a little head-rush iced by some euphoria. Each to their own, as pathetic as it may be, but I could only pity non-smokers in instances such as these.

A single beer and a solitary cigarette served me just fine and I was soon ready to head back to *The Other Foot*. As strange as it may be, what I most craved in this tropically warm climate was some stodge. Beyond that actually, what I most craved was a Fray Bentos steak and kidney pie and mash or something. Not having eaten anything but healthy (albeit not particularly fresh-seeming) fruit and paprika crisps all day, I felt as though I was deserved some feeding. A lentil curry was a cheap and fulfilling find, and was healthy. Eating this delicacy almost felt like sacrilege given my level of sobriety and the fact that it was still fully light.

Still hungry though, and as if to undo any good for myself that I had done, I soon ordered from some shack the tastiest kebab that I've ever tried (and I've been to Turkey before, if you'll excuse my shameless namedropping). It implicitly provided the rejuvenation and feeling of being overly sated that I had so desired. Finishing any food always leaves me feeling as though my skin glistens—with grease rather than any radiance—and I've become shiny, again with perspiration rather than any radiance. Anyway after sprucing myself up and returning to my hotel, it is a blessing to discover that nobody in the large glass-walled dorm room has English as their first language. The remainder of the evening is enjoyably spent on the ground floor of my hotel drinking beer—with only a couple of cancer sticks in between—and playing numerous games of pool; even winning a couple of them, which is far out of my usual billiard characteristics.

After what felt like the longest and deepest sleep since this trip started, I have to remind myself that the day that I wake up to has any premise. It is towards the beginning of my shower that I remember that I am to be meeting Daphne this afternoon. With this thought, I can surrender my feeling that I ought to do something of much worth for the rest of the day, as meeting Daphne shall surely be a memorable occurrence in itself. As little sense as I realise that this makes.

As I finish my most basic breakfast, I run into a couple of the guys—hardly recalled their names then, let alone now with any confidence—that I had fun playing pool with the night before. They were going to go to a waterfall just an hour or so away from our hotel apparently. Whether or not I could fit this in before meeting Daphne later was rather irrelevant, given how little I had any desire to join, having sampled Ella the day previous. I wasn't deliberately dissing waterfalls, saying that they all look the same or even that they're not worth seeing; anyway, I just couldn't be bothered.

What had caught the corner of my beady little eye was a copy of the Virgin and the Gypsy by D.H. Lawrence. I can't seem to recall whether I've read this particular book, and I take this mostly as a confirmation of the fact that I'm not so young anymore, rather than indication that I'm a reader without much retention. I'd definitely enjoyed Lady Chatterley's Lover along with Sons and Lovers, but this little number… Oh yes, it's actually one of that large number of books that I've begun to read—often enjoying and getting more than half way through—and shamefully just never finishing. That doesn't even mean that I disliked it, just something else that came up in my little mind that had it shelved, literally. Well it's only short, so I could easily plough a great deal of the way through it before being united with Daphne.

Drinking lashings of coffee at a café just opposite my hotel means that I am feeling well wired by midday. More than content nonetheless. I noticed that I received a text from Daphne half way through my reading session, which gave the name of a drinking den (which I think read as 'the Fountain Gate' in the language of the country where we were visiting) that she highly recommended. She estimated that she'd arrive there around 3pm. This struck me as probably the most inconvenient time food wise, but hey ho.

The hours flew by, and before long it was about time for me to be going to set off to go and meet my relative. Why *Brief Encounter* again sprang into my mind I do not quite know; I've never even seen the film and it was hardly like we hadn't spent significant time in each other's company in the past.

There was something that felt most surreal about meeting a senior relative who I hadn't seen in quite a while in a country thousands of miles away from home. It was a good job that we were related, as I'm sure that my breath still reeked of coffee, although I was hoping that wine would dilute the pungent coffee breath that I had. Without having brushed my teeth, It must've still stunk somewhat.

There I was, composed and sat munching dried roasted peanuts and drinking from the Sauvignon blanc bottle that I had ordered for the two of us to share. Daphne was certainly a drinker who could open a bottle and finish it at a greater pace than anybody else who I have had the pleasure—or chore—of drinking with. To be fair, she liked beer as well, along with anything else that she could give her liver practise on, though *obviously* I deplore any gender assumptions being made, and it seemed a safe bet that we would both favour wine as a choice of drink. I'd texted Daphne of my whereabouts on the first floor balcony of the Fountain Gate (or whatever it was actually called) and returned to the D.H. Lawrence that I'd borrowed from the hotel.

At not too long past 3, a beaming Daphne came over to me and trilled 'Hey babe!' as she gave me a squeeze. She's in a turquoise loose cloth dress of white floral prints, which all looked pretty agreeable. In spite of her age, she succeeded in pulling off a trendily short peroxide haircut, complete with espadrilles and as many bangles as you could count.

'You look well!' were the first words out of my mouth, which were followed almost immediately by a 'no need to sounds so surprised… It's what being single does to you isn't it!'

'But you've never looked that bad though…' I reply, of course with reference to that fact that ever since I'd known her, she has always had some significant other tucked around her shoulder. Normally her type involved somebody who she could walk all over and be hen-pecked into place. I draw a painful comparison between Phoebe and Daphne, and my suspicion that I could be perceived as Phoebe's lynchpin to go to when there's nothing else. This is just not true though. Daphne's men may be disposable door mice, whereas Phoebe and I go way back, and I make as many—if not the bulk—of the big decisions we take. Defensiveness is the attitude that society moulds me into as the male who feels like the one always on the chase in a relationship.

If manning-up means suppressing all feelings in exchange for a subservient girlfriend who adheres to all of my wants and desires, then this does not appeal to me in the slightest. A relationship may be great, but I'd only be satisfied in the knowledge that I'd be able to fully survive and make my existence function on my own.

The flippant allusion that I make to Daphne's wide array of partners thankfully goes unnoticed as she nonchalantly remarks that 'cor, it's a real shame that I never got to see your Phoebe this time...'

It's something I always find strange when independently minded women such as Daphne choose expressions that imply that Phoebe's some possession of mine. Perhaps I'm just reading too much into it.

'Yeah she had to arrange to go all of a sudden, for some reason that I didn't overly pry into...'

'You did right not to ask too much Darren. She'll have had her good reasons, and I tell you, she worships the ground that you walk on!'

This was certainly an example of Daphne taking it upon herself to lay down a rather unqualified opinion, yet I'd be lying if I didn't say that it felt reassuring to hear. Pleased as I was by what she was saying, she had to go a step further 'you know I don't really believe in tying the knot, but if two handsome young things were ever fit to get married...'

I quickly interject with a 'no need to go all Austen on me!' I laughed it off, and Daphne joined in before adding 'just saying that these things don't come along often and it should be cherished while they last, babe' I'm not quite sure when or how 'babe' became absorbed by Daphne's vernacular, but I certainly didn't approve of this expression being used by my aunt. Who am I to judge though? 'You're hardly one to talk though are you given your history!'

This was an incredibly bizarre and uncomfortable conversation for a twenty-something (not that any age would really have made this sort of dialogue any more justifiable for either of us) to have with his aunt. It just did not feel like the appropriate sort of exchange to be having, but it gave me that horrible feeling of dread as to where it may be going. Credit where credit's due, nothing about this conversation felt as though it were awkward. Yet an awful feeling suddenly came over the pits of my stomach that the 's' word may even get brought up given another bottle or two of wine; which we were almost certain to glug.

'Well you'd be surprised' offered Daphne and 'oh shit, this was all I needed'. Some rusty rose tinted specs coming on to bore me with. Luckily at that moment she propositioned me with a packet of smokes that she'd extracted from her huge pink felt handbag. Daphne took a cigarette along with offering me one. 'Cheers' I gratefully responded before slightly wincing as I opened the packet of *Vogue* slim cigarettes and sparked up with her gold zippo lighter.

Well I hope that it was obvious that we were related to one another, as an image of Daphne as a fag-hag couldn't be more intricately and wincingly be conjured in my mind. What did I care anyway; white wine and a slim cigarette did seem to complement each other like birds of a feather anyway.

Unprompted Daphne continued with 'Caius was his name and I was around your age actually'. Not only did he sound like some sort of Mills and Boon Character (obviously I wouldn't really know!), but I can't say that I had much desire to know anything more about him; though this option of averting the conversation had long since ceased.

'I just let him drift through my fingers and never committed to the poor guy… Now I understand that he's an architect who earns shed loads of money and has an apartment in Paris, a gîte in the countryside and a seaside home'

'Did he marry somebody else then?' I enquire 'Course he did', she said. And it's all my own stupid fault…'

Going with the vacuous expression that my wondrous aunt is albeit all too capable of using, I was half tempted to say 'well there must have been a reason' and I wouldn't have been at all surprised if Daphne had told me that he was actually gay. That'd be a prime example of one of the unfortunately less-than-infrequent times when comedy could be easily extracted from one of her many tragedies. But no, what she continued with was 'if I'd only had the courage to go and move to Paris with him back then, I'd have had a different life. Okay we might have buggered about like most people, but at least we'd have had a go…'

This divulgence caused me much surprise. It was the first time that I'd ever heard Daphne sound at all vulnerable, as sentiment had just never seemed to be the sort of thing that she'd much valued to herself, or at least she certainly never felt the need to share it with any other people. Ha, I suppose that, in some ways, I should have felt honoured to be one of the few people—my dad definitely would never have been close enough to her—to whom Daphne had ever delivered this news. He may have even met Caius with Daphne, but would have likely deemed this as unworthy information to bother storing in this memory, as in fairness Daphne had introduced more than a giant's handful of lovers in my lifetime, let alone my dad's.

As with so many other things at this time, my on-going ruptured relationship with Phoebe was conjured in my mind. And I was by instinct attempting to draw some comparisons with Daphne's anecdote. I could see some clear parallels between both Daphne and

Phoebe's flakiness and lack of commitment. Perhaps it was supercilious and even slightly macho-sounding to construe that, in refusing to confirm her devotion to her fella, Daphne had prohibited herself from chances of the best quality of life that she could find. Still, as unashamedly blasé and assuming as it may sound, I was more than convinced that Phoebe and I could have an incredibly exciting, eventful and fulfilled life in which we could rely on nothing but one another.

We'd both taken the remainder of our cigarettes in pensive silence and appreciation of the beautiful environment. One of those stark moments of reflection—leading to realisation—slapped me in the face as I noticed Daphne's numerous liver spots, along with the way that her well yellowing fingers appeared to have long moulded themselves into some sort of clasping cigarette holder.

The quirkiness of the situation (a guy in his late twenties having fun drinking and smoking with ancient relative thousands of miles away from home) had its appeal at times, though in other instances it did just seem to be plain weird. Not that I even cared who observed the situation. In some ways it was just the sort of relaxation that I needed. I felt a sense of perfect balance in being in the company of this capricious relative; always there, but infrequently present throughout my life.

It was in some respects a fitting end to my trip. Having enjoyed the shreds of decadence and drama, it was as though I'd now inadvertently returned to the familial nest in the company of an elder relative, and now I felt in many respects ready to retreat back into my own nest.

11. Day 24: Homeward Bound

So this little adventure was about to close. The several days' separation from my usual lifestyle and my daily meet-ups with Daphne were exactly what I needed. It was the perfect format for me to digest my love-life shenanigans; mulling around the quiet resort by day—along with the odd visit to some place of interest nearby—with a meet-up with Daphne for a meal and a drink by night. The drinking sessions were so long by anybody's standards that the need to do a great deal for the whole of the rest of the day was pretty much written off anyway.

Also, my hostel had a small outdoor pool attached, with the added miraculous extravagance of one of those poolside bars. This felt astonishing, given that the hostel was so quiet. The only other people that I saw in the pool throughout the whole time was a group of half a dozen or so British business people, rightly delighting in a jolly part of their trip. A tall and gangly guy with wispy dark hair is the only one that has in any way imprinted upon my memory. And he only captured my attention because he kept having to hitch up his clearly oversized, vibrant orange-coloured swim shorts; hopefully they were borrowed last-minute, but his appearance nonetheless managed to annoy me.

The strangest thing was that the music system—which generally played no music that I'd ever recognise—would sporadically blast out short interludes of 'Smack My Bitch Up' by the Prodigy. Loudly. In the right context and with the right people, this holiday song would be something to celebrate. Although I did quite enjoy just how ill-fitting the song seemed to be in this context, it certainly failed to incite any conversation or cheerfulness with anybody around. Apart from a few vague displays of some acknowledgment, there was absolutely no communication between any of this group and me. Still, this seemed to be what we all wanted.

The atmosphere mirrored the beige-coloured tiles surrounding the pool, complete with the staleness that seemed to permeate the place from the excess of sun exposure and cracks all over. I had uncovered a copy of *Naïve. Super* by Erlend Loe from the bottom of my rucksack, which until I had begun to horde all of my stuff together for my final pack, had been far too submerged to gain my attention. A friend had given it to me several months ago with the recommendation that it had helped him to 'sort shit out'. Be this as it may, and as much as I was enjoying the read—I can't say that I got that far in before my flight back home—this trip had strangely in itself help me to feel sorted, although things in my life were in some ways more all over the place than they had ever been.

Don't ask how, let alone why, but despite Phoebe's arrival and sudden ambiguous departure, I began to feel more liberated than at any other point in my memory. Maybe it was just the holiday having worked its trick successfully, but I felt far calmer and more relaxed than I had done at the beginning. I had certainly succeeded in gaining perspective; nothing at all really mattered in terms of anything. Least of all Phoebe and I; we'd go where the wind took us. In the time since our parting, I still loved and wanted to be with her to the same degree as before, but I wouldn't try to cling to something I could never have. I suppose that it could be compared to bereavement: I'd never ever forget or wish any less to spend all of my waking moments alongside Phoebe, although doesn't everyone live without something that they want?

Not to be deliberately flippant, but my good fortune in life is perhaps most revealed by the fact that losing Phoebe really would be the biggest drawback to my entire existence… Only given the quantity of my life that I spend with Phoebe in my reality back home in London, nothing will fundamentally change whatever the outcome.

I've long been mature enough to never actually take anything too seriously, though in some way, this trip—or be it the excess of sun inducing some light-headedness—seems to have pushed me forward by imbuing me with a healthier attitude to life. That is, that nothing at all matters a great deal. Of course I'll still aim to work hard and play harder, but overall I just felt rejuvenated.

I'd the time of my life whilst Phoebe was with me and, if anything, I was enjoying how sage it made me feel. I could almost overlook the fact that it was so seamlessly cut short, with no definition of our future together, and just focus on the joyous time that we'd both experienced. It was one of those instances where I didn't really care so much what the future held. I had become relaxed enough to be un-preoccupied by anything.

The prospect of beginning my new job and being reunited with all of my separate enclaves of friends in the near future was certainly reassuring, yet it was also exciting to have no real idea of what the future held. Well aware that this period of happy indifference was bound to have to come to an end soon, I was more than happy to live within it whilst it lasted.

The only issue that had started to increasingly bother me over this final section of the holiday was the fact that I started to have elevated discomfort in urinating. Not quite like needles pricking all around my nether regions, but that's probably the closet description that I could have at times. Genital herpes was the last thing that I needed—as with every one of the many carriers, I suppose—especially if it were a grotesque price that I was forced to pay for a small slice of paradise with the love of my life. I wouldn't say that I was a hypochondriac, but it really would add insult to injury if I'd caught an incurable cold-saw from the love of my life.

Especially if it had to be the lasting present of insignificantly significant James. Don't get me wrong, as shameful as it may be, I'd only relish the thought of him having herpes. Or anything whatsoever the matter with him and his pesky, flabby young body, really. I just tried not to think about it; there didn't seem any real point in getting it checked out, as I should touch down in Heathrow almost within the blink of an eye.

Daphne and I bid each other farewell on my penultimate day in Sri Lanka. Given that my flight wasn't until the early hours of the morning, it was a relief to know that I wouldn't have to check into, and potentially leave something behind at, any other hostel.

It was before 7 o'clock in the morning when I decided to leave for Sigiriya. A tour was easy enough to find, and paying enough money for the extortionate luxury of an air-conditioned taxi was more than worth the brass. Sigiriya was amazing, and I don't even feel as though I'm being hyperbolic in claiming this. Of course my experience of exploring the charming palace of ancient history was tainted by the twinging sadness that I was not able to share its beauty alongside Phoebe. She'd love it. 'Always next time' I thought.

At least the entire day came without the accompaniment of any rash or vile discharges, and I could urinate in comfort again. Little panic over. The only slight negative aspect of my choice in going to Sigiriya—and it was a highlight of my trip—was that I'd not be exploring some of the desolate scenery of the Island's north. Had I gone there with Phoebe, we'd have been able to bask around in the nude, which I love doing. Phoebe being with me would also probably have meant an end to me being able to claim that there is no photographic evidence of me having done this since I was about 2 or 3 years old.

There is nothing much more to be said about this life-affirming experience, other than that it can be a liberating joy, though I was hardly in much hurry to repeat it. This is as sand manages to get in just about every crevice that you wouldn't even know existed, and despite trying to be careful I had always managed to come away with a slightly shrivelled and slightly sunburned penis.

As much as I never mind baring all, going for it alone, in the absence of Phoebe, was far from something that I could much bother with anyway. I more than contemplated it though. But I certainly would never exchange this for the choice that I made. And at least I didn't have to fear so much that I'd somehow end up getting a stiffy—quick running into the sea was my backup plan for this—or, even worse, that I'd end up bumping into my auntie Daphne. I mean, it is just the sort of place where she'd probably go, but the prospect in itself is just too dreadful to even contemplate.

Coming away from Sigiriya, I was almost looking forward to returning to home life, with or without Phoebe, with relief that I'd soon be returning to some routine of normality. I even now had some excitement about the new job that I was about to commence in Whitechapel.

Any positivity that I might have felt was heightened by the fact that—in what seemed almost fictional given my luck and her track record—I received a message from Phoebe reading:

"Hey, my love, you're heading home tomorrow, aren't you? Cannot wait to see you again. Even though it's just been a few weeks, I've missed you so much. I'll explain everything! Are you able to meet at Elizabeth Hall rooftop garden at the South Bank Centre on Thursday night? If it's not raining…Xxxxx"

This was, in fact, a thorough description for Phoebe, and the amount of elation that the receipt of this message caused could not be overstated. Still, I tried not to be overly optimistic. She could even have taken James back for all I knew. Only at least I would be treated to her company and we could get to the bottom of all by then. The main thing, though, is that the thought of seeing her gave me the most active butterflies in my stomach, and if this didn't confirm the depth of my feelings for Phoebe and unerring desire to be alongside her, then I don't know what would.

In the evening, I had my first ever experience of an actual phone chat with Daphne. Turns out that she had loved her nature trip and, believe me, she had plenty to say about it. Whether it was because I was feeling increasingly unreserved knowing that I'd be leaving this country in several hours' time, I shared with Daphne about Phoebe's message.

She gave hardly any reaction or response, which I found almost funny. It was as though I was merely telling her something incredibly obvious, and she soon resumed talking about all of the 'so dignified looking' multi-coloured birds that she'd seen during the day. If anything, this acted to me more a confirmation of the fact that, to Daphne, there was no doubt that Phoebe and I would end up together, although it could just be that she didn't much care. Saying goodbye to Daphne, she assured me that 'I know you'll be all right…just be lucky!'

My flight was frustratingly delayed for about 3 hours (had loads worse, but still annoying). I remember killing time whilst waiting around and even chortling to myself that it was on this exact same holiday that I had been forced to endure Stephen and all of his nothingness. It was validating to think of all of the experiences that I'd been through and of the full and unprecedented way that my life had moved since.

This short episode of travelling never really had its own distinctive purpose, but it had certainly achieved more than I'd ever bargained for. I had confirmed my comfort in my own (however sun-kissed, ha) skin. More than anything else, though, rekindling my relationship with Phoebe was an unexpected yet incredibly blessed experience, and as bumpy and long-and-winding as our path may be back on home turf, it was something that I more than needed to fulfil. Maybe it's just my sun-drenched brain talking, but I cannot ever remember feeling more assured or secure in all of the decisions that I have made in this life. Of course whatever happens, as I've said, Phoebe and I shall probably just bugger everything up like everybody else seems to, but at least we'll be able to have our own go and cock it up and end up hurting each other in our own ridiculous way. At least it'd be on our terms.

Two

Day 1: So Naïve

Here I am now, in my early thirties complete with an all-too-rapidly receding hair line—which I'd ten times rather exchange for a few grey specks—and a marginal beer belly. Or if I'm feeling optimistic (or indulging in the adequate amount of denial), I've just filled out a little bit. And I choose to shave my hair on a 1 or 2 all over—depending on the season…as if a few millimetres of hair make any difference whatsoever to overall warmth! I've become a bit sturdier as I go to the gym to bulk up several times a week.

This is not the life I ever foresaw. Still, what in God's name is? Life as always could be better and it could be an *awful* lot worse couldn't it?

It's now been just about 3+ years since I last felt the need—or time gave the opportunity, which in fairness is more accurate—to record any of my boring goings on. It's probably easiest if I just go on from roughly where we left off in my life, when I was free of any real responsibilities or commitments.

To think that I went around calling people bright-eyed and bushy-tailed when I had no limits on my swagger or any of the weight of life on my shoulders…

This ellipsis was unintentional. Mildred had found her way upstairs and apparently felt the urgency to spray Phoebe's perfume—which, for whatever unbeknownst reason, was left on the mosaicked coffee table in our living room—all over whatever she could find. This was dealt with in my usual charm—aggression—charm—way of trying to do the best job of parenting. I mean, she needs to learn that you can't just help yourself to things that you see without asking permission, yet there's no way that she could understand the value of Phoebe's carelessly-left-about Gucci perfume.

We ended up making a joke of it and laughing as we resumed playing a bit of 'rough and tumble' using the cushions of our tired looking William Morris printed sofa. As it has now done one time too many, it all ended in tears. This was due to nothing more than a small carpet burn that came from skidding against our thin red rug on the pine floor of our small bay-windowed living room.

Although I'd kissed it better and did my best consoling her, I was soon becoming tired of the obvious crocodile tears; no way was I giving in to her requests for another mini-chocolate éclair. Mildred and I were almost—well, as close to it as we could ever really come—to the verge of falling out, when Phoebe's arrival home deflected the situation, and our pride and joy could soon be read to, bathed and tucked up in bed.

Well, this is what I'm pretty certain is going on now as I take advantage of another opportunity to write. Joint non-conjugal roles are things that we tend to do pretty well, though normally I prefer to read to Mildred whilst Phoebe can feed her some tortellini or something. I actually do the bulk of the cooking generally (as the tortellini may illustrate), though we surely have to set the example to our daughter that we all have do a little bit of everything.

Understanding the logic of a child and the spontaneous, sporadic and fairly frequent ridiculous-seeming demands is at times akin to trying to figure out that the so-called 'rush hour' has no real bearing to the actual length of time.

It's a bit of a quandary that I have barely turned 30 and seem to have succeeded in climbing a mountain that I never had any real intention of escalating. I certainly haven't done this at my own pace, as any of you of have also indulged in having children will instantly appreciate. If I've learned anything, it's that nothing in your life is worth having a morsel of control over if you are going to live up to live up to the expectation being a successful parent.

I'm increasingly haunted by how much our reliance on technology highlights the destitution of the modern world and how, at times, it really felt like we'd gone beyond ourselves; a hunter-gatherer life must have been far simpler and fulfilling. Perhaps we could attain a sense of reward through genuine relation to other people and form judgements beyond how many devoid Facebook likes that something has received. Of course, catching up with my social media is the first thing that I always have to do in the morning, and I hate the world and myself because of this. Then I go back to as real a world as it can be with all of this instantly accessible information. Still, without any optimism, I'd feel incredibly hypocritical in raising Mildred without all of this technological assistance, so I guess that you just have to take it for what it is.

The whole concept that I am now a father even carries extra weight for me, and this seems like an ideal opportunity for me to fill you in from where we left off. This was when I was young, supposedly carefree and based in some far-flung corner of the world, untarnished by any real responsibility. Anyone who knows me well will appreciate that I have never at all been without worries and angst, although I was seemingly ticking along in as decadent and feckless a way as I could afford. Having just told my iPhone to put on an alarm for tomorrow morning at 6:30, I'm back to ruminating how best to convey developments in my life once I'd touched down in London Heathrow after my month-long adventure.

All that I vividly remember about my returning from travel is that I'd overlooked the proximity of my return to work and was disconcerted by the fact that my new job seemed within touching distance.

Meeting Phoebe was predictably still my most pressing concern during this period, though first I had to start my new job along the Whitechapel end of Commercial Road as early as the Monday after landing. At least there'd always be plenty of cheap Indian food for lunches, I thought. Instinctively, I never much liked this job, or any of my colleagues, from the second I started to when I handed in my notice just 4 months or so later. That's a different little story, though, which I'll cover another time.

Perhaps my preoccupation with the fact that I'd be meeting Phoebe in the evening after my first day of work in my brand-new job was an early omen, which would lead towards my consistent disaffection with the vocation.

We'd opted to meet in the Alwyne Castle on St Paul's Road around Highbury and Islington for 8 that evening, instead of the South Bank. As ridiculous, and even emasculating, as it sounds, the fact that Phoebe had been the instigator of having some food left me with some added optimism, as it meant that this wouldn't be a hit-and-run situation where Phoebe drops some bad news that'd be uncomfortable for me to hear.

The weather was being more-than-kind for early September, and I was able to complete my predictable wait for Phoebe to arrive with a pint of Doombar in one hand and the G2 in the other. This wait was of no real length of time—hadn't even been given a chance to bugger up the crossword—when I was approached by a serene-looking Phoebe. We were both still in our work clothes, with our badges still on, as we squeezed each other; Phoebe's black sunglasses and greater retention of her deep summer-glow seemed to carry the optimism and perfection of our couple of weeks travelling together.

I was indulging in a deep stare at Phoebe's exquisite glamour, with her white short-sleeved blouse, tight-fitting rouge knee-length shirt and high-wedged light espadrilles making a reappearance. This was with her rouge nails, bulky metallic earrings and necklace.

'Bottle of white wine to suit the weather? And you can help me out with this 50g of Drum full-strength tobacco—complete with the standard twigs in it!—that Duty Free insisted that I buy, before it inevitably all goes stale with the amount I smoke…'

There was a brief moment of silence after this was said. This in itself was a rarity as neither of us was by any means the type to waste time in our consumption of vices.

'Well, I just can't drink or smoke now, so you just sit yourself back down and I'll go get myself a sparkling fizzy water' (the patronisation was extra-affected, which made me smile).

This knocked a bit of the wind out of my sails; Phoebe was my favourite person to disinhibit myself and have a great time with, and a drink only ever helped us with this.

'What, don't tell me that you're part of the club now?!' I half-joked upon hearing these words.

Phoebe was wearing an expression that I can't say I've seen before or since. This was completely the wrong joke for me to make, and she was conveniently en-route to the bar by the time that I had finished uttering this expression. To be fair, I didn't really think that much more of the remark, as the idea that Phoebe would ever allow herself to get pregnant was just so far out of the question.

We both wanted to get so much more out of life and do so much more before kids came onto our horizon, whether or not we were each other's respective partners by the time that this could ever arise.

It was fully dark and the temperature was noticeably now dropping, and I followed Phoebe inside, as there was absolutely no point in us staying outside if she wasn't able to help me smoke myself to death tonight. She beamed at me from across the bar as I ordered myself another pint and picked up a couple of food menus.

We migrated to a table at the Alwyne Castle's indoor food section. Phoebe had soon found her way to sitting next to me and certainly wasted no time in getting down to business.

'Shit, this is so awkward. I've been petrified of telling you this. Darren, I'm pregnant. And you're the father. There's just no correct, right or easy way of telling you this is there?'

'Damn right there's not!' I bellowed, though this was without much thought or meaning as I was just in pure shock. In my mind, it was more likely that Phoebe was joking than that I could actually be the father of the little embryo apparently inside her. 'At least this helps resolve my mystery of why you so suddenly had to return to London.'

My world came crashing down as the idea of me actually being the father of this baby was too absurd to even contemplate. I'd had the audacity to cynically predict that Phoebe was going to latch on to me and we'd end up having to rear this child as a collective. If it was some nonentity who she'd had a one-night-stand with sometime, then I'd potentially contemplate the idea of Phoebe and I forging a relationship out of this, but something in me feared that this was James' little wretch, which was just not something that I could ever entertain.

It was after another pause, which seemed uncomfortable and to last for longer than necessary, that Phoebe cemented my doubts with the dumbfounding revelation that, 'Obviously, I'm afraid that this means that you're going to become a dad. This must be so startling to you and I'll respect your decision if you don't want to be a father yet.'

Again, I paused for a little bit before uttering that, 'I don't think that there's any question of whether I'm ready or not. Reality's reality, and if I've ended up becoming a parent, then of course that's what I'll become.' Before continuing my rapid stream of conversation, an inquisitive streak took hold of me and I tried and failed to be diplomatic with a: 'But isn't it a bit premature, given when all of our holiday sex was, for you to be so sure that you're expecting my child? Please don't read into that they wrong way.

She aptly responded in the blunt style to which I had become so accustomed. From one of our first close conversations involving her menstrual cycle causing her to suffer from bloating as a teenager, we've never strayed from anything but absolute directness. 'Well, I've had a period since I last faked an orgasm with James, and I haven't started once since we've rekindled. You know that I'm usually pretty regular. Read into that whatever you will.' To think that my slight concern had shifted from Phoebe having been infected with an STI from James, to the bleak prospect of her carrying his child.

This had the potential to be read cryptically; perhaps James had excelled himself once at least. Though I'm sure that this isn't what she meant by any stretch. The stereotypical 'but we were careful…' ejected from my lips. In reality, I wore a condom for the first couple of times, but then, given the sort of trusting relationship that we had, when Phoebe led me into it for our third time without so much as requesting that I wore any sheath, I just presumed that she was all under control. I'd firmly believed that a baby would be the last thing that she'd want for about a decade. Also, seeing as she'd been on the pill before she even became sexually active due to a trace of light acne, I automatically assumed that she was willing to have sex with me without wearing any protection because she was on the pill.

I was especially perplexed as I took into account that we'd both had near-brushes with sexual health before; well, Phoebe's mild case of thrush is hardly extensive enough to be technically called an STI, but nuns never seem to get it though, do they? Phoebe soon continued with: 'That's why I'm not necessarily expecting you to take any of the responsibility for this child; it's almost completely my fault; I was well overdue my contraceptive injection. I'd got the dates wrong.'

In many ways, my gut reaction could not have been juxtaposed to what anybody, including myself, could have expected. There was no feeling of dilapidation and destruction, but rather one of some ashamed self-satisfaction, relief and even affection. Don't get me wrong, going in for the indulgence of having a child couldn't have come further down the list of things that I would have wanted to do within any of the foreseeable; if ever. Instead, the traditionalist and even at times oppressively large sentimental side of me came out. Not in doing something as ridiculous as reducing Phoebe to the possession of my wife, but I strongly felt that: 'First, you need to stop blaming yourself for anything. If we are to become parents together, then I think that we should be a couple living together and the works.'

What I meant by 'the works', I do not know, but I was just in the midst of digesting some of the most revolutionary news that I'd ever directly faced. Me and my close mate, Freddie, had discussed several times our (though mainly his) unprecedented fears of making one of his long string of flings pregnant, and we couldn't see it as foresighted to bring a child into this ever-more repugnant and self-absorbed world.

I appreciate that it could have been said at any time that the world is in for self-destruction caused by its citizens—overwhelmingly men—and we've survived, but now we've just gone so far beyond ourselves. As can be seen in the overwhelming figures suffering from depression, we can clearly almost no longer cope.

With the divisions in wealth ever-escalating, growing up in a post-Thatcher world appears to be largely engineered towards indulging the individual and pursuing instant gratification in the pursuit of wealth. This is then met with that appalling notion that this just has to be dealt with, as there is just no going back. Pretty much like the delusion that it is in any way possible to distance yourself from technology now that the revolution has swept over us all. People have become incapable of seeing the emotional void and sense of loneliness and underachievement created by this movement engineered to fuel capitalism and a sense of entitlement and self-worth. Manipulative and self-advancing sociopaths just aren't the sort to feel the need to express their gratitude and joy that all that individualised technology has enabled them to do. The brutality is that we're all thrown together in a supposed connectable world but in reality this means that we're all so alone.

With this in mind, you may see me as the classic self-righteous hypocrite, complete with all of their delusion, in rearing (with love and affection and all of that) a child of my own. The pretentious defence is that I believe the way the world is going is not unavoidable by any stretch. By no means do I want to mould Mildred into anything that it is not of her own choice or accord, but I'll always bring her up to question everything and not settle for the world as it appears. Without denial, I can say that part of the reason why I was so welcoming of Mildred at such a young stage of my life must have been to subconsciously deflect some of the feeling of inadequacy in having achieved seemingly so little through my own existence.

As somebody who needs to have a strong and consistent focus, although it was something that happened inadvertently, becoming a father was certainly the right path for me to take. When else could I have belonged to a catalogue front cover family? Joking of course, though I think the fact that the mothers glance at me as the young dad 'Tiny Tots' on a Thursday afternoon proves that I've still, nearly at least, got what it takes. So, am I a full-time house father then?

Of course I'm fucking not. This would kill us all in our family. What happened was, I left my umpteenth job in the charity sector and did a PGCE in teaching history (even though my most advanced qualification in the subject is at A Level) and now teach at the Bridge Academy around Haggerston. Being able to cycle to work is an added perk to a job that I love, and I can't believe that I wasted so many years doing a job that I didn't much enjoy. Beautiful old hindsight, eye. It's certainly far from the best school, and the word 'challenging' could easily be used to describe it, but it gives me that positive old sanctimonious glow at times. The 3 days a week that I do there is certainly enough though. Too much more would drive me insane. Phoebe does 2 or 3 days a week of counselling, which complements this incredibly well. Ha, I feel like I'm in danger of making it sound as though we're the perfect cereal box nuclear family, but jeez we're certainly a way away from whatever that is.

Mildred jointly belonging to the pair of us is unquestionable, though there is no definitive proof of her paternity. Although I was of course the modernist father who accompanied Phoebe to all of the antenatal classes and intricately monitored every step of the pregnancy, there is, at times, an unspoken, dark, overhanging cloud concerning our daughter's fatherhood.

Although I've consciously chosen to avoid too much intricate analysis, my reckoning points to Phoebe's due date being marginally premature to what it would have been from when we rekindled our relationship. It is ambiguous though. For this reason, I've never raised the issue. Instead, I have just embraced Mildred as my daughter and I have devotion for her beyond the extent that I ever thought it possible. Biology's surely a secondary matter anyway. It all gets far too Jeremy Kyle when too much emphasis is placed on fatherhood. Judaism may have been ahead of its time in terms of basing a child's faith on its mother, as this is the only parent of which you could be certain, but for a new-age atheist, it feels rather primitive to much care.

Of course, if it were ever to be confirmed that Mildred was somebody else's father, I'd have to separate from Phoebe. This would be catastrophic. It's not that I am content living a lie, but rather that I am more than satisfied with the way that things are, and there can be no reason to question Phoebe's definitive assertion that I am the father. I see no need to needlessly rock the boat.

Phoebe's promiscuity has always spiralled my own, and I continue to find this more appealing than threatening. Experience should surely be sought after rather than feared. Of course, we're exclusive now, though I can't say that I'm overly concerned that I'd feel too great a sense of betrayal by whatever may go along discreetly behind closed doors. This is by no means advocating any kind of open-relationship type arrangement. All that Phoebe and I really seem to care about is that each other are happy, and any relationship seeking anything else must be a fallacy.

It's not worth thinking about too much, but I'd be lying if I said that I weren't a tad dubious at times about what would happen to

Phoebe and I if we were not so immersed in the young life that we've brought into the world.

It always seems far too easy for me to be subsumed by parenthood and then curtailed by the responsibilities and constraints that it places. Instead, I have just chosen to see it as opportunity—believe me, once you have your own child, life cannot ever have the same meaning as it had before—and to me, having a child is the happiest sort of crisis that you can have. It is great for now, whilst we have such a young family, though part of me dreads to think what'll happen when we inevitably—as we'll always encourage freedom and independence of thought above all else—become an empty-nest family.

As I'm admittedly somebody who needs to have a focus, it'll be my responsibility to devote my energy to something else once we are less hands-on with our child. It'll be more than a birth, that renaissance for Phoebe and me, as we've never shared everything with each other as an item in our own right. A bit like my own parents, I suppose.

The age at which the pair of us chose to grow up together through having our daughter may have been about right for our parents' generation, but puts us out of sync with the vast majority of our friends. You can almost cut a dividing line from when we were at school; you either became a teenage parent, or you went to university and lived life before maybe settling down after the age of 30. It's fitting that as we have always been something of outsiders, Phoebe and I fill a void somewhere in the middle of these two groups.

We've made a strenuous effort to maintain our friendship circles and still do the odd bender from time to time (though for us to both be able to go out is almost unheard of). But our friendship circle has become more solidified and, if anything, more varied, which is something that we both relish. Most of our friends who are parents of Mildred's contemporaries are older than us, though we've also rekindled with many of the lost school acquaintances who had children when they were teenagers. Only distantly though. We go to the playgroups and stuff to ensure that our daughter has enough interaction with children her own age. But mostly, we socialise with our same circles of friends as before. We've always had a small cluster of old-timers who are equal friends with us both, and we've by now cherry-picked people from both of our circles with whom we have now become really close. The fact that we are the anomaly, rather than the norm has actually enhanced the attraction that people have seem to have for spending some time with us.

Some are still engaged in long-term relationships—where we can apparently set a precedent for their own settling down—and for others we seem to merely offer a welcome alternative to their unstably chaotic and fun single lives. I'd be lying to say that I'm not envious of their decadent-seeming existences, although we took a turning, and it is unavoidably accurate to say that I couldn't even imagine much reward in a childless life anymore.

Here I am, living not so much as a mile away from with my original E5 postcode in Lower Clapton. Although I'm more than happy with my current location—I can easily cycle to school of a morning 3 days a week—it is far more circumstantial than nostalgic that we've ended up here. Like most of the best things in life, luck's got as much to do with it than anything else. Miriam Laith is a mate (to use the term loosely) of mine from the UEA, and now that she's working for Hackney Council, she was able to make the best of our situation (and the Tories hadn't been in power for long enough to insist that we committed the obscenity of getting married). We were fast placed on the top of the priority list, and we soon moved into our Victorian two-bedroom terraced Council House—one of the few council properties saved from Thatcher's purging of this vital resource. Who knows for how long this will last, as our house would be of the sort worth at least around £500,000, to give an aptly conservative estimate.

Within a couple of months of learning that Phoebe was pregnant, I handed in my notice. Otherwise, I'm sure that I would have wallowed in a job that I didn't much like—just above the level of not being able to stand—and then inevitably drifted to some other similar job that I'd have more or less equal feelings toward. Instead, I took up a PGCE in Secondary Education at Goldsmiths. This especially suited me as I was still living in Peckham at the time.

Given how much of a bombshell the fact that we were to become parents was to Keith and Sandra (along with Phoebe's parents Ray and Cathy), they couldn't have handled it all better. My folks had, after all, been in the same position when they were significantly younger than me, so weren't in much position to show negative judgement; it could only be an instance of the pot calling the kettle black. All I can say is that I saw their protective parental instinct come into play. Outwardly, both of my parents had always gotten along like a house on fire with Phoebe during whatever fleeting meetings that they'd had over the last number of years. I'd be a fool, though, not to have detected that they could both feel a little wary of the pull that Phoebe had always had over on me and the fact that I could easily be taken for a ride. This is probably because the depth of my feelings for her is beyond what most people have the pleasure or misfortune to experience; but then that's what they all say.

Mum probably just couldn't wait to become a nanny, and Dad only had an issue with the fact that I chose to quit my job so soon after finding out that I'd have a family to support. Whilst I can see things from his perspective, the fact is that he's still pretty much from the 'job for life' generation. It's also likely that he, subconsciously at least, has some resentment for the fact that he had to toil for so many years—never much enjoying his job, living for the fact that he was able to put bread and water for me on the table. It's a 'made my bed and I'd better lie in it' sort of thing.

But without being all defensive, it wasn't as though I hadn't laid out a viable plan for the future. Not only would teaching probably bring in more money long-term than my charity sector job, but I should actually get something out of it. To Dad, it was out of mere indulgence and decadence that I opted to enter into a career that I might actually enjoy, as to his instincts this was in itself antagonistic to the purpose of work. To this day, it is one of those unmentioned elements of my life, even now that I am, according to OFSTED, a supposedly 'outstanding' secondary school teacher.

Although he respects what I do as a job, coming from the patriarchal mind-set that the male should be the breadwinner, the notion of me having decided to limit the amount that I work to 3 days a week is harder for him to understand.

It was upon Phoebe divulging that she was pregnant that living arrangements took precedent. I couldn't do things by halves, and I think that it's fair to say that we both had to have an all or nothing attitude if we were ever to have a go at being a family.

The first thing was for me to complete a PGCE and get qualified at being a secondary school teacher and for Phoebe to become a flourishing counsellor. We were soon liaising and plying off as much urgency and pressure as possible on our old friend, Miriam Laith, to find ourselves our own home. Phoebe moved back in with her parents in the Walthamstow side of Highams Park (well, it was an E17 postcode and within the parliamentary safe Labour constituency, so definitely more of the former) with the healthy pragmatism of saving some money. I stuck in my house-share in Peckham.

Upon meeting my 3 new drab housemates, I was incredibly glad that I had a focus beyond being trapped within this tedium. Luckily, being something of a glass half-full person, living with people for whom I felt little emotion upon meeting or leaving, this ended up being an ideal situation. I probably spent as much time intruding upon the welcoming hospitality of Phoebe and her parents as I did living in my Peckham flat share anyway.

Everyone was always incredibly friendly, and without being too arrogant, Phoebe's parents seemed thankful that their second daughter (unlike the eldest, who had long been married to some douchebag in California) had me in tow. It was always the perfect, happy, relaxed atmosphere to surround our little foetus!

As my charity job in Whitechapel was salaried, it wasn't exactly as though I could work every hour of overtime that God sends, though I would have if I could as this new life of mine gradually started to seem like less of a fable. This was my focus.

Being able to distance myself from my well-meaning line manager, with her incredibly narrow black-and-white way of seeing the world, would be another bonus of leaving my job. I only announced my upcoming fatherhood to my colleagues given that I cheekily presumed that the charity sector would be more than willing to offer me paternity leave. In making this plan, though, I'd overlooked the fact that I'd already enrolled onto my PGCE place, and because I hadn't worked in the company for long enough, receiving paternity leave was just not viable. So much for the benevolence of charity. In fairness, I could understand their point.

Not that this made any difference, as no line manager has the ability to actually listen to anything that you're saying—no matter how much they think they do—which you probably understand if you've ever worked in an office. They simply ask closed questions, and you never actually have any real ability to voice any of the rounded opinions that you may have. Of course, in whatever job—even if you're self-employed—tensions and hierarchies are always in place—though in the educational profession (or in my experience at least) it all seems far more open and based on genuine teamwork.

Now, you can likely understand how being a single parent has to be one of the hardest positions in this world. Collaboration is something that is relied upon. Trust in each other has to be the fairest exchange for the ever-fading passion that you unavoidably end up with. More banal, mature discussions unavoidably constitute the bulk of your conversation. You begin to inescapably conform to the middle class convention of exerting the pretence (that you can't help but actually believe) that you have a clue who the best doctors, playgroups, books to read and toys to play with etc. are for your child's rounded development.

In the case of Phoebe and I, this definitely has over spilled into us each of us seeing the other as more than tiresome at times. Traits that I'd used to have found endearing, such having to hear her belt out Gloria Estefan's 'Dr Beat' to the radio whilst I was trying to do marking at home, are now just infuriatingly embarrassing. The idea from a favourite Smith's song that 'Nothing's changed, I still love you, only slightly less than I used to' monopolises my thought process. We both get on each other's nerves now, which never used to happen, but at least, overall, we seem to find it as funny as it is.

With this, I'm beyond much caring about the feelings between Phoebe and I, since as a family unit, I don't think that we could be more devoted and committed. It'd be unhealthy if my feelings towards Phoebe remained the same as they once were. The way I see it, that the important thing is that we have remained devoted to each other, and there are times where our love, admiration and passion for each other remain consistent.

As long as glimmers of love continue to exist, then all's fine… how can you ever truly love somebody that you don't hate and resent at other times? We still have sex often enough. And we're due to have another child—planned this time—in another five or so months.

Being part of the whole 'we'll love it the same whatever it is' brigade, we at first hadn't bothered to find out the sex of the baby. Only when our boring pragmatism took hold did we eventually enquire. As we have only 2 bedrooms, learning that we'd be expecting another girl was a welcome relief, as they'd be able to share a bedroom for longer and we could stay put for the foreseeable. We'd got a good deal on our Victorian council property, and although single sex schooling wasn't what either of us felt to be ideal, Clapton Girls Academy does now offer great education. At least I recognise that I am forced to be a parody of myself, by cheapening the wonder of having another girl so much.

Things are all pretty set for us now, and everything's in some order. We earn just about as close to enough money as capitalism will ever allow us to feel satisfied. My paternal granddad would be turning in his grave—if he weren't cremated—to think of what luxuries we manage to attain for ourselves. Our summer holidays, for example, we have either a 2-week jaunt to either visit Phoebe's sister in California or a camping holiday in Brittany in northwest

France; definitely more than a few steps up from my dad's childhood trips to Essex's Jaywick or Clacton-on-Sea. Our expectations have risen from a donkey ride and stick of rock.

We've all been blessed with fine health. We don't drink to anything near the extent that we used to and so rarely take any recreational drugs; we go to the gym and only smoke on family holidays, as for us it's a fine example of teaching our children of delayed gratification. In fact, all's well ordered, and we're enjoying our lives enough in a conventional sense. Facing and thinking this makes me hate myself and feel depressed in equal measure.

Whatever happiness and unhappiness that flourishes in me now is absolutely nothing any better or any worse than what I should have experienced if I'd continued in my previous transient existence. Friends would always have said—and I swear I'm not bullshitting or trying to flatter myself—that I was pretty gregarious and, if anything, I still feel that I am, so not much has fundamentally changed as far as my biorhythms are concerned.

Although I certainly used to carry an ample degree of insecurity, since Mildred came into this world, I really can't say that I give enough of a monkey's about what anybody thinks of me. I suppose, though, that I have retained enough sanity to at least be concerned a bit.

Of course, I've carved out a certain relationship with the world, and I still want that to stay as consistent as possible. Though with the perspective that I've gained, I'm not all that bothered what others really think. This extra layer of maturity—or delusion—would most likely have taken a hell of lot longer to build without having become a father.

Having children can't help but make you a little loopy; whilst they're new-born at least. Going back to when I was alone in the house with Phoebe by my side for the first time ever, and going around the house stark-bollock naked—as I still continue to do if I can get away with it—I thought nothing of going to collect a parcel from the front door. Completely oblivious to what I was even doing. Oops. No wonder the postman looked so threatened and cagey.

Without a doubt, there are times when I can't help but feel slightly threatened. From finances to Mildred's almost questionable paternity, all of these have to sink in as factors that I'll always have to deal with. The judgement that I've formed of James had convinced me that he'd be filing for custody at some point in years to come, as soon as the world susses out his true character, leaving him older and lonelier and in search of worth. Now, though, I'm confident that he would be laughed out of court in all his arrogance—and perhaps with the confidence in mistruths that only stupid beings can ever possess—from the moment that he places any direct claim to Mildred's paternity.

The paternity issue, though, has gone from becoming increasingly irrelevant to being side-tracked completely. From the moment Mildred entered the world, our bond was cemented and never felt as though it could be any stronger, especially due to the increased resemblance between her face and mine. This shall probably be the closest thing that I'll ever be offered to a fairy-tale ending, as it conveniently overlooks all of the slog of life on the way.

'You're the spitting image', I often hear when I'm with Mildred. Our 'porcelain' lips (as we get told) especially appear to be identical. Whatever that even really means.

To think that I'll be choosing to go through all of this again when Mildred's sibling is born. We've yet to think of any names, as this makes it far too real to be contended with. We both want this child so much, and we don't want this pregnancy to be lanced with any more pressure. We will probably look to see if we can move before too long anyway. Now that we both earn good money, we may either go into the private housing sector or simply up the bedrooms in the council house that we live in. Walthamstow's a possibility, as it's nearer to our parents and there are enough decent schools. Talk about the cyclical nature of life. No rush though, as we're all seemingly happy enough where we are.